Tim Willocks ... ... ied
medicine at ... ... ied
in 1983 and ... ... the
author of thr... ... ... *ood-
stained King*

Praise for *Bad City Blues*

'A catalogue of relentless sadomasochism and psychological degradation, redolent, in parts, of Jim Thompson or Charles Willeford' *GQ*

'A gothic melodrama updated to contemporary New Orleans ... A natural, instinctive, highly visual writer with a particular gift for erotic interludes ... animated, passionate' *Guardian*

'A fine, plot-driven yarn' *The Times*

'Tim Willocks is the man. He's the best writer I've read in years ... his books are so intelligent and well-written' *Loaded*

'Until this man put pen to paper, Raymond Chandler was probably the only English writer with the talent, the wherewithal and the sheer bottle to write a convincing hard-boiled contemporary American crime novel ... He simply tells a powerful story like it is ... a superb thriller' *Glasgow Herald*

'Willocks has an amazing talent ... At his best he reads like Mailer, Robbins, Vachss and Ellroy combined' *Time Out*

'Willocks writes like the Archangel Gabriel using a pen that's been dipped in the devil's semen' *Loaded*

'A writer powering through on adrenaline. Deeply inlaid in his novels, along with the ferocity of the sex and violence, is an old-fashioned code of honour ... It's the electrifying pace of his writing and its unashamed, unfashionable rawness which grabs you' *City Life*

'The violence is explosive, the sex erotic and the atmosphere as fragrant as a sewer ... a cracking read' *Nuneaton Evening Telegraph*

BAD CITY BLUES

Tim Willocks

ARROW

Published in the United Kingdom in 1998 by
Arrow Books

1 3 5 7 9 10 8 6 4 2

First published in the United Kingdom in 1991 by Macdonald & Co
(publishers) Ltd, London & Sydney

Arrow Books Limited
Random House UK Ltd
20 Vauxhall Bridge Road, London, SW1V 2SA

Random House Australia (Pty) Limited
20 Alfred Street, Milsons Point, Sydney,
New South Wales 2061, Australia

Random House New Zealand Limited
18 Poland Road, Glenfield
Auckland 10, New Zealand

Random House South Africa (Pty) Limited
Endulini, 5a Jubilee Road, Parktown 2193, South Africa

Random House UK Limited Reg. No. 954009

A CIP catalogue record for this book is
available from the British Library

Papers used by Random House UK Limited are natural, recyclable
products made from wood grown in sustainable forests. The
manufacturing processes conform to the environmental regulations of
the country of origin

ISBN 0 09 918422 2
Printed and bound in the United Kingdom by
Cox & Wyman Ltd, Reading, Berks.

Dedicated to

LESTER F. WILSON

and

In Memory of MARK NELSON

In the desert
I saw a creature, naked, bestial,
Who, squatting upon the ground,
Held his heart in his hands
And ate of it.
I said, 'Is it good, friend?'
'It is bitter, bitter,' he answered.
'But I like it
Because it is bitter,
And because it is my heart.'

Stephen Crane
Black Riders III

PROLOGUE

MEDELLIN, COLOMBIA

The American stopped on the edge of the sidewalk as a shatter of bright sunlight caught his upturned face. There could be no mistake, thought Luther Grimes. It was him.

The morning traffic was bumper to bumper and when the American saw his chance he threaded his way between the press of battered cars and smoke-belching trucks to sit down beneath the awning of a cantina on the far side of the street. While he waited for his coffee he shook a cigarette into his mouth from a red pack and lit it with a match. After the first drag he paused to pick a shred of tobacco from his tongue. His hands were big and darkened by the sun and his black hair was cropped short at the back and sides. He was dressed in a soiled white shirt, one button open at the neck, and a baggy black linen suit. The suit was shabby now but the American wore it stubbornly, as if he wouldn't be sure of who he was without it.

At a glance he looked well enough, especially on that squalid, dirt-poor street, but there were hollows under his cheekbones that said he was pounds lighter than he should have been; and when the sun had caught his face for that instant down below, the paleness of his eyes – that pale Northern blue – had been hidden by deep sockets gouged even deeper by despair.

Luther Grimes, standing naked at the window, stepped back and turned his face away as the American looked up through the smoke haze towards the façade of the old hotel. The retreating movement made Luther feel cowardly and sneaking, qualities he did not generally feel to

1

be part of his nature. You bastard, he thought, and wasn't sure whether he meant himself or the man waiting for his coffee across the street.

His pride took him back to the window and he watched as a barefoot boy in raggedy shorts tried to sell the American a brightly coloured bird tied to his finger by a string. Tell the boy to go fuck himself, thought Luther. But sure enough the man dug into his pocket, gave the boy some money and refused to take the bird. As the boy skipped away the man's composure fractured at the edges and he bent forward and slowly rubbed his face with both hands in a gesture of unspeakable weariness.

Luther felt a tightness spread from his throat, up through the sinuses behind his face. When it reached his eyes an unconscious reflex pushed the feeling back down and the tightness faded. It was time to get out of this country. He loved it because it was so fucking uncivilized but he'd made the money he'd come for and he'd be a fool to push his luck. His body stiffened as he felt the girl, also naked, come up behind him and press herself against his back.

'What's the matter?' she said, in Spanish. Her hands reached around his waist and stroked the hair on his belly.

Her gentleness set him on edge and his muscles tensed but he didn't want to hurt her by shrugging her off. Caught between the sight of the American and the gentleness of the girl he felt restless and somehow trapped and the words came out without thought.

In Spanish he said, 'Am I a good man or a bad man?'

It was a stupid question and he felt stupid for asking it. He'd got by for twenty years without even thinking it; now wasn't the time to start.

The girl squeezed him tighter and said, 'It doesn't matter. I love you.'

The answer filled him with a familiar sense of fury and disgust and without speaking he pulled her over to the bed and fucked her violently from behind with the fan ticking softly in the air overhead. She made the sounds he

2

expected her to make, grunting woman-sounds com-pounded of reluctant satisfaction and muted distress, sounds he'd uttered himself on occasion but not for half a lifetime and never with a female, and he envied her deeply and knew he would never understand it. He forgave her in his head because she was young, but too many times had he struggled with himself in the flaccid cunt of a thoughtless and selfish lover and shards of contempt needled his heart. When he came it was with an angry, solitary, guilt-ridden ejaculation that left him obscurely dissatisfied and confused, but as he finished and withdrew and shoved her aside he knew at last what to do about the man drinking coffee across the street.

He stood up and towelled sweat from his chest and thighs with a sheet he pulled from the bed.

'Put some clothes on,' he said. 'Quickly. There's an old friend waiting to see us.'

He ignored the question in the girl's look and glanced out of the window to check that the table outside the cafe was still occupied. Then he started to dress with crisp, controlled movements. His clothes were expensive, a lightweight suit in pale grey-blue silk, a white aertex shirt, lace-up boots in which he could walk for a month without seeing a blister or kick a man's skull in without worrying about his toes. He stuck a passport and a money-clip of US dollars into his shirt pocket and shoved a wad of crumpled currency into his pants. His hair was long and black, and he scooped it together in his hands and tied it behind his head in a pony-tail. Before putting on his jacket he slipped into a shoulder holster holding a short-barrelled Magnum revolver.

The girl was ready before he was and was dressed to break hearts as usual in a white silk sheath. She said she only wore the dress because she knew the sight of her nipples pleased him, but Luther didn't believe her. It was going to be hard to leave her behind to some coke-guzzling millionaire but he would do it. For her sake. Maybe. Anyhow, that was for later. Now it was time to do what he should've done a long time ago. No more running. No more bullshit games. The girl was combing her hair in the dressing-table mirror. Her name was Anna and she was fifteen years old.

'Let's go,' said Luther.

By the time they got down to the street the American had gone.

Through the billows of car exhaust and the smoke of street-corner cooking fires Luther could see that the table was empty and there was no sign of the dusty black suit on the teeming sidewalks.

In English, Luther Grimes said, 'Motherfucker.'

Eugene had looked like he hadn't got more than a few days left in him. Luther felt in his pockets and found a cigarette. That was the difference between them, he thought. He'd learned early on to hold himself way down inside, to lower the shutters before things started to hurt. Eugene always set himself up for the gut-punch, begged for it even. Always looking for something that wasn't there. Like, maybe, love. Fuck that shit. He lost the thread of his thoughts as a small brown hand tugged at the hem of his jacket.

The barefoot ragged boy, using all the doe-eyed charm he could muster, was offering him the bird for the beautiful lady. Luther looked down at the boy without smiling and took the string from him, looping the end around his own index finger. The bird's feathers were raggedy, like the boy, with a lot of green-blue and yellow. As Luther pulled on the string the bird fluttered up into the air, tugging frantically against the knot around its leg.

Luther reached into his pants pocket and pulled a banknote at random from the wad. The note was dog-eared and torn but both he and the boy could see that it was green and had a portrait of Benjamin Franklin on the front. The boy probably couldn't read the words and sure as hell didn't recognize Franklin but the number was easy enough to identify. One hundred American dollars. More money than the kid could expect to see in two years. The kid knew that the gringo had made a mistake and would put the bill back into his pocket but, in the end, he was still a little kid and he just couldn't help his bent shoulders and sunken chest from swelling out at the thought of a desperate and wonderful dream coming true.

Luther handed him the bill.

The boy grabbed it in his fist and crammed fist and money into the pocket of his shorts. As he did so he backed off to what he thought was a safe distance. He opened his mouth to say something then stopped as Luther started to wind the string around his finger, slowly rotating his wrist, drawing the cheeping, struggling bird down into the palm of his hand. When the string ran out Luther closed his fist around the bird and started to squeeze. All the time he kept his eyes on the boy's face.

The boy looked away from the bird and stared at Luther. He was a tough-looking kid but even the tough can bleed inside and tears came into his eyes.

The boy said, 'I want to buy my bird back.'

Luther stopped squeezing. He could feel the bird's heart pulsing rapidly against his fingers.

'How much?' said Luther.

Slowly, the boy pulled his fist from his pocket, his head fighting hand-to-hand with his heart. After a long pause he stepped forward and held out the portrait of Franklin and the loose change Eugene had given him. Luther looked from the money to the boy's eyes.

'That all you've got?'

The boy nodded. 'Everything.'

Luther shook his head.

'Not enough,' he said.

With a single quick jerk of his fist he crushed the bird to death and threw the crumpled mass of feathers into the gutter.

Anna, watching the scene from behind Luther's shoulder, made a whimpering noise and ran up the steps into the hotel. Luther kept his eyes on the boy and nodded. The boy, after a moment, nodded back and ran off down the street holding his money.

Anna was a woman and would never understand, but the boy did. The boy understood very well. Luther scanned the street again but Eugene wasn't to be seen. He'd missed his chance to end it. They both had. He shrugged and flicked his cigarette butt into the road. Next time, then.

He walked back up the steps that Anna had taken.

Next time he'd let it happen.

CHAPTER ONE

Callilou Carter swung her car through the iron lacework gates of the driveway and pulled up on the gravel in front of the house. As she cut off the engine and lights, her body felt lifeless and sick. She wanted a cigarette but she'd already smoked too many and her mouth tasted gummy and foul. Instead she closed her eyes, and rested her forehead against the steering wheel to listen to her nerve-ends scream. Beads of sweat trickled down between her breasts and made the dress she was wearing cling to her belly. She tightened her fists against the pain.

'Jesus Christ.'

For a fifth of a gram of decent cocaine she would have sold her mother's eyes. Cicero Grimes had warned her that this might happen. She just hadn't expected the need to be so sudden or so cruel.

Gathering her strength, she scraped a strand of hair from her cheek and hauled herself from the car. It was an hour after sundown but the hazy blue dusk brought little relief from the rotting heat. August in Louisiana wasn't her favourite time of year and Louisiana wasn't her favourite place. But she wouldn't have to take it for much longer. As she walked across the gravel to the house, she could feel the damp patches on her dress getting bigger. She climbed the steps to the front door and took a key from her purse.

Cleve's home – she'd never thought of it as hers – was as bloated and fake as he was: all bogus stone columns and fancy plaster work designed to make him feel wealthier and more important than he already was. White trash made good. Like she was. Or like she would be, come tomorrow. The thought made her feel better. As she let herself inside, a gust of air-conditioning coated her arms with goose pimples and she shivered. Suddenly the house felt wrong.

For a start it was dark and Cleve didn't like the dark. He said it turned his thoughts to sin. Callie walked down the corridor, switching on the lights in each room and calling out Cleve's name. When he didn't answer she thought maybe he was over at the church and some of the tension eased from her shoulders. But he was there, all right, squatting in the kitchen like the cockroach he was, with glassy red eyes and a hard-on, and Callie thought, *Shit*. Why did he have to wise up tonight, after all this fucking time?

Cleve was sitting at the breakfast bar in a white cotton vest and silk candy-striped boxer shorts. One half of his face was covered with tropical coconut shaving foam and some of the foam had melted and run down his neck into his chest hair. The other side of his face was stuck with half a dozen scraps of blood-stained toilet tissue. For a moment he didn't seem to notice her standing in the doorway; then he blinked once and turned his head to stare.

His pupils were dilated with an other-worldly glaze: the same glaze that came over them in the pulpit when he relayed messages from the Creator. In his left hand he clutched a black leather Bible with his initials printed on the front in gold. In his right he held a snub-nosed revolver. The right hand shook as she looked at him. The revolver pointed at the sweat stain over her belly.

'May God in his infinite mercy forgive you your iniquities,' said Cleveland Carter. His voice trembled with the wrath of the righteous. 'And may he forgive me also for what I am about to do.'

Callie mastered an overwhelming desire to defecate and smiled at him.

'Cleve, honey-baby, what's the matter?' Her voice was

concerned, wifely, supplicant. Beneath the supplication was the iron self-control that had so far protected her from assholes.

'Wherefore, O harlot, I shall judge thee . . .'

Callie held on to the smile. Fuck you, buster.

' . . . as women that break wedlock and shed blood are judged.'

She'd tried to anticipate this. For two years she'd charted the labyrinth of his mind and strolled around it with a whip in her hand. In public, on the gruelling social round expected of the vice-president of a big city bank, she'd allowed him to play the big shot so they could justify a big shot lifestyle. Sweet and submissive and as sexy as all hell, she'd even bent before the more divine whims that Cleve indulged as preacher at the 'Glory Be' evangelist church. On their wedding day, on one of his inspirations, she'd washed his feet with her hair in front of the congregation. The pious had nodded with approval and proclaimed it the perfect marriage.

They were right: Cleve was her last pimp and customer both. Before the world he was her master. In private she kept him on a leash and kicked him; and Cleve, panting with anguish and unrequited lust, still awaited the day when the Almighty would permit him to spill his seed into her body instead of onto the floor, or the bedsheets, or her feet. While the price had been right it had beaten the shit out of lying on her back in a Galveston motel while sad men in clean underwear grunted between her legs, but now she was onto something better. Independence beckoned and she didn't need asking twice. She watched a bubble of saliva swell and burst between Carter's lips.

'I will give thee blood in fury and in jealousy.'

Callie held out her arms and walked over towards him.

'Leave Deuteronomy until later, honey, and let me kiss you.'

Carter stood up from his stool. 'Keep your filthy distance, obscene whore.'

9

Callie stopped two feet away from him. She ran her hands down her flanks and bit the inside of her lip. This wasn't like him. She tried not to stare at the gun.

'The stench of adultery is rank upon your breath. Its foulness nauseates me.' He waved his revolver in the air. 'I gave you the chance to purge yourself and you threw it back in my face. Now prepare to make acquaintance with your Lord and master.'

Callie steeled herself and changed tack.

'Cleve!' She was Miss Stern. 'Stop being a jerk-off and put the gun down.' She reached out and grabbed a handful of cock through his shorts. 'I want this inside me and I want it now.' His cock swelled rapidly in her hand.

Carter flushed red and raised his face to heaven. 'O God, the woman whom thou gavest to me, she gave me of the tree, and I did eat.'

With a grunt he slammed the Bible across the side of her head and she went down. Patches of blackness speckled with coloured dots shimmered before her eyes. The Bible fell to the floor beside her and she felt his hand in her hair, pulling her to her knees and twisting her head back. She wanted to cry out but didn't. Cleve had never hit her before. Never. She swallowed a wedge of fear that threatened to choke her as the barrel of his gun hovered an inch from her right eye. Cleve's face, his lips white, lowered towards her.

'Who is he?'

He shook her head savagely. She screwed her eyes shut and held her breath as clumps of her hair came loose in his hand.

'Tell me, bitch. Who've you been with?'

She grabbed his wrist to stop him. Carter's voice was a shriek of psychotic jealousy.

'His name. His name! *I want a name!*'

He drew back the hammer of the revolver and for the first time Callie believed that he would kill her. She was suddenly too scared to lie. Trying to keep the scream out of her voice she said, 'Cicero Grimes.'

Carter let go of her hair and she opened her eyes. From the flies of his shorts a magnificent purpling erection craned towards her. Callie had always looked on Carter's huge cock as one of God's crueller jokes. At that moment it offered the only chance she had. She grabbed it in her right hand and pulling hard, leaned forward to suck him.

'Thank God for Jesus!' said the Reverend Carter.

With a strangled gasp of ecstasy and dismay he ejaculated copiously over the front of her dress. She let go of him and he staggered backwards to lean against the breakfast bar, wheezing for air. For a moment he seemed unable to breathe; then he regained some composure and said, 'Even the mercy of the Lord burns!'

He dropped his gun on the bar and clasped his hands together. Eyes closed he bent forward holding the doubled fist against his lips. Callie got to her feet and rubbed her scalp. She'd done it. She'd won her second chance. Her fingers were just closing around the gun barrel when Cleve grabbed hold of her hair again.

Men are afraid of the dark.

Legs crossed, naked and huge, Clarence Jefferson sat sweating in the tight, airless space-without-light and stared in front of him, seeing nothing. For thirty minutes each day he sat here in the basement storage room and tried to keep his mind as black and empty as the walls around him. This was where he tried to approach the raw experience of his own existing: to know the weight of his body, the perspiration collecting in the creases of flesh at his waist, the damp heavy air moving through his nostrils. It was the hardest work he ever did, watching his mind without watching it, taking hold of it when it strayed, leading it back time after time to sit in the void and be.

Men are afraid of the dark.

Once again he cleared the thought away. Silence. Emptiness. Then a string of word-images.

11

RED ... DUST ... FIRE ... TWILIGHT ...
BONES.

The sequence repeated itself – red, dust, fire, twilight,
bones – and Jefferson let it be without asking what it
meant. His watch bleeped twice and the images disappeared. He rose to his feet and stretched, first towards
the ceiling against the tension in his lats, and then hands
palm-down against the floor, tugging against the stiffness
in his hamstrings and spine. He stood upright and shook
his head. His body was ready for the heavy physical work
he would put it through but the word-story lingered
inside his skull and left a sensation of tightness behind his
eyes. Unusual. He reached out and opened the door,
shielding himself against the light with a forearm. Maybe
the tightness was due to the storm that was threatening
from the south. Or the stress of policing the summer riots.
He shrugged. Maybe it was just a sixth sense trying to let
him know that out there in the City something bad was
waiting to happen. He smiled, huge and naked, and went
to put on some sweat pants and track shoes.

Out there in the City there was always something bad
waiting to happen.

Cleveland Carter closed the bedroom door behind him
and made his way down the stairs feeling God-like. His
breathing was effortless. His limbs tingled. He had never
felt so potent, not even in the midst of his most blistering
sermons. Still dressed in his underwear he went into his
study and found Clarence Jefferson's number. The
thought of calling in the police made him pause. Instead
of dialling he fell to his knees and put his hands over his
face.

'O my Father, I thank thee for taking pity on me, who
has sacrificed his life to thy greater glory. Hide me from
the secret counsel of the wicked; from the insurrection
of the workers of iniquity. Help me perform works of
righteousness in thy name.'

Less pious thoughts crowded his mind, forcing out the soothing words. What would Jefferson do? He'd heard things about the Captain he'd rather not believe. But it was too late for doubts; he had to place his trust in the law. To do otherwise meant anarchy and chaos. Dear God, how could she? Drugs. Robbery. Blackmail. Mixing with homosexuals and niggers.

He blinked hard twice. At least he hadn't killed her. The faith of his fathers living still, in spite of dungeon, fire and sword, had stayed his hand. If he could help bring the villains to justice he would be happy – providing a scandal could be avoided. Discretion was essential. He was certain Jefferson was the man to handle it.

The other man in his thoughts was Cicero Grimes. Dr Grimes. Hardly surprising that a doctor should be steeped in evil when so much of their craft was devoted to vileness. Contraception. Artificial insemination. Abortion. Darwinism. At least there had been no adultery. Her involvement with Grimes was criminal, not sexual. He'd been wrong to doubt her. She was weak, as were all God's children, but she truly loved him. She had not fornicated. She had sworn it and he believed her. Like Jesus, he could forgive.

In the past she had punished him as was fitting, for Satan had cursed him with a prodigious libido and God, in his wisdom, with the exquisite penance of premature ejaculation. Tonight, in the aftermath of her confession, the Lord had allowed him to penetrate her for the first time and he'd sown his seed on fertile soil; or at least within the outer third of her vagina. The memory induced fresh movement within his shorts. He had at last consummated their marriage and henceforth all would be well. That was more important than the money.

But only just.

They had to get it back at all costs. Blessed Jesus. A million dollars. Maybe considerably more. As he reached for the phone he heard a car start up outside the window.

Callie's car. Panic seized him and he ran out of his office and down the corridor to the front of the house.

'Callie!'

He flung the door open in time to see the tail lights of her car disappearing into the night. He ran down the driveway screaming her name. Lumps of gravel slashed the soles of his bare feet and he stumbled and fell and landed on his shoulder with a cry, just beneath the brass sign in the garden that said 'Gethsemane'. Tears scalded his eyes and his breathing became tight again.

'My God, my God, why hast thou forsaken me?'

A monstrous sense of injustice threatened to crush his chest. He clung to a name.

'Captain Jefferson.'

Cleveland Carter clambered to his feet and painfully picked his way back to the large white house. Bitter tears rolled down his cheeks. He loved the Lord. What had he done to deserve this trial?

And who in the name of God was Cicero Grimes?

CHAPTER TWO

Clarence Jefferson was halfway through his thrice-weekly power lifting routine when the Reverend Carter called. He worked out in the garage at the back of his house. Jefferson could not bear the chromed weights and mirrors that filled most commercial gyms, nor their clientele: sun-tanned oafs pumping up their egos so that they could show a triceps dimple on the beach or whilst undressing in front of girlfriends who wouldn't notice or boyfriends who would. Narcissism depressed him. Power made him happy. Heaving huge masses of metal through the air with no other object in mind than to be able to heave even more appealed to him. He felt that it brought him closer to some understanding of the human condition.

When the telephone rang he was just completing a warm-up set of five-hundred-pound squats. He backed up between the squat stands and lowered the bar into the cradles, panting softly. The buckle of the leather belt about his waist was covered by a roll of fat. He grunted as he released the belt four notches. Beneath the fat his abdominal muscles were like sections of steel pipe.

Most people thought he was just another born-again redneck. Others learned better.

Years before, when he'd first manoeuvred his way into vice, he had invited a number of pimps to discuss terms with him. His demands had set a new standard in police greed and they'd laughed. One of them had done more than laugh; he'd tried to lean on the new captain. Ambitious. In retrospect perhaps even rash. The act of dislocating a man's shoulders takes more in the way

15

of strength than technique and is spectacularly brutal, which was why Jefferson chose to demonstrate it on the pimp. But afterwards it had been difficult to make himself heard above the screams, so he'd squatted behind the squirming body and placed the heels of his hands against either side of the pimp's jaw. Flexing his pectorals and anterior deltoids – and whatever lip muscles he'd needed to smile with – he'd brought his hands together and caved the bastard's face in. The pimps had given the Captain what he'd wanted. And for Clarence Seymour Jefferson, getting what he wanted had become something of a habit.

He had no plans to break it.

When he heard Cleveland Carter on the telephone he assumed that the call was meant for his wife. She had the sort of shrill pseudo-operatic voice so beloved of religious choirs and was involved with the 'Glory Be' church, a flock of sheep's assholes with more money than sense who believed they needed Carter's hysterical rhetoric to get them through the eye of the needle. Jefferson was grateful for his wife's devotion. It reduced the amount of time he felt obliged to spend with her. And when, of a sunny Sunday morning, he lay enjoying cut-price fellatio from the lips of the city's sweetest whores, he derived an added piquancy from the knowledge that Eleanor was at that moment standing by the altar and leading the faithful in rendering 'His Hand In Mine'.

He was surprised then when Carter pleaded, with an urgency bordering on panic, that Jefferson come over to his home at once to investigate a criminal event of the most godless nature.

He had spoken to Carter on half a dozen occasions and considered him a Bible-beating clown with the moral sophistication of a Colorado beetle, characteristics which made him ideally suited to receive the power and wealth which society had lavished upon him. Carter was a vice-president of the Louisiana Mercantile Trust Bank and number one hatchet man for the shareholders. It wasn't difficult to picture his bloated face sweating with the effort

16

of crapping on the have-nots. Jefferson made it his business to know things about such figures.

If he remembered correctly, he had a series of colour photographs of Carter's boss insinuating his tongue into the anus of a thirteen-year-old nigger boy.

As far as he knew, Carter had no such pecadilloes. He'd saved a Galveston prostitute from damnation and on instructions from the Lord – no doubt transmitted via her luscious nipples – had subsequently married her, but that was not a secret. In fact Carter often mentioned the event in his tedious and verbose sermons as evidence of his semi-divine status. So as he showered and changed, Jefferson wondered just what Carter's problem could be and why, if he was the victim of a crime, he hadn't simply called the department.

Jefferson put on a pair of khaki slacks and from his wardrobe of Hawaiian shirts selected one which evoked the dazzling blue of Pacific skies. It was made of 100 per cent pure rayon and sported a pattern of palm trees, dancing girls and sea birds that only repeated itself once in its passage around the fifty-six-inch width of the shirt. The shirt hung down nicely over the .357 Colt Python he wore in a belt holster over his right hip. He popped a speed loader full of shells into his pocket and left the house without saying goodbye to his wife.

Carter lived on an azalea-lined street in what he liked to call an *ante bellum* house. Jefferson assumed this meant it had been built just before the Vietnam War. A big white house in a big white suburb full of big white people: moderately wealthy American Dreamers who spent a large proportion of their six-figure incomes trying to convince themselves that they were very wealthy. Jefferson had always found the self-confidence of the rich to be a hollow nut, easily cracked and containing a void. These people didn't even have that. Fear of losing their place, the quintessential characteristic of their class, oozed from every landscaped garden and triple-locked door. The iron gates to Carter's house were open and as he drove up the driveway, past the ludicrous sign which named the house 'Gethsemane', Jefferson reflected that his contempt for them was so profound that he was not even moved to disgust. He parked his Eldorado around the side of the house where the car was not easily visible from the road and found Cleveland Carter waiting at the front door as if for the Second Coming.

'God bless you for coming so promptly, Captain,' said Carter. He spoke in his Sunday-best deacon's voice and puffed out his narrow chest in an attempt to appear dignified. But the scabs of fresh shaving cuts marked one side of his face and his hand trembled as he held it out for Jefferson to squeeze. Jefferson squeezed and Carter winced and coughed.

'Come inside.'

The house had been decorated by someone who had spent a lot of time watching millionaires in soap operas. Polished wood and gold-plated door fittings, a chandelier in the hallway, thick carpets in reds and purples. Oral Roberts would have approved, if not the Nazarene. Jefferson found it revolting. His wife had decorated their own home in a down-market version of the same style.

'This is a very nice place,' said Jefferson. 'You've done well, Reverend. Congratulations.'

Carter inclined his head. The gesture was meant to convey modesty but shrieked with pomposity. 'You are kind. Material possessions are, of course, inconsequential trivialities when compared to the unimaginable glories heaped upon the righteous in the everlasting hereafter. But at the same time we must not scorn earthly riches if God so chooses to favour us.' His voice trembled with sincerity. 'Remember that money is the most tangible sign of the Lord's specific love.'

'Amen to that,' said Jefferson.

'We'll talk in my study.'

He led the way down the hall, limping slightly on both feet, and showed Jefferson through a door. The study was standard upper-middle-class American in its furnishings:

18

mahogany table, leather upholstery, wood panelling, bookcases. Jefferson scanned the bookcase with interest. Instead of the expensively bound and permanently unopened classics normally supplied with such furnishings, this library looked well-used and consisted of such titles as 'I Need To Talk To Someone, God', 'Exercising Your Authority Over Satan' and 'Thank God I Have Cancer'. There were also volumes by such born-again veterans as Eldridge Cleaver and one of the Watergate burglars. On the wall facing the desk and the window was a portrait of Carter in a dark suit, temples greying with distinction, holding a Bible in his right hand and wearing a stern but benevolent expression on his face. The background was of a sunlit rural landscape with a white country church in the distance. Behind the figure of Carter, between him and the church, was a flock of sheep.

Jefferson sat down in front of the desk. 'What can I do for you, Reverend?'

Carter, from behind the desk, sighed and shook his head.

'The peace and tranquillity which has long blessed this house has been shattered by the hand of an iniquitous woman and her pack of villains. The tale is so sordid that I suspect that even you, a professional in the field, will be shocked by what I have to say.'

Jefferson suspected that the sermon was Carter's only means of verbal communication. He cut him short.

'I think I can handle whatever you've got to say. Tell me what happened as simply as you can.'

Carter leaned forward in his chair.

'As you know, Captain, before I met my wife she made a foul living of sorts by selling her body. It isn't difficult to imagine what led her down that road. An atheistic upbringing, teenage petting parties, cigarettes, cable TV, denim jeans and the contraceptive pill. After my first wife died, God rest her unblemished soul, I spent several years alone, devoting myself to the service of God both at the bank and in the church. Then one fateful day I spoke at a baptismal meeting up the coast in Galveston. Callilou was at the meeting. I suspect she had gone along to feed her prejudices about our work, to snigger and mock, but that day the Holy Spirit entered me and I spoke with such divine passion that the poor child, as I then perceived her, was on the spot converted to the way of Christ the Redeemer and took baptism at my own hands.'

'Very gratifying,' said Jefferson. Callilou Carter was a handsome woman. Seeing her rising from the river in a wet shirt would have moved the Holy Spirit in anybody.

'Indeed. There is more rejoicing in Heaven when a single sinner repents than . . .'

'I've got the picture,' said Jefferson. 'And shortly after she was washed in the blood of the lamb, God spoke to you again and you married her. Eleanor often commented on the joy it gave her to see you two working together for the greater glory of God. But I take it something has gone wrong.'

Reverend Carter shuddered. The ability to shudder at will was probably important to a populist theologian.

'I'll get to the point, Captain. You must, of course, be aware of the robbery which took place at my own bank earlier this year.'

'Yeah,' said Jefferson. 'I'm aware.'

Jefferson felt his anus tingle with excitement. The Mercantile Trust job had been the smoothest bank robbery in the state's history. Over a million dollars had been cleaned out of the safe deposit boxes. Millions more in jewellery had been left behind. The bank's own cash reserves – less accessible in the main vault and more easily traced into the bargain – had not been touched. The thieves, a team of five, had tunnelled into the bank from the sewers, directly into the basement which housed the safe deposit boxes. The precision with which the thieves had isolated and neutralized the alarm systems specifically protecting that part of the bank, whilst ignoring those covering the main vault, had made it a certain inside job. The alarm systems were too sophisticated to penetrate by

20

exploratory means but if the details of the systems were known then bypassing them was simply a matter of applying technical skills which, while specialized, were not uncommonly available.

The case was still open. Jefferson was not involved but he knew the procedure. Repeated questioning of bank and security personnel, perhaps some covert surveillance, lists compiled of criminals or suspected criminals known to have the expertise to do the job, finding and interviewing those men, checking alibis. Thousands of man hours. Interstate liaison. Mindless tedium.

It was the sort of police work that Jefferson had always avoided. Seven months after the robbery there had been no arrests. No one had shown up spending money they shouldn't have had. Informants knew nothing. The mob, upset at missing their share, had looked as hard as the police. Like ITT and Gulf and Western, the mob didn't like independents. Jefferson had not been surprised at the lack of results. A gang who had the discipline to leave all that jewellery behind rather than take the risk of fencing it weren't going to advertise themselves. But no one had been hurt and public concern was minimal. When people saw a job like this reported on the news a lot of them whistled and thought 'Good luck to them.' The rest didn't care. The insurance companies would hike their premiums, but they would do that anyway. Interest faded and the police effort wound down.

Now here it was, sitting at his feet.

Carter's story was easy to anticipate. To save time and the strain on his own patience, Jefferson condensed it for him.

'I think I know what you're going to say, Reverend. Mrs Carter was your personal assistant at the bank, that I know. My guess is that she fed the plans of the building and the alarm system to the thieves and you just found out about it tonight.'

Carter looked deflated. 'Yes,' he said. 'That's correct, I'm horrified to say.'

'She had access to that kind of information?'

'Good God, Jefferson, during the thousands of hours she and I have spent together she could have picked up all sorts of things. I can't remember. She said it wasn't her idea. I trusted her. Of course I trusted her. She was my wife. She was a Christian.' His voice lost its contrived stateliness and became shrill.

'It's important that you remain calm,' said Jefferson. 'For the moment it doesn't matter how she got the plans. How did you find out?'

'A week ago she became very belligerent and, I might say, suspicious in manner. She told me to stop watching her and to keep my friends at the church off her back. Her language was foul. I didn't know what to say. Later that same day, Friday, she said she was going to stay with her aunt in Galveston for a few days and left.'

'Was this a sudden change in her behaviour?' said Jefferson.

'The overt aggression and suspiciousness seemed sudden, but in retrospect her behaviour has been odd for months. Sometimes highly strung, irritable and agitated, at other times over-cheerful, hyperactive, extremely charming in fact. Preoccupied as I've been with the bank and the church, especially since the robbery, I thought little of it. While she was away in Galveston she rang twice a day and on several occasions she sounded odd, perhaps upset or ill, but insisted that she was fine. Three nights ago a revelation suddenly overwhelmed me: she was committing adultery. Probably had been for months. The conviction was so absolute that I felt sure that Jesus himself had conveyed this knowledge to me. I was devastated.'

Carter was speaking with his eyes fixed on his hands, which he wrung together on the table in front of him. Shame and embarrassment poured off him like sweat.

'She came home two days ago,' said Carter. 'She seemed well, better than for some time. I waited for her to say something, to confess, but she said nothing. She was sweet and considerate and has hardly been away from the church or my side. Somehow I lacked the courage to confront her.' Carter faltered. Jefferson thought he was going to break into tears but he caught himself and went on.

'I began to doubt myself. I prayed desperately for guidance, a sign. But there was nothing until tonight. She received a phone call and wrote down a number. She wouldn't tell me who it was from and was rather aggressive when I pressed her. She left the house for an hour against my wishes. I had no doubt that it was her lover and she had gone to speak to him in private. I tried to be calm, I tried to act as our Saviour would. Violence has never played any role in my life, Captain, but when she came back my wrath was so great that she told me everything.'

'Is she still alive?' Jefferson's tone was sharp. If Carter had killed her in a cuckold's rage the trail stopped here.

Carter tried to summon up some dignity but could only manage pompous bluster. 'Captain, I am not a murderer. I confess that I threatened her with a pistol but I was in control. I merely wanted to frighten the truth from her. She's alive and all too well, though I don't know where. She tricked me and escaped whilst I was calling you on the telephone.'

Callilou didn't sound like the type to cave in to a fake threat, not from a thick slice of country ham like Carter. But if he'd started to get seriously crazy she might well have spilled her guts.

'People can be found,' said Jefferson. 'Finish your story. What did she tell you?'

'Well, she denied adultery. A year ago she started seeing an old girlfriend and began taking drugs again. Cocaine. I suppose I underestimated just how essentially depraved a creature she was. I blame myself for not seeing that. My prayers and guidance could have made all the difference. Naturally her addiction brought her into contact with criminals. One of them, a man she called Luther, found out who she was, or who I was, and started blackmailing her. Unless she helped him set up the robbery he would expose her drug habits to myself and the press and police.'

Carter shook his head. His expression was both sad and bewildered. 'She must have been terrified that she would lose me, lose our life here together. Marrying her was not an easy step for me, Captain. Many friends advised against it. But my love was so strong, so pure that I knew I had God's blessing. And now . . .'

Jefferson almost pitied him. Carter was helplessly infatuated by the woman. Her erratic behaviour over the months was compatible with a cocaine habit but the blackmail story was obviously an arm's length of bullshit.

'We know how they did the robbery,' said Jefferson. 'Did she tell you who was involved and what happened to the cash?'

'She mentioned only two names: "Luther" – I don't know if that is a surname or a Christian name – and "Grimes". Grimes is the doctor she consulted with her cocaine problem. While she was supposedly in Galveston she was really at his clinic. The drugs plunged her into some kind of paranoid delirium and she talked to him about the robbery. From that point on the good Dr Grimes seems to have forgotten the meaning of professional ethics.'

'A million bucks is all the ethics most people ever need, Reverend. What's Grimes' part in all this?'

'He virtually tortured her until she told him where the money was. You see, the thieves had figured that Callie was the safest person to hold onto the money until they decided to split it between them. She's had it all this time, right under my nose.' Carter took a handkerchief from his pocket and blew his nose.

'Dr Grimes,' prodded Jefferson.

'Yes. She took the money to Grimes tonight. He has it all. She said she was glad to be rid of it. She was free of the drugs and free of the money. She could return to her real life with me.'

Jefferson grunted. 'So where is she?'

'God only knows, Captain. I told her that we had no option but to inform the police. There was no question of my acquiescing in anything illegal. She begged me not to. Afraid of going to jail. I told her that if you handled the problem – you being a devout member of our own congregation and a man who would understand the need for discretion – a scandal could be avoided, perhaps the family name kept out altogether.' Carter smiled ingratiatingly.

Jefferson smiled back. Reverend Carter's views on law and order, as expressed from the pulpit and in such magazine articles as 'Castrating the Gay Menace' started with long jail sentences for homosexuals and cunnilinguists and got steadily more punitive from there. Jefferson was touched by his new faith in criminal rehabilitation.

'Well, anything is possible under God, Reverend.'

'Almost the very words I used,' said Carter. 'She seemed to agree with me. After an unusually intense display of physical affection she fainted. Or, I'm afraid, pretended to. While she recovered I left her alone in her bedroom and came down here to call you. Moments later I saw her car driving away. I couldn't believe it. I broke into her room, praying that I was wrong, but she'd gone. I didn't know what else to do but wait for you.' He raised his hands in a gesture of helplessness.

'Calling me in on this was the right thing to do,' said Jefferson. He used his most reassuring voice. 'Now tell me one last thing. This man, Grimes. Does he call himself Cicero Grimes?'

'That's him. Cicero. One of pagan Rome's most fiendish minds.'

Jefferson ignored the observation. 'Were you expecting visitors tonight?' he said.

'No. I have some paperwork to do. I'd planned an early night. Tomorrow is Sunday and I usually spend most of the day at the church. There is always so much of the Lord's work to be done. You and I are soldiers in the same cause, Captain. If we were to relax our effort for a moment the whole world would be swamped by a scum-tide of criminality and perversion.'

Jefferson frowned. 'Is your presence at the church essential?'

'Not exactly,' said Carter. 'I dare say they could get along without me for a day if I had an important reason for not being there.'

'Good,' said Jefferson. 'It would be as well if you kept the day clear tomorrow. This business is unlikely to be solved tonight. I may need your help and it could take up quite a few hours of your time. I want you to call whoever you need to and tell them that you won't be available for a couple of days. Naturally you won't mention anything that has happened tonight.'

'If you really think it's necessary, Captain.'

'I do. Make the call.'

With a dismissive wave Jefferson sent Carter from the room. Being subconsciously steeped in St Paul's philosophy that slaves should obey their masters, religious personalities, in Jefferson's experience, tended to be particularly pliable in the hands of any authority they perceived as higher than themselves. Carter gave an involuntary half bow as he left.

Jefferson was satisfied that, given a few irrelevant embellishments of his own role in the drama, Carter's account was honest. That Callilou Carter was a gifted liar was equally certain, but the Reverend was too confused to think straight. How much of Callie's story was truth and how much invention was not important in itself. The location of the money was the truth he needed to uncover.

He stripped Carter's account down to the few facts it contained. Callie and a man named Luther were involved in the burglary of the bank. Where they were he did not know. The money, perhaps all of it, was still around. Where it was he did not know. Cicero Grimes was somehow involved. That was all. It wasn't much. But Jefferson savoured deceit with the same sort of pleasure he derived from the smell of his own flatus.

26

The aroma of this affair was rich.

Grimes represented the only concrete lead. Jefferson knew the doctor by sight. He didn't look like a medical man. He didn't have that air of preening self-satisfaction that was the badge of his profession. And his neck and his forearms were too thick. Grimes' face was pugilistic in its outlines but fine in detail. His eyes were the colour of a winter sky in Minnesota: almost grey but really a pale, pale blue. Looking into those eyes Jefferson had sensed a personality not easily swayed by fear or avarice. He had such a feeling rarely enough for him to trust it when he did. That Grimes was involved in robbery didn't ring true.

Grimes lived in an abandoned fire station in the Channel surrounded by crumbling slums that the young professionals hadn't dared move in on yet. He detoxified drug addicts, a group for whom Jefferson had not a shred of pity. Grimes had treated four police officers that Jefferson knew of. The department also called him in from time to time to help deal with hostage situations, in which Grimes had shown a talent for negotiating with crazies. He had a background in forensic psychiatry and unlike most of the corrupt and liberal-minded scum in that profession he went out of his way to establish the legal responsibility of criminals for their actions. He was tough, played by his own rules and didn't appear to give a hoot about money. Why he endangered himself to help hostages Jefferson couldn't know until he knew him better. He was a wise enough student of human nature to know that of all possible reasons people might have for taking such risks, altruism was the least likely. Whether Grimes did it for kicks, in atonement for some inner guilt or in the hope that some day one of the crazies would gun him down, Jefferson didn't know. But it would be interesting to find out.

Jefferson spent most of his time dealing with human vermin, from the likes of the Reverend Carter to the street shit choking every gutter in the state. This was different. He looked forward to dealing with Grimes with some pleasure. First he had a few threads to tie up. He stood up as Cleveland Carter came back into the room.

'I've done as you asked,' said Carter. 'I'm at your disposal for the next thirty-six hours.'

Jefferson smiled at the Reverend's choice of words. 'Earlier, you mentioned a gun,' he said. 'I'd like to see it.'

Carter looked puzzled but said, 'Certainly.' He left the room and returned a moment later with a snub-nosed .32 Colt revolver in nickel plate. Carter handed it to Jefferson who covered his hand with a handkerchief before accepting it.

'Did your wife ever handle this weapon?'

'She may have touched it tonight. I don't remember,' said Carter.

'I'd like to see the room she escaped from. Do you mind showing me?'

Carter shook his head. 'Of course not. Follow me.'

They went upstairs to the first floor. Carter led the way down a corridor and stopped before a door. The door was ajar and there were splinters on the floor where the lock had broken out of the frame. It had been a good strong lock. Carter must have been in an advanced state of mental distress to go through it like that. Jefferson slid the pistol into the pocket of his trousers and pushed the door open with his elbow. The room was medium sized, equipped with a single bed, a dressing-table with a mirror, a walk-in closet, and a chest of drawers. The doors of the closet hung wide and several dresses had fallen from their hangers and onto the floor. The top drawer of the chest was also open and some of its contents scattered. The curtains at the window were drawn back and the window raised high.

'Do you sleep in separate bedrooms?' asked Jefferson.

Carter shuffled inside the doorway. 'Occasionally. Callie suffers from migraines and sometimes prefers to be alone.'

Jefferson walked over to the window and spoke over his shoulder. 'And you have no children.'

'That's correct.'

'I don't blame you,' said Jefferson. 'Why make the world a shittier place than it already is? Myself, I had a vasectomy three months before I got married.'

He smiled at the expression on Carter's face and poked his head through the window and looked down. Nothing to hold on to, but it was an easy enough drop for a young person running for her life. The window was on the opposite side of the house to where Jefferson had left his car. Below the window was a strip of grass and a gravel path. In the poor light he couldn't be sure but thought he could see tears in the turf where her feet had landed. If she'd hung from the sill by her hands before dropping, there would be fingerprints on the paintwork. If her prints weren't on the murder weapon it would give the boys in homicide something to think about. But not enough to make them doubt the rest of the evidence.

Using the handkerchief again Jefferson pulled the window closed and drew the curtains. The curtains were made of velvet.

'I could've saved myself the trouble, you know,' said Jefferson.

Carter gave him a puzzled look.

'The vasectomy I mean,' said Jefferson. 'Eleanor's got that ripe, heavy build that makes anal intercourse irresistible.'

Carter's face writhed.

'She don't like it none,' said Jefferson. 'But then she don't have too much choice, do she?'

Without haste he drew the .32 from his pocket and shot Cleveland Carter once through the centre of the chest.

Carter spun into the wall, smashing his face against the plaster, and fell to the floor where he quietly exsanguinated.

Jefferson dropped the pistol where he stood, drew the curtains and opened the window again. The sound of the shot should not have carried far. A single bang can draw attention, but people rarely recognize the sound.

They wait and listen – for another such sound, or a scream, a crash, a commotion. When they hear nothing else they shrug and go back to watching TV.

Moving lightly on his feet Jefferson stepped around the body, taking care not to tread on any drops of blood. Carter had lost several litres into the shag pile of the carpet and Jefferson did not bother to check for a pulse. He judged, with satisfaction, that the bullet had probably ruptured the aorta where it curved up and away from the heart.

Before he left the room Jefferson put his right hand over his own heart and sang in a coarse voice:

> 'If the good Lord ain't willin'
> To say what we're doin'
> Then the Devil have mercy on me.'

And then he was laughing in an empty house.

CHAPTER THREE

It was midnight on the Mississippi Delta as Eugene Cicero Grimes barrelled down the West Bank Expressway heading for the bridge and home. He did not hear any chimes but the thunder rolling in from a storm far to the south provided a fair substitute. The thermometer was still pushing 92 degrees and the City – as scarred and old and stinking as ever – sprawled gasping in the bend of the river as it sweated out the end of one day and prepared itself for the next.

The heat didn't bother Cicero Grimes. He liked sweating. It was the three-hour drive on bayou country blacktop that had left him feeling tired and pissed off. He should have spent the time lying on damp sheets with a pitcher of julep by the bed: listening to Miles Davis play 'Lonely Fire' while he savoured the sounds that Callie made when she went down on him. But life was compromise. He couldn't expect to organize a murder without making some kind of sacrifice.

The thought was sickeningly glib and the anger flooded his mind. Suddenly he hated himself with a black passion. He was fucking his insides bloody with a blunt instrument of his own making. He knew it but he didn't care. Let it all burn. He wasn't going to live in a cage anymore.

The thought reminded him of his father and the fact that the old man had been expecting him for dinner four hours ago. Grimes didn't want to see him. Not tonight. He didn't want to deal with the old bastard throwing his weight around as Grimes knew he would; as he always did. But the obligation was too ancient and too deep and

31

there was a good chance he'd never see the old man again. Think about it, he thought. As US 90 began its long swing towards the bridge Grimes cursed himself, took the next exit and headed for the Point.

Grimes pulled a cigarette from the pocket of his black suit jacket and tapped the end against the hub of the steering wheel. As he worked his way through the old neighbourhood he occasionally caught a glimpse of electric lights flaking the soft black water. The river was lazy and docile now but it hadn't always been so. That's why they'd built the levees, to hold back the waters of the Big Muddy when she went on the rampage. First with the elbow-grease and blood of the convicts and slaves and dirt-poor scum whose names were lost to history, then later with their machines and spillways and pumping stations, they'd even caged the river itself.

There were times when Grimes would've pulled the levees down and let the river wash them all into the Gulf, but for him the City was the last habitable spot on the continent and so, much as he hated what they represented, he acknowledged that he needed the levees as much as anyone else and was glad that they were there.

Headlights flared behind him and a horn sounded. In his side mirror he saw a bloated face leaning from the window of a truck and heard a loud voice asking why didn't he take his hand off his dick, buddy, and get out the fuckin' way? Grimes looked at the traffic lights in front of him: red had turned to green. He did not move. The voice shouted again. 'Hey, fuck-face, I'm talking to you.'

The insult was routine enough. There was no need to take it personally. But at that moment he couldn't help it. He threw his cigarette through the window, grabbed the door handle and burst from his car. The smell of exhaust fumes and hot asphalt smothered his face. Scarlet heat dripped from his brow. Random noise and the glare of headlights needled his senses. He walked towards the truck with his arms swinging loose and heavy. Moist air clung to his fists. He felt his chest swell with adrenalin.

The truck driver jumped to the pavement from his cab, carrying a tyre iron in each hand. Go for it, you redneck bastard. Please. As Grimes got closer his mind's eye saw them both frozen where they stood, carved in stone with their fists raised. He could have ruptured the truck driver's liver, or maybe broken his legs and draped him over the hood of his truck to wait for an ambulance. Instead, when the truck driver lunged at him, Grimes caught the swinging fist and applied a wrist lock and arm bar. A stream of obscene suggestions poured from the trucker's mouth and the tyre irons fell to the pavement.

For a moment white light bleached Grimes' mind and he tasted the satisfaction – no, the pleasure – it would give him to finish the move and break the elbow in two. Then the whiteness cleared and the bad moment was gone. He eased up on the driver's arm and marched him back into his truck. The driver sat rubbing his wrist and looking down at Grimes in bewilderment.

'Sorry, friend,' said Grimes. He tried to sound sincere but only felt stupid. 'I guess anyone can act like an asshole in this heat.'

'Shit, buddy.' The driver grinned nervously. His accent was as thick as corn pone. 'My wife tells me I act like an asshole all the time.'

Another horn blared, this time from behind the truck. The driver jerked a thumb over his shoulder.

'Listen to those cocksuckers,' he said. 'You'd think they all had something important to do.' He put the engine into gear and said, 'Listen fella, the heat y'all got inside your head ain't got nothing to do with the weather. I don't know who's meant to catch it but next time try and make sure it's the right guy.'

Truck drivers.

Grimes said, 'I've got some things on my mind.'

The trucker nodded. 'It shows, man. Stay cool, now, y'hear?'

'I'll try.'

Grimes raised a hand and got back behind the wheel of

his car. The light had gone through several cycles and was green again. He drove straight on, his hands shaking as he dealt with the aftermath of the adrenalin surge. He shook his head at himself and turned into his father's street.

George Grimes lived in a shotgun house – one room stacked behind the other like compartments in a train – in the old Ward 15 district. A long time back the royal turds who'd run the colony for King Carlos had kept their slave pens here on the Point. Later it became a decent residential neighbourhood then slowly decayed until, by the 1930s, moving up north to find better things had seemed like a good idea to an unemployed youngster like George Grimes. Now the young professionals were moving in and spending their dollars on renovating the nineteenth-century houses. Some of the houses, over on the Point itself at a safe distance from the drab ghetto around it, were very fine; but George Grimes' house was the kind you'd expect an old ex-convict who refused any help from his sons to be able to afford: the same kind he grew up in – draughty in winter, stifling in summer and cramped all year round.

By the time Grimes stopped outside his hands were steady again. He hoped that the fight with the trucker had helped cool the venom simmering in his blood; but if anyone could turn up the heat again it was his father. Grimes didn't seem able to share a cold beer with him on a sunny Sunday afternoon without at some point wanting to cut his own tongue out. Promising himself to avoid conflict he locked the car and went to ring the doorbell.

There was a noise inside and then his father opened the door. George Grimes was sixty-nine years old, and with his full head of iron-grey hair, his broad, stubborn shoulders and the military bearing of the class '46, he remained a fine figure of a man. As usual, the white shirt he wore, frayed cuffs and collar and all, was clean and freshly pressed and the creases in his pants were like knives. Grimes remembered going to a union meeting with his father when he was a boy and hearing someone say that George Grimes had the warmest smile and the coldest eyes they'd ever seen. He didn't smile so much anymore and he wasn't smiling now, but the steel-trap gaze was still icy and Grimes felt himself shifting uncomfortably on the stoop.

'You're late,' said his father. The softness of his voice heightened the accusation and he turned his back and walked into the parlour without waiting for an answer. Grimes followed, trying to hold on to his promise.

'I'm sorry, Dad.' He tried to make the apology sincere without showing weakness. 'I got caught up in something important, something that couldn't wait. I forgot about supper. No excuses. That's just what happened.'

George Grimes replied with a deliberately ambiguous grunt. Grimes held his tongue and looked about the room. The parlour was sparse and tidy with the neatness of a man who'd lived alone for many years and decided early on that neatness was important. It was furnished with a sideboard, a couple of easy chairs, a shelf of books by Melville and Jack London and C. Wright Mills, and a black and white TV set. Against one wall was a pine table with the flaps opened out to make it big enough to serve dinner on. There was a checked cloth on the table with two places set and a dish of fried chicken congealing in the middle. In a number of other dishes were cob corn, sweet potatoes, butter squash, all carefully served, all cold and dappled with sweat. None of it had been touched.

A bad feeling took hold of Grimes' stomach. He'd been here before: him in the wrong, guilty as hell; his father raising a flag on the moral high-ground like John Wayne at Iwo Jima. Try, at least, he told himself.

'You should've eaten without me.'

His father picked up a glass of bourbon standing by a bottle of Wild Turkey on the sideboard and sat down more heavily than he needed to in an armchair.

'No need to,' he said. 'My appetite just kind of upped and left on me.'

Grimes didn't feel like eating but he took a chicken leg from the dish and bit into it. It was cooked with a lot of butter and black pepper and tasted good.

'This is great,' said Grimes.

His father shook his head. 'I can't eat it cold. Upsets my digestion, especially at this hour. I'd never get to sleep. But you can help yourself.' He loosened up a little. 'Fix yourself a drink too.'

As Grimes finished the chicken and wiped his fingers on a paper towel his father said, 'So what did you have to do tonight that was so damned important you couldn't find time to call me?'

Grimes kept his voice neutral. 'I had to take a trip out of the city at short notice. A favour for a friend.'

'Oh. Where to?'

'A couple of hours west down US 90.' Grimes couldn't see any harm in telling him that much but the information made his father stiffen in his chair.

'That's Cajun country.'

'I guess so. Can't say I ran into any.'

Grimes poured a large measure of Wild Turkey into a glass and swallowed a mouthful. Without ice it didn't go down so easy and he shuddered and said 'Christ.' His father was pinning him down with his eyes.

'Look, it's just a deal, Dad. No offence but it doesn't concern you.'

'You have to lie all the time to be good at it. You don't. You've found Luther.'

Grimes drank more bourbon, hoping it would loosen the knots pulling on his guts. 'I don't want to talk about it.'

'Don't, son. Let the dead bury the dead. Leave it alone.'

They were both trying, Grimes knew, but the rogue chemicals were already getting away from them, the knots getting tighter. Grimes breathed deeply and said, 'I don't know where Luther is. If he's living in the Cajun country it's a coincidence.'

Almost a coincidence. It was true he didn't know where

Luther lived but it didn't surprise him that the decaying farmhouse Luther had chosen for the split should be in the same part of the state. George Grimes wasn't convinced.

'You're lying.'

'I don't lie to you. I may not tell you everything that's on my mind but I don't lie.'

'It's written all over your face.'

'Don't start pushing, Dad. You'll lose. This isn't your business.'

George Grimes stood up from the chair and pushed. He didn't know how not to.

'Not my business? Jesus Christ, boy, you're my family. Leave it be. I know you. I know Luther. I trod the same bloody turf as he did. Get within twenty feet of him and you'll die . . .'

'Dad . . .' But he couldn't stop him. It was the same old contest, will against will, rage against rage.

'Two wrongs don't make a right, goddamn it, I should know . . .'

The last of Grimes' control ran through his hands like water.

'Listen!' He blasted through his father's aged cliches. 'You don't know jackshit about wrongs or rights or me or Luther or any goddamn thing else. It's just the same as it's always been – you treading on my face, telling me what to do and how to do it, never listening to what I say, what I need. The last time I asked you for something I was seven years old. Some cocksucker from the neighbourhood had bloodied my nose. I was crying. I was scared. I was ashamed. All you said to me was "Why didn't you hit him back?" That's all. "Why didn't you hit him back, you little yellow bastard?"'

'Jesus, what?' His father reeled from the accusation and the feeling behind it, trying to recall the incident and failing. 'I never called you a yellow . . .'

'That's what it felt like. You never wanted to know what mattered to me. You still don't. Well now you're on your own, old man, and better off that way. So leave me a-fucking-lone.'

Grimes raised the glass to smash it, caught himself, set it down on the table instead. He felt blinded, could hardly breathe. The urge to destroy something was paralysing. His mind spun as he struggled to cope with the destructive impulses in his limbs. The only peaceful option he could find was to leave, now, and deal with it later alone. He made for the door.

'I love you, son.'

Jesus. Grimes stopped at the door and rested his forehead against the wood. He'd never heard him say it before.

'I love you both.'

For some reason Grimes thought of the frayed white shirt collar and the trouble taken to iron it, and intense sadness constricted his chest.

Behind him his father said, 'I just didn't want you to turn out like me.'

Grimes raised his head and pulled the door open. Without looking around, fighting for his voice, he said, 'I love you too, Dad.'

Grimes realized that he'd never said it before either. Then he walked out and slammed the door behind him and stumbled back towards his car.

CHAPTER FOUR

The air in Sweetbread's Bar was dense with smoke and the smell of male bodies exuding alcohol and sweat. A fair crowd had escaped the suffocating humidity of the street to drink Dixie beer and listen to Sweetbread's B.B. King tapes, and their heads bobbed in dim brown alcoves and across small marble-topped tables. Behind a wooden partition at the back of the room a nickel-ante poker game had been in progress since noon.

As Jefferson walked in he recognized a live recording of 'Sweet Sixteen'. Despite the rattle of drunken conversation and the poker players' litany of check and raise, King's vocal histrionics were unmistakable and Jefferson experienced a twinge of nostalgia, an emotion to which he was not accustomed. It vanished as he spotted Joe Gags sitting on a stool at the bar.

Joe was wearing a National Rifle Association baseball cap and staring at his drink with a sour expression. Good boy. Jefferson had called him twenty minutes earlier from headquarters where he'd spent an hour trawling the computer for information on Cicero Grimes.

As Jefferson shouldered his way through the crowd he felt the attention of many eyes upon him, suspicious and unwelcoming. At the far end of the bar Sweetbread detached himself from a customer and moved towards Jefferson as if on wheels. His black face was smooth: experience had left no dents in it. The dents were on the inside where no one could see them, not even Jefferson. If Sweetbread was anxious to see Jefferson at the bar –

and he had to be, for he was not an asshole – he wasn't letting anyone know it.

The seat beside Gags was occupied by a slim thirty-year-old in a lime green silk shirt and a grey fedora. Neither the shirt nor the hat suited him. Jefferson stood beside the slim man and stared at his face without blinking from a distance of six inches. After eleven seconds the man picked up his drink and vacated his seat. Eleven seconds. A genuine tough-guy. Jefferson settled onto the stool, ignoring Sweetbread, and smiled at Gags.

'Joe Gags,' he said. 'The Man with the Golden Arm. Let me get you a drink.'

Gags looked up from his bourbon. He seemed unhappy. Unhappiness came kind of easily to most people when Jefferson insisted on them meeting him at short notice. Gags emptied his glass and pushed it towards Sweetbread. 'Same again,' he said.

Jefferson kept his eyes on Gags as he said to the bartender, 'Give me a beer. And don't serve me any of that Dixie shit, boy. Dos Equis will do.'

Sweetbread's face remained impassive as he served the drinks. He was about to pour the beer when Jefferson snapped his fingers twice and pointed at the glass.

'I'll take it straight from the bottle. Oh, and boy, do me a favour. Turn down that monkey music.'

When the drinks were in front of them Sweetbread stood waiting for a moment. Jefferson spoke to a point six inches to the side of Sweetbread's head. 'You want something?'

'No, sir.'

Jefferson knew Sweetbread would have enjoyed working him over with the lead-weighted billy he kept under the bar, but he'd also be happy to know that this business didn't concern him. Jefferson turned back to Gags, and Sweetbread shifted away to watch them from a distance.

'Why the hell are we meeting in a shine joint?' said Gags.

'I heard they were having a special on pork chop sandwiches.'

'Shit.' Gags did not smile. 'You play poker, Captain?'

'No,' said Jefferson. 'Not my kind of game. I'd have to learn how to lose gracefully.'

'I'd play every day if I could. I love it,' said Gags. 'I ain't good enough to make a living from the game but I still love it, you know? Saturday night is poker night unless I'm on duty. Tonight I'm not. I'm on my third beer when I find myself sitting in a nice pot, over a hundred bucks, at seven card Hi-Lo with a fucking Garcia on the first five cards. A pat six-four low. The fucking phone rings. A certain party needs to see me. No it can't wait. Be at Sweetbread's in fifteen minutes. Jesus. I go back to the hand. It's declaration time. I've got the cinch low and you know what? I'm so fucking preoccupied by what the party on the phone might be after that I fuck up. By mistake I declare high instead of low and lose the whole fucking bundle. The guys were still laughing when I left.'

'That's only the second saddest story I've heard this evening,' said Jefferson. 'The saddest would really make you bust a gut. All I need from you, Joe, is a little harmless information. You can be back at your game in an hour with an extra hundred bucks to play with.'

'It wasn't so much the money that hurt as the situation. You have to play to appreciate just how much of an asshole a mistake like that makes you feel. What do you want to know?'

'Talk to me about Cicero Grimes.'

'So that's why you pulled me down to this shit-hole.'

Sweetbread's stood just across the street from Grimes' apartment.

Gags looked at Jefferson for a moment, then at his own fingernails, and then shook his head. 'I can't do it. Grimes is a friend. He saved my life.'

'He saved your life for money, Sergeant. It was his job. I had an inflamed appendix taken out when I was in the airforce. That don't mean I owe some fucking debt of honour to the surgeon, whoever he was.'

'That's not the same,' said Gags. 'No one else could have helped me. And anyhow, like I said, he's a friend. Just hearing you ask about him makes me want to call him and tell him to leave town. You may not rate me very high, Mr Jefferson, and I know I ain't clean, but I sure as hell ain't going to sell his ass for no hundred bucks.' With difficulty he looked into Jefferson's eyes. 'Not for ten thousand.'

Jefferson laughed in his face. 'How Mama Gags must be rejoicing up there in Heaven, knowing that her little Joey's found religion at last. Goddamn, boy, you make me feel humble. We've never had a close relationship, you and I, and I dare say you'd sell me out sooner than you would your special buddy, Grimes, but we've been useful to each other in the past. I'd hate to have to spoil that sense of mutual respect and co-operation. Some unpleasant things might come out. You might find yourself isolated. You still keep that cute picture of the wife and kids on your desk?'

'You scum-sucking pig,' said Joe Gags.

'Be warned, son. Don't make me blitz you.'

Jefferson tipped the bottle of Dos Equis to his lips and swallowed twice.

'Grimes may not be in any trouble. If he is, what I want from you won't make things any worse for him. I just want some background. You don't want to help, okay. I'll just make a couple more calls and my problem is solved. But before you leave just ask yourself how eager you are for a change in life style.'

'Jesus, why all the heavy breathing? Grimes has never broken the law as far as I know. Not seriously anyhow. If he isn't at home I don't know where you'll find him. What the fuck else you wanna know?'

Jefferson relaxed. For a moment he'd been worried that Gags was going to be difficult. 'Like I said, I just want some background, a few facts that will give me the flavour of the man. I want some idea of who I'm dealing with. I want to know what makes him tick.'

'Well for a start don't let that MD shit fool you. He's got enough hairs up his ass to weave a whole Indian blanket. I've trained him in karate for seven years and he's tough and he can take pain. That's important to him, being tough. He needs to prove to himself over and over that he's got guts.' Gags shrugged. 'I always get the feeling that he's never quite convinced.'

'Has he convinced you?' said Jefferson.

'You remember that siege over in Iberville, in the project? Year before last.'

Jefferson nodded. He had thought about it earlier when Grimes' name had first come up. A crack junkie had barricaded himself in a roach hole apartment with his sister, her three kids, an automatic shotgun and two gallons of gas. He'd poured the gas over his relatives and threatened to cremate them and then gone on to shoot and wound the two patrolmen who'd been first on the scene to investigate. The SWAT team had sat staring through their scopes for three hours without seeing so much as the tip of his dick. The captain in command wouldn't authorize gas or stun grenades because of the gasoline. Instead he'd called Cicero Grimes and asked him if he would go in. Grimes had done so, unarmed. Thirty minutes later the junkie had walked out crying on Grimes' shoulder. There were a lot of people in the department who shared Gags' respect for Grimes. Jefferson found the thought obscurely irritating.

'So he's got a certain kind of balls,' said Jefferson. 'I want to know what kind he doesn't have.'

'He's no hard-ass, if that's what you're getting at, even though he'd like to think he is.'

'Why's that?' said Jefferson.

''Cause he's scared of hurting people. There's all kinds of violent shit bottled up inside him but he's frightened of it. A few times in sparring sessions I've seen him on the verge of letting it out but he stiffens up, you know? Like he's just seen something that scared him. A man can't be a real hard-ass if he's scared of causing pain.'

'You're not telling me as much as you could do, Joe. So he got a temper that he's scared of letting rip, and he needs to prove he isn't yellow. So what? Why make that the first thing you say about him?'

'Fuck, Captain, I ain't no analyst. How would I know what makes him tick?'

'You're beginning to get on my nerves, Joe. That's unwise. I want it all laid bare. Anything he might feel bad about, anything that would make him want to make amends. I smell guilt all over this guy. Maybe he hasn't broken man's law but somewhere in his life he's broken God's.'

'When he was bringing me down from heroin we spent a lot of time together.'

Gags fidgeted on his chair and tried not to look at himself in the mirror behind the bar.

'We talked a whole lot but that was personal stuff. What I've told you so far, that's from my own observations. What he told me himself is private, confidential. I can't betray that.'

Jefferson pushed himself away from the bar. 'You're dead, buddy boy. Get yourself buried.'

He was halfway to the door when Gags stopped him with a hand on his shoulder.

'You're breaking my balls,' said Gags. 'Okay, so I got some things that maybe you can use. But I got to know what's involved.'

Jefferson gave him a smile that was eighty per cent sneer. 'My right hand hasn't seen my left in twenty years. I thought we were playing at grown-ups now. You can't make conditions with me. You fucked up once before, remember?' Softly he added,

> 'There was a little man,
> and he had a little gun,

44

and his bullets were made of
lead, lead, lead.'

'You ever think about that lady, Joe? Her sitting in her wheelchair in the sun wondering what her little girl would look like today if only she were still alive?'

'Fucking hell,' said Gags.

'Yeah. I pulled you out of the drowning pool. I'd hate to have to throw you back in. Don't be a two-time loser, Joe. The consequences could be severe.'

Gags' face was the picture that was worth a thousand words, contorted by the struggle between conscience and self-interest. Jefferson had witnessed the spectacle countless times. It never ceased to entertain him.

Offhand he couldn't remember a single occasion when conscience had won.

As they walked back towards the bar a while later, Gags with a weary tread, Jefferson threw one arm across the man's shoulders and patted him gently on the back.

'Don't take it too hard, Joe,' said Jefferson. 'None of us is the man he'd like to think he is.'

Jefferson signalled Sweetbread for two more drinks, looked at Joe Gags and smiled.

Maggie Crane sat next to Jefferson in the front of his car. He'd squeezed her name and address from Joe Gags. Like Joe, she was less than delighted to see him. Jefferson took a handkerchief from his pocket and handed it to her. To his mind it was a pretty gallant gesture but she didn't even thank him. Instead, through the tears rolling down her face, she called him a dirty name. He'd heard the name before and it didn't bother him.

Maggie cringed down in the passenger seat as he raised his hand.

'Big tough guy,' she said.

There was a painful swelling on the inside of her left arm where he had pinched her with his thumb and forefinger.

'You said we were going to headquarters.'

'I lied,' said Jefferson.

'I want to go there,' she said. 'Even you wouldn't beat up on me in HQ.'

Jefferson smiled. The naivety of the general public was a constant source of pleasure to him.

'I've got rights. I want a lawyer.'

'You people spend too much time watching Hill Street Blues.' Jefferson shook his head. 'Listen, Maggie – you don't mind if I call you Maggie, do you? – there's no need for this. I have no interest in you personally at all. On a scale of one to ten, a stinking ex-hippie nobody like you is a minus three. But if you cause me a problem, a witness and I are going to find enough smack in your apartment to nail your pretty little ass for dealing. Then tomorrow a couple of my men will find some more stashed in that record store you run.'

He snapped his fingers.

'Your pathetic little world comes apart as easily as that. I don't believe Grimes can mean that much to you.'

'He's a nice guy.'

'Nice? What the fuck is "nice"?' He put just enough psycho into his voice to make her cringe again.

'Christ, I don't know, he's just, well, good to be with when he's in the mood. He doesn't care about things you're supposed to care about, like killing yourself to get ahead or eating in fancy restaurants. He doesn't put on a front.'

'Everybody puts on a front. How did you meet him?'

'I had a problem one time, a couple of years ago. He helped me out, we got to know each other.'

'So the good doctor likes to fuck his junkie patients. That's "nice".'

'I wasn't a patient. It was my brother who was hooked. In the end Grimes couldn't help him. Danny killed himself. It was a bad time.'

'And Grimes did a powerful job of consoling.'

'Look at it any way you like,' said Maggie. 'You can

46

make it into something dirty if you want. It wasn't dirty
to me.'

'I bet it wasn't, honey. What do you know about his
past?'

'He trained to be a surgeon at one time, in Chicago.
Chicago's where he grew up. He got fired for calling his
boss a crook. His boss was doing a lot of operations that
Grimes thought were unnecessary. After that he spent
some time in Nicaragua helping the Sandinistas wounded
in the fighting, the children and the refugees, you know?'

Maggie sounded impressed. To Jefferson it smelled like
a stack of pious bullshit.

'Why would an intelligent American care what happened to a bunch of stinking peons?'

'I wouldn't expect someone like you to understand it.
It's got something to do with ideals.'

It was a thought. She bought the idealist line too, the
same as Gags. Maybe they were right: it could just be that
the doctor was that dumb. But Jefferson doubted it.

'What did he tell you about his family?'

'His father lives over on the Point. Grimes sees him
every month, I guess. Once, when he was drunk, he told
me he had a brother, then he turned strange and never
talked about him again.'

'Did he tell you his brother's name?' said Jefferson.

'No. I think he was sorry he'd mentioned him. Grimes
gets kind of morbid sometimes. Locks himself in that
firehouse for a week and blasts himself on speed and Wild
Turkey and won't answer the phone. I don't know why.
He never let me get that close. Or anybody else as far as
I can tell. One time, when I used to have a key to the
place, I found him kneeling alone and naked in his
bedroom, drinking from the bottle and talking as if
someone else were there. Violent, obscene talk like he
wanted to hurt whoever it was he was speaking to. It was
scary. But the weird thing was the walls of the room. They
were covered with shit. Real shit, I mean, smeared all over
the room. He was clean but the shit was everywhere. It

still makes me shiver when I think about it. I never told him what I'd seen and he never mentioned it. Next day he was fine again and the place was all cleared up.'

Jefferson tapped his teeth with a fingernail. He didn't think about what Maggie was saying to him. He didn't analyse. He just absorbed the images into his mind and trusted them to work on his instincts.

He didn't get anything more from Maggie than he'd got from Gags on Grimes' career. When he came back from Nicaragua Grimes settled in the City and completed a residency programme in general psychiatry at Tulane, then a fellowship in forensic psychiatry. Again the fascination with criminality and violence. When the fellowship ended Grimes resigned from the faculty and isolated himself in his firehouse in the Channel, doing his eccentric addiction work and occasionally turning out for the department. And now somehow he was involved in this Carter affair. Jefferson's interest hadn't been so aroused in a long time. He had one last question for Maggie.

The Eldorado was parked two blocks from Sweetbread's. Through the windshield Jefferson saw Artie Mann come trotting down the street towards them. Jefferson wound down the window and Artie pushed his scrawny face in, panting lightly. His breath smelled of tobacco and Mexican junk food.

'He's here, Cap.'

'Don't call me "Cap", Artie. Is he alone?'

'Yessir.'

'I'll be along in two minutes. You get back there now.'

Artie trotted off again. Jefferson took a twenty from his pocket and pushed it into the waistband of Maggie's jeans. She looked at him with loathing.

'For a cab back home,' he said.

This was a lie. Money, pure and simple, was the best method he knew of soiling a person. He'd made sure Joe had taken the hundred, too. He leaned across in front of Maggie and opened the door. As Maggie started to climb out Jefferson pushed her back into the seat and held her down with one hand on her belly.

'One last question,' he said. 'And don't be afraid to be frank.'

He extended the middle finger of his hand between her thighs and pressed it against her vulva. She stiffened her body but had more sense than to fight. Jefferson grinned and waggled the finger up and down.

'How does Dr Grimes like to have himself a time?'

CHAPTER FIVE

The neighbourhood stank of burnt rubber and rotting garbage, and Grimes' regular parking spot was blocked by the smoking shell of a Volkswagen microbus. Torched by kids, he guessed. Maybe the owner had paid them a few dollars so he could collect on his insurance. Maybe they did it because they liked to see things burn. Either way Grimes didn't blame them. They hadn't chosen to be here; he had.

He left his car halfway down the next block and stretched his legs. The sounds of a night too hot to permit much sleep drifted through the haze. Distant sirens and drunken shouts, domestic anger and breaking glass, TV gunfire and a blues guitar. Voices dying with a dying fall, he thought; and children squabbling in overcrowded beds; and the sighs of lonely women in cheap summer cotton leaning from their windows and dreaming of home.

The walk took him past boarded and broken windows, past walls built from crumbling brick injected with filth and despair, past overflowing bags of trash heaped by the street-lamps, past dog turds sweating in the heat of the night. Overfed rats squatted in the yellow light and stared at him without blinking. A garbage man had been stomped to death for fifteen dollars and change and a digital watch he'd got by saving gas coupons, and his colleagues were on strike. The bureaucrats in Public Health would complain, the garbage men would insist on protection, and the police would shrug. No one who could do anything about it really gave a shit about the garbage. As long as the assorted ethnic underdogs who lived in the neighbourhood – the blacks and Vietnamese and Cubans and Central Americans – remained docile and provided bodies to service the District, the system stayed happy and nothing changed.

The City was a crazy-woman's quilt of brilliance and squalor, joy and sadness, regeneration and decay. Unlike the younger, blow-hard towns squealing for attention on the East and West Coasts, or the dour, tight-lipped bully squatting on the shores of Lake Michigan, the City had been around for too long and seen too much to feel the need of putting on any particular front. It was a mixed bag of the whole damn world, shaken together and emptied out onto a tongue of land at the edge of the continent where, with luck, the rest of the country wouldn't take too much notice.

The Channel was a tough neighbourhood. It wasn't a no-go zone like Iberville and some of the other Federal Projects, but it was tough. Yet no one had bothered Grimes on the street for years. It was partly the close-cropped hair, the jutting bones in his face and the heavy arms that swung wide of the side of his body and made him look like a retired boxer. Or so he sometimes fancied. But it was also because he was known as a medical man who would check out a bad belly-ache in a kid without sending a bill, or talk someone's husband out of cutting his own throat, or hers, or stick a few sutures in a flesh wound without informing the cops. And so even though he didn't belong there the neighbourhood recognized him in its laconic way, and made him feel a little bit less alone.

During the drive from his father's house, over the bridge into the City proper, he'd tried again, hard, to understand the nature of the fury that lingered like an ague in his bones. Sometimes he just couldn't get the balance right, couldn't even out the yin and yang. The years he'd spent in pyschiatry had given him insights, had supplied the stunted dwarf on the blind giant's shoulder with another set of lenses, but in the end they were just

51

clever words that only brought an illusion of comfort at moments of calm. When the giant started raging it was all the dwarf could do to hang on for his life.

In his progress from butcher to shrink Grimes had dealt with the armless, the legless, the gut-shot and insane with a coolness under fire that had impressed even himself. He was good at what he did and people admired him. But to himself it often seemed a grotesque lie. When he stepped outside the protection of the role, when he got close to those that mattered, he couldn't always control the promptings of his own inner nature. Thinking about the problem, talking about it, got him nowhere. He knew where to find the white whale, he thought, but where was the harpoon you could ram into your own head?

Until Callie had broken into his life in the middle of the night with a mouthful of obscenities and nipples he would've killed for he'd just started to believe that he was, after all, capable of some sort of tenuous relationship with the world at large. He'd even started to quit thinking about Luther and the past. Then he'd let himself fall in love. He knew that to do so invoked the wrath of vicious gods but he'd done it anyway and now here he was, tearing bloody pieces from his own heart and savaging his father who deserved something better. The thought completed the circle and once again the blackness rose in his gullet.

The firehouse reminded him of his failure to adjust. It had been built on the street corner in the 1890s and abandoned in the seventies when the service had been modernized. Grimes had bought a cheap lease with big ideas for rebuilding the interior: putting in a sprung wooden floor for a gym, an apartment for himself above that, living quarters on the top floor for clients – all that good shit – but somehow he'd never managed to get it together. Time, energy, motivation. On the old concrete downstairs he had some weights, a bench and some squat racks, and a heavy bag hanging from a girder. Most days he did ten three-minute rounds on the bag but lately it

52

hadn't made him feel any better. Upstairs on the first floor he had two bedrooms, a living room, kitchen and a big bathroom with a massage table next door. But the top floor remained full of trash and the basement full of rats. He'd been there four years and one day he'd get it all fixed up. But not today.

On the outer wall of the firehouse, above the folding glass doors that used to give access to the engines, a local philosopher had sprayed the words 'EAT. FUCK. KILL.' in red paint. The paint had faded in the sun. As Grimes crossed the street he noticed a man standing under a lamp-post outside the firehouse. The man was staring up at the slogan and moving his lips without speaking.

The man was white and thin. He was in his mid twenties and would be ugly all his life. Grimes had never seen him before. He had the look of someone who'd spent a lot of time degrading himself to survive and wore a baggy T-shirt with 'FUCK IRAN' printed on the front in fading block capitals. Without turning his head he watched Grimes approaching from the corner of his eye and took a cigarette from his pocket without removing the pack. He probably spoke with his hand over his mouth and ate his dessert before his meal too. A shitbird. On prison visits to assess psychotics Grimes had seen dozens like him. The letters on his shirt could as easily have read 'EXCON'. The shitbird pretended to notice Grimes as he walked past, and smiled. His teeth were brown. He had a narrow face and thin blond hair; his eyes were milky and intensely stupid.

'Where y'at, brother? Hey, listen, you got a match?'

He spoke in a swaggering downtown-ese that shoved a toothpick up Grimes' nose. He realized it was unnecessary, but the Wild Turkey had increased the isolation and savagery of his soul, and with one hand he grabbed the shitbird by the face and shoved him hard against the lamp-post. The cigarette crumpled into the shitbird's lips and the back of his head hit the metal column with a hard dull clunk.

'Listen, sackashit, you don't have any brothers in this neighbourhood,' said Grimes. 'So go fuck yourself.'

The petty spitefulness of the insults gave Grimes a certain peevish amusement. It was the sound of the words he enjoyed more than any intention behind them and he continued with gusto.

'If you're still standing here in five minutes' time I'll punch holes in your head big enough for rats to nest in. And you know why?'

With difficulty the shitbird shook his head.

'Just because I can do it.'

Grimes let go and the broken cigarette fell to the ground. The shitbird raised his hands, palms outwards and backed away. Damp tobacco clung to his lips.

'Jesus, Doc, no offence meant . . .'

Grimes turned his back on him, suddenly nauseated by the game. He opened the door to the firehouse and climbed the stairs to a second door that was sheathed in sheet metal. He opened the lock with two keys, stepped inside and slammed the door shut harder than he needed to. He walked through into the living-room, snapping on the lights.

As usual it was shit city. The furniture was old and soft and second-hand. The lighting was muted and provided by lamps with fabric shades. Scattered on the floor by the sofa were some of Callie's clothes and a dirty shirt of his own. The smell of sex clung to them. Or maybe that was his imagination; it was days since she'd left and seemed like months. He took a bottle of Carta Blanca from the icebox and sat down on the sofa to drink it. The coffee table by the sofa was a jumble of cups, beer bottles and boxes of half-eaten pizza. From where he sat he cleared a corner of the table by shoving things aside with his foot and rested his heels in the space. He took a swallow of beer and tried to feel a little less jaded before he attempted to go to bed. He shook a Pall Mall from a red pack on the table and lit it. A decent night's sleep would wind him down.

On the floor six feet away the telephone rang. He grabbed the cord and pulled the phone towards him. He picked up the receiver without altering his posture.

'It's me,' said Grimes.

'Jesus Christ, Grimes where've you been? I've been trying to reach you all night, you bastard.'

Callie sounded close to tears. He had never known her cry, even when she'd thought the mob wanted to trim her toes with bolt cutters.

'I've been checking out the farmhouse like you told me to, remember? What's the matter?'

There was a long pause and, reluctantly, Grimes began to feel bad again. He could feel her teeth grinding at the other end of the line.

'Cleve knows everything,' she said, 'that's what's the matter. When I got back from calling you this evening he went completely apeshit. Said he was going to shoot me. If you'd seen his eyes you would have believed him too. I'm still not a hundred per cent, Grimes. I'm still jumpy from the drugs. Jesus, I didn't have to be paranoid. Cleve looked like he was having one of his fucking visions. I had to tell him about the money.'

Grimes bit the first joint of his thumb. The shitbird.

'God, I don't even have a cigarette left,' said Callie. 'If there was a line of coke here not even you could keep me away from it.'

Grimes inhaled his own cigarette more quietly, feeling as intensely stupid as the scrawny scumbag outside. The shitbird had called him 'Doc'. The shitbird was supposed to be a complete stranger.

Grimes said, 'Listen, Callie, there's something I have to check out right now. Can you hold for a minute?'

'Be quick.'

He went over to the window and scanned the street. The shitbird was nowhere in sight. It didn't make Grimes feel any safer. He returned to the phone and said, 'Are you hurt?'

'No, I'm okay.'

'Are you alone? Can you talk?' he said.

'There's no one else here.'

'Okay, take your time,' he said. 'Tell me about it.'

'Cleve's been acting weird ever since I got home,' said Callie. 'When Luther phoned tonight Cleve's lips went kind of white and I could see he was struggling not to pop, you know, but he couldn't stop me leaving. After I'd spoken to Luther and then you I didn't want to go back home but there was stuff there I needed if we're going to go away.'

'Sure. What happened when you got back?'

'Cleve was sitting in the kitchen in his underwear. "I want a name," he says and shoves a gun in my face. Lots of crazy Bible talk. All I could think about is how a thousand assholes a year shoot their wives for cheating on them and don't feel bad about it till afterwards. By now he's got that far away look in his eyes, the one he gets in church, and he's calling on Jesus to turn the bullet aside if he's making a mistake. When I realized he thought he could shoot me and still get into Heaven, I knew I was dead. What else could I do?'

Grimes sighed. For a moment he tried to imagine how a born-again fruitcake like Cleveland Carter could become such a big wheel in the Business District. Then he recalled successive occupants of the White House since Nixon went back to California and it wasn't so hard. What else could she have done? He asked her.

'What did you do?'

'I knew that if I could convince him there was no sex involved I had a chance. I gave him a tale about Luther blackmailing me into giving him the bank's alarm system.'

'Blackmail?'

'To keep my cocaine habit and Cleve's church off the front pages. You should have seen his face when he realized that the robbery he'd been huffing and puffing about for six months was my fault. I made him believe I'd wanted to tell him a thousand times but was just too scared of what would happen.'

'What else?' said Grimes. 'Does he know you have the money?'

'No.'

'Does he know that I'm involved, know my name I mean?' said Grimes.

'I'm sorry, Grimes . . .'

'Fucking hell, Callie.'

He was angry and frightened. It wasn't just him and Callie and Luther any more. He felt the whole city close in around him.

'Fucking hell is right,' said Callie. 'Look, I had to make him think that he had it all. No. That makes it sound as if I thought about what I was saying. I didn't. The cocksucker hit me. I was so terrified I let him try to fuck me and he actually managed to do it. That's how far off his head he was.'

'Jesus.'

'You think I was thinking about you? I just wanted to stay alive. After that he suddenly came over as sweet as honey, told me as long as I hadn't been unfaithful he could forgive me. Then, sweeter still, he asks me do I know where the cash is and it's on his face as plain as day that he's got ideas about getting a piece of it for himself.'

She paused. Grimes found the pause obscurely threatening. 'What did you say?'

'I was scared, confused. He still had that gun in my face and that giant prick of his hanging over me, drooling for more. I told him you had it.'

There was another pause while she waited for him to react. Grimes wondered why he wasn't already dead or in jail. At that moment both alternatives had their attractions.

'It gets worse,' said Callie.

'Just keep going,' he said.

'He got mean again after that. Said the only thing to do was to bring in the law. By then he knew how close he'd been to murder and wanted the whole thing taken out of his hands. I begged him not to. Think of the bank, I told him, think of the church, the scandal. So he thought about it. Then he said, "Mrs Jefferson's husband is a policeman." She runs Cleve's church choir. "Captain Jefferson is an intelligent man," he said, "and a Christian. He'll understand the need to be discreet." Grimes, I tried like hell but he wasn't going to change his mind. I can read him like a prayer-book. He was feeling guilty about giving in to the temptation to keep the cash so suddenly he's Mister Law-and-Order again. Jesus what a hypocrite.'

Grimes had stopped listening. His face felt stiff and numb. He considered leaving the building but he couldn't see how it would help. If others were involved they were already here. Shitbird, for instance. To run would be to panic. Panic was disaster. Jesus Christ, though. Clarence Jefferson.

Clarence Jefferson was the last guy in the world he wanted to fuck with.

Grimes said, 'Go on.'

'Managing to screw me for the first time since we got married must have gone to his head cause he started to try again. All I wanted was out, Grimes, and you can "Jesus Christ" all you like. Anything was preferable. So I told him to go get cleaned up and make his phone call to Jefferson. I figure at least he won't be calling to confess to my murder.'

'I'm sorry for getting angry,' said Grimes. 'You did the right thing.'

'Thanks. While he was gone I locked the door, grabbed what I needed, climbed out the window and drove the hell away from there. I've been in this crummy hotel for four hours now waiting for the cops to pick me up. I'm too scared to go out for cigarettes. You got any good ideas?'

A great weariness had descended on Grimes. It occurred to him that he was probably well out of his depth. He said, 'Have you got rid of your car?'

'Yeah. I came here in a cab. The driver probably thought I was a hooker. I don't think he got a good look at my face.'

58

'Okay, listen carefully. Don't call here again. Don't tell me where you're staying, there may be someone listening to this. I'll see you tomorrow night, as we arranged. You know when and where. If I'm not there you'll have to handle Luther on your own. Don't worry about the cops. I don't think they'll be looking for you, but leave the hotel now and find somewhere else for the night. Don't let anyone know where you are. Jefferson's a big bag of boiled potatoes who likes to make people sweat. He's so crooked they say he shits turds the shape of pretzels. If you'd seen him you'd remember. He looks like Orson Welles on a high-cholesterol diet.'

'I've seen him in church. Even before I'd done anything he made me feel guilty every time he looked at me.'

'If Jefferson knows there's a million bucks at stake he'll want a seat at the table. He won't involve the department unless he has to.' Grimes stopped talking.

A very large man stood staring at him from the doorway of the living-room. The man wore an electric blue Hawaiian shirt patterned with sea birds and dancing girls, and a Panama hat with a black band. He removed the hat and held it over his stomach. Grimes guessed his weight at three hundred pounds – maybe more depending on how much muscle lay under the flab – and his height at some inches over six feet. His hair was short and wavy and his mouth bowed and sensuous. Like many huge men who'd spent a lifetime amongst people smaller than themselves he exuded an air of physical force and confidence that was either reassuring or intimidating depending on the circumstances.

Grimes felt his bowels turn to water.

Clarence Seymour Jefferson.

Jefferson smiled at Grimes as if he were delivering bad news to someone he didn't like, and padded over to an easy chair. He sat down, placing his hat on the floor beside him, and laced his hands across his belly. The fact that he seemed so immediately at home made his invasion all the more menacing. With a gesture of his head he indicated that Grimes should continue his conversation.

'You still there, Grimes?' said Callie.

'Do just as I say, Callie. If Jefferson turns up at any time and you get close enough to kill him: kill him. You've got a gun. Don't speak to him. Shoot him and make sure the bastard is dead.'

Grimes stared straight into Jefferson's eyes. They were a moist brown colour. The fat packed around the sockets obscured the whites so that the irises looked like rat droppings set in pink plastic.

'I have to go now, Callie. I'm afraid you're on your own now.'

'Grimes, what's wrong?'

'Bye, baby. Remember what your Mama told you: stay away from that dope.'

Grimes put the phone down. He said to Jefferson, 'I paid a lot of money for that lock.'

Jefferson shrugged. 'It'll keep out the street trash alright. You shouldn't worry. Anybody good enough to open it wouldn't be making a living in this shitty neighbourhood.'

His voice was like melting toffee.

'You and me got things to talk about, Dr Grimes.'

Jefferson stood up smoothly. Most people rising from a soft chair put a hand on the armrest or on their knee to help themselves up, or at least rock their body forward for momentum. Jefferson stood straight up, perfectly balanced. It was a demonstration of strength and body control that Grimes found less than comforting. Jefferson saw Grimes taking note and smiled again. From beneath his shirt he produced a .357 Colt Python with a ventilated barrel.

'Stand up, Doctor.' Jefferson pulled a face full of mock regret. 'I'm afraid I'm gonna have to put you on the rack.'

Grimes obeyed. He couldn't think of anything else to do and he couldn't think of anything smart to say. He couldn't even swallow. Fear lay in his throat like tenacious phlegm.

When Jefferson gestured with the gun and said, 'Over against the wall, arms and legs spread wide. Like you've seen it done on TV,' Grimes obeyed him again. Jefferson cocked the pistol and jammed it into Grimes' armpit.

'I sure don't want you to die just yet, Doc, so if this gun goes off while I'm frisking you you're gonna live. But you won't be able to pick your nose and scratch your ass at the same time before the next presidential election.'

The body search was rapid and thorough. Jefferson found nothing and stepped back. Grimes turned his head to look over his shoulder and watched Jefferson put his hand under his shirt again and pull out a bag made of coarse black cloth. At its neck was a drawstring. Jefferson held the Magnum close to his hip where it couldn't be grabbed or knocked aside and stepped forward again. Without speaking he used his left hand to pull the black bag over Grimes' head.

Darkness enveloped Grimes and he felt the drawstring pull tight about his neck. For a moment there was silence. Then he felt something brush close to his head, sensed thick lips pushing against his ear through the cloth, and heard Jefferson whisper four words in his caramel voice.

'Welcome to Bad City.'

CHAPTER SIX

The bag round his head dropped him into a void without air or light or sound. Somewhere in the void his bowels tossed on a black ocean. His internal organs were splitting and bursting and the ruptured cells leaked a foul liquid that corroded his bones and muscles. He could not move. He could not even scream. This was the real thing. Jesus. He felt as if he were going to fall face first into a pile of his own shit.

Fear at this level was a physical event. He concentrated his thoughts on his body. He was not breaking apart. The weakness in his limbs and bladder and bowels, the turmoil in his belly, the sweating palms and dry mouth: these were the physiological effects of adrenalin, unpleasant but harmless. He wasn't going to die. He would not be killed while the bag was on his head: Jefferson wanted him to talk. The bag was his protection.

He regulated his breathing and the fear subsided. He was back in control, of his bowels if of nothing else.

But the pain in his arms grew. He was standing about four feet from the wall and leaning forward onto his hands. His wrists and elbows and shoulders throbbed to the rhythm of his heartbeat. In the aftermath of his panic he welcomed the pain. Pain could be explained, studied, endured. As long as it diverted his mind from fear, pain was an ally.

Time passed.

He had no idea how much time. The bag on his head became soaked with sweat and the moisture of his breath. It clung to the contours of his face and made his skin itch intensely. Because of the drawstring at the neck little ventilation came up from below and he had to suck air straight through the double-layered fabric. He had to abandon his controlled breathing. His triceps no longer throbbed but hummed with a liquid ache. He could feel nothing below the circles of fire at his wrists. Cramps pulled across his chest and his shoulder blades. His spine seemed bent by a malignant disease. He had to move. He had to.

Slowly, Grimes edged his feet towards the wall so that he could stand more fully upright and take some weight off his arms. Four inches, six, eight. The ligaments in his back wept with gratitude for the change in posture. He stifled a groan that might have alerted Jefferson and with small movements began stretching the different muscle groups, squeezing their waste products back into the bloodstream.

A sheet of light dazzled him. Then a wave of pain swelled from his right rib cage and broke across his brain with a roar. He dropped to his knees, heaving for breath, struggling not to vomit into the bag. He fell over sideways. Blood rushed back into his joints and muscles and new pain oozed through him in concentric rings. The bag muffled his cries. Pain and disorientation muffled his thoughts. Several seconds passed before he realized he was sprawled on the floor.

The floor. He was no longer standing. For a moment the sense of release was so intoxicating that he was grateful for the blow that had knocked him down. Then, out of the blackness, another blow fell in the same place, and another. The edge of a meaty hand. He pulled his knees up to his chest, covered his ribs with his elbows. A finger and thumb pinched his Achilles' tendon and squeezed. Agony coursed up his leg and he struck out with his foot. The kick found open air. Roaring with frustration he struggled to his knees, lashing out left and right hooks with his fists. His left arm hit the wall. With both hands he ripped at the constriction round his throat but his fingers were blunted stumps without sensation. A finger-nail came loose as he tore at the fabric, trying to loosen the drawstring. Rage pushed him from his knees to his feet. Standing made him feel less helpless. He could kick and punch. He could fight.

A huge fist blasted him in the belly. He dropped his arms and tensed his abdomen and survived. A second punch following immediately on the first doubled him over. Gasping for air he lunged forward with his head and hit what felt like the wall of a padded cell. He threw his arms out and grabbed two handfuls of rayon. He drove his knee upwards and hit the padded wall again. The snorts of a crazed animal echoed in his ears. The sounds were his own. He flailed upwards with his fingers trying to find an eye to gouge, a lip to hook and tear, a handful of hair, a throat. But then the padded wall in front of him was gone and he felt his arms being folded behind him and jacked up between his shoulder blades. Someone screamed. Metal bracelets clicked about his wrists, one, two. Hands big enough to encircle his upper arms lifted him from the floor and flung him into the wall like garbage. He smashed the side of his face and saw more lights but he did not fall.

There was a pause.

He leaned his chest against the wall and breathed in desperate gasps. Hysteria beckoned invitingly. He swayed on his feet, balanced between rage and terror. Before he could fall either way an implacable mass of flesh pushed against his back, his buttocks, his head, compressing him slowly into the wall. Within a few seconds his rib cage was immobilized and he could not breathe. Bright lights, patches of primary blue and red, sprang across his vision. He felt himself rising, accelerating upwards, now at out-rageous speed, through a blackness flecked with fluorescent green particles. Liberation. He was laughing. He was free.

He was dreaming.

Callie lay naked on a pine table, face down, a white towel between her body and the wood. A second towel, folded three times, supported her head. They had been working out and her skin was flushed with blood and glowed pink through her tan. Here and there a muscle flickered under the skin. With her features smoothed of tension he wanted her worse than ever. It was her third day and Grimes had been falling in love with her — no other phrase would do — since the first time he'd seen her high-boned face.

It wasn't the kind of love that had much to do with happiness or rapture or flying to the moon. No chance of that for Cicero Grimes, he thought. No. It was the dark anguished yearning that gnawed like starvation at his belly and filled him with anxiety and pain. Maybe he'd been waiting all his life to fall in love with a whore. He liked the idea. Otherwise there was no real reason for it that he could see. Everything he knew about her was bad; but he wanted her anyway and fuck the consequences. His chest tightened with tenderness. You asshole, he thought. He breathed deeply and shook the tenderness off.

His hands glistened with body oil. The oil was scented with synthetic sandalwood. Standing by her head at the top of the table he laid his hands on the nape of her neck and began to massage the muscles with his thumbs. His hands felt strong. His throat was dry. His stomach and balls ached. As he dug out the knots in her back and shoulders his heart rose and fell on a long undulation of desire. He wanted to fuck her. Instead, he told himself that he just wanted to make her feel good. His fingertips brushed her breasts where they swelled from beneath her body. Gently, gently. His head swam. It seemed like a long time since anyone had let him be gentle with them. He took a deep breath, held it, released it, and went on.

He slid his hands down her sides and under her waist, digging his fingers into the flesh of her belly and drawing them back towards his in a slow movement. She groaned and he felt a tremor under his hands. He reached down again until pubic hair crinkled under his fingertips and repeated the movement. This time he felt her flesh tug against the lips of her cunt. Another tremor. His cock throbbed. It felt too good. He wasn't sure he could handle it.

Without hurry, without breaking contact with her skin, he moved from the head of the table so that he was standing at her left side. With one hand he tipped another spoonful of oil into his palm, warmed it and worked it over her buttocks. A droplet of oil gathered in the niche of her anus. Spreading her with his palms he dipped his middle finger into the droplet and, without penetration, moved its tip in a slow circle. Callie breathed a word into the towel beneath her face. It sounded like 'Jesus'. He moved his free hand onto her legs and she moved them apart and bent her knees a little. At the top of her thighs her labia glistened in the sunlight falling from the window.

Grimes paused, held back by a dulled sense of professional ethics and the awareness that he was a fucking fool. But this was what he wanted. There was nothing those bastards could do to him that mattered. And even if there was, he didn't care.

Callie sensed his hesitation. Through the yellow hair hanging across her face she said, 'I haven't felt good in a long time, Doctor. That's what I'm paying you for. Make me feel good again.'

Grimes said, 'I don't know.'

He felt stupid. Gross professional misconduct, they'd call it. A flagrant breach of ethics and trust. Guilt pierced his conscience. The guilt made his cock throb harder.

He stroked her labia and felt his entrails tingle as he introduced one finger into her vagina and then another. He moved with the same rhythm he'd used to work her muscles. At that moment all her energy, all her strength, was focused in that space, or so it seemed to him. He pushed in more deeply while his thumb massaged her anus. She lifted her face from the towel and opened her mouth silently and he felt her insides squeeze his fingers. He slid his left hand under her body and pulled her nipple taut against her skin and she squeezed him again. With delicate movements of his ring finger he rubbed her clitoris. When finally she came she cried out once and shuddered and for an instant Grimes fancied he caught a glimpse of her inner life. Then it was gone.

His own inner life was a fog of lust and confusion. He was horny. He was guilty. He was scared. This wasn't right and he knew it; but fucking never had been simple. He never knew what to think; or what anyone else was thinking. When sexual intercourse was on the agenda it was always easier to do than to think and the essential depravity of the situation appealed to him.

He slid his arms beneath her body and turned her over onto her back. He was rougher than was necessary. There was anger in his head too. Bad. She didn't seem to mind. Her head hung from the end of the table with the folded towel cushioning her neck and he could not see her face, only her chin pointing away from him, framed by the muscles of her neck. He bent over her breast and took her nipple into his mouth and pulled it with his teeth. The nipple was thick and textured. Her hand wrapped round the back of his head and pushed him downward across her belly. He parted her pubic hair with his fingers. She tasted tart and he inhaled her smell. His tongue flickered over her clitoris whilst his fingers stroked her lips. Her nails dug into his scalp as she lifted her hips up toward him and squirmed, rolling her head from one side to the other but holding her cries inside. She came in a rush and rolled onto her side and doubled forward, pushing his head away. She put her fingers on his wrist and held his hand still. Her eyes stared at him from above flushed cheekbones. His lips glistened with moisture and he rubbed the back of his hand over his mouth. She held out one hand towards him.

'Take your clothes off.'

Grimes looked at her and realized with the perverse joy of surrender that he'd do whatever she asked him to. He pulled off his shorts and jock-strap and the sleeveless sweat-shirt he was wearing. He stood at the foot of the table and pulled her towards him. A pearl of semen already glistened at the tip of his cock. She wrapped her legs about his waist *and the pearl dissolved as his glans met her cunt and slipped inside.*

Organic smells mixed with the scent of fake sandalwood. She was warm and soft and he fucked her with long, slow strokes. It was nice but should have felt better than it did. He wasn't too surprised. This wasn't the first time that sexual ecstasy had escaped him. She lay there and let him fuck her and he looked upon her pleasure and wondered why he couldn't lose himself as she did. She didn't have to do much more than pant and for her it looked better than nice. But she could have been faking, like the sandalwood. He felt his erection fading and thought about Maggie. Maggie, who had lain underneath him in the same bubble of pleasure – or fake pleasure – without caring – or seeming to care – whether he could get inside it or not. Yes. And the others too. He concentrated and his erection returned. He expelled a few drops of semen but didn't come. His cock felt like a part of a machine. She became too wet and he couldn't feel her enough.

She protested as he withdrew his cock, then moaned, pleading but with a hint of apprehension, as he turned her over and pressed its tip against her anus. She bore down and he slid in. Better. Sort of better. He fucked her for a few minutes more, her cries of satisfaction pushing him further and further away from her, then he ejaculated, feeling too tense to enjoy much more than relief. His cock slithered out. He dropped down to his knees and rested his head against her legs, drained by a sudden sense of isolation and waste. The sunlight hurt his eyes and he shut them. Callie made a noise above him and moved on the table. She said, 'That was terrific.' But her words seemed far away and what the fuck was 'terrific' anyway? The lights grew brighter, burning through his closed eyelids. He tried to raise his arms to shield his eyes but the arms were chained behind him and he could not move.

'Talk to me, Doctor.'

Grimes woke up and waited for the pain to close him in.

CHAPTER SEVEN

Someone pinched the inside of his thigh. He squirmed away and opened his eyes for a second. The light burned. He registered a fat face shining with sweat. Somewhere on the floor lay two hundred pounds of pain. He didn't realize that the two hundred pounds were him until two pairs of arms lifted them from the floor and he moved too. The arms sat him in a chair. Ecstasy flowed through him. He loved the arms. Voices floated above him.

'Bring me two glasses of water.'

'Hey look at that, man. He's got a hard-on.'

'Shut your stupid mouth and do as I say.'

An indefinite period of time floated by and then someone poured water on his face. Or some kind of healing potion. Sections of his nervous system that hadn't been in contact for a long time started exchanging messages again. He wanted to rub his face but his hands were still chained behind his back. Someone else's hand wiped the mixture of sweat, water and mucus from his face with a cloth. The cloth was soft. The hand was gentle. He opened his eyes.

Jefferson smiled at him. 'Here, Doc. Drink this.' He lifted a glass towards Grimes' face.

The rim of the glass was cold against his lips. He bolted the liquid in gulps. When he had finished Jefferson took the glass away. Grimes looked at the wall in front of him and saw a framed photo of Warren Oates wearing a dirty white suit and holding a soiled canvas bag and a .45. So he was still in his own living-room, sitting on the sofa. The shitbird sat in an armchair eating a peanut butter and jelly sandwich and looking at the pictures in a karate magazine. He had a bottle of beer wedged between his thighs. Jefferson sat beside Grimes on the edge of the sofa holding an empty glass. He put the glass on the table.

'That feel better?' said Jefferson.

Grimes said, 'Make yourselves at home.' His voice sounded thick, the irony unconvincing.

'You know who I am,' said Jefferson.

'Yes.'

Jefferson smiled. 'You must be scared.'

'I'm scared,' said Grimes. 'But I've been scared before. I think I can handle it.'

'Good for you. You've learned some Hollywood tough talk, you don't whimper and I'm told you've got some kind of a black belt. You say your dick's bigger than mine, okay, I believe you, but don't get over-confident. This is a new country for you. I mean I know you're a ballsy kind of a guy but balls won't help you here. What you need is to use that fancy brain of yours. You keep cool, answer my questions, show some intelligence, we'll get on fine, maybe even make friends. Get in my way and you'll go down like a sock filled with shit. Now, from the top. How did you meet Callilou Carter?'

'I put an ad in the Lonely Hearts.' It was stupid but he needed to find out what he was dealing with.

Jefferson shook his head. 'Shit, Grimes, you're gonna have to take better care of yourself than this.'

Jefferson grabbed the front of Grimes' shirt and tore it open with an abruptness and violence that told Grimes all he wanted to know. In the same movement Jefferson took hold of the lapels of Grimes' jacket and dragged the shoulders down over his arms. Grimes choked as Jefferson's left forearm locked across his throat, pinning him to the back of the sofa. Jefferson licked his lips. He seized hold of Grimes' left nipple between finger and thumb and half lifted him from the sofa. Grimes felt as if he were about to lose half his chest. The pain was extraordinary. Instead of fighting it with his mind, where it would fuel

70

his fear, he let his nerves gape open and took the pain into his body. His body struggled and thrashed but the arm across his throat was phenomenally strong. Just as Grimes was about to start screaming Jefferson let go of him and backed off. Grimes sat breathing heavily and stared at the cop without blinking.

'You can do without this,' said Jefferson. 'Next time I might have to tear your dick off. Mrs Carter, please.'

Grimes sat up and shrugged his jacket and shirt back onto his shoulders. He wanted to tell Jefferson to fuck his mother, to do his worst, to do him the favour of his life and tear his goddamn dick off, but it was too early. He had to rest between rounds, pace himself, think each step through. He couldn't think of a good reason not to answer the question.

'I found her here, downstairs in the gym, handcuffed to a three-hundred-pound barbell. She was as crazy as two waltzing mice. Paranoid. It was three o'clock in the morning and she got me out of bed by screaming "Go suck your cock you mother-fucking bastard" at the top of her voice. By the time I got down there she was alone. Someone had broken in through the glass doors and left her chained up with a bag of clothes and an envelope containing a letter and a thousand dollars in cash. The letter said she'd been going crazy for two days and could I take care of her. So I did. That was a week ago.'

'You still have the letter?'

'Here in my jacket pocket,' said Grimes.

'Artie, make yourself useful,' said Jefferson. 'Come and put your hand in the Doctor's pocket.'

Artie put his beer and magazine on the floor and walked over to Grimes. There was a sneer of peevish enjoyment on his face as he jerked open Grimes' jacket and pulled out a folded sheet of paper. Artie handed the letter to Jefferson. Jefferson did not take it.

'Read it out to me, Artie.'

Artie unfolded the sheet and stared at it awkwardly. He shrugged apologetically at Jefferson.

'I don't read too good, Captain.'

Jefferson jerked his head impatiently. 'Give it back to Grimes. You read it.'

As Grimes took the letter Jefferson sat watching him for a reaction. Grimes tried to keep poker-faced. It was difficult.

'*Dear Dr Grimes,*' he read, '*Please take care of this woman. You don't know her or me but I know about you and I know you can do it. Callie has been taking a shitload of cocaine these past few months. I don't know exactly how much but a lot and every day. It didn't seem to do her any harm until two days ago when she started to go nuts, by that I mean out of her fucking skull, excuse my French. She thinks I want to kill her, which isn't true, and that the cops and the Mafia have been tailing her and tapping her phone and watching her house. Today she tried to stab me. Tonight she can't sleep because bugs are crawling all over her body and she is going totally apeshit. She's never been like this before, Doc, maybe it isn't the dope, I don't know, but you got to get her well and fast. Sorry to bust in on you like I'm going to but it is an emergency. Here is a grand, if it isn't enough there is more, I guarantee you. Don't call the cops in on this, she wouldn't want you to, I guarantee you that, too, but I know you are not the kind of a jerk-off that would do that. Thanks again, Doc, and please do your best. The key to the cuffs is in the envelope with the money.*'

Grimes lowered the letter. 'It's signed *A friend*,' he said.

'What was wrong with her?' said Jefferson. He took the letter from Grimes and glanced at the squared block capitals of which it was composed.

'She had a paranoid delusional disorder induced by cocaine,' said Grimes. 'It happens. She didn't want to stay until I explained that if she didn't I'd have to take her to a hospital or, if she refused that too, get the cops to take her. She decided I was the best of a bad deal.'

'So she wasn't so nutty after all.'

'She wasn't completely without insight but she was ill

72

enough. Once I'd shown her some certificates to prove I was a doctor and not a button man for the Mafia she felt a bit better about staying. These illnesses are terrifying. The episodes caused by cocaine are short-lived. Take away the drug and most people get better within three days or so, which is what Callie did. I just gave her small doses of Haldol to ease the distress.'

'And by that time she had a stranglehold on your scrotum.'

'No.' Grimes' face felt hot. He hoped it didn't show.

Jefferson shrugged. 'Who's this "friend"?'

'He means a friend of hers. Like he says in the letter, I don't know him.'

'You know when I was growing up we were told that whenever you tell a lie it adds years to the time you got to spend in purgatory.'

'You can't lie to the Captain,' said Artie Mann. 'He's got ears. He hears things.'

'Keep it shut Artie and sit down. Who's the author, Grimes?'

'I'd rather not say.' He tried to prepare himself.

'You'd rather not say.' Jefferson, still sitting on the sofa, put a hand on Grimes head and stroked his hair gently as if he were some kind of domestic animal. Grimes tried to ignore it but Artie's leering face amplified the humiliation he felt. He pulled his head away but Jefferson slid the palm of his hand onto the nape of his neck and dug his fingers into the muscles on either side of the spine. Grimes' skin crawled.

'Look, Doc.'

Jefferson gave Grimes' neck a little squeeze. Pain shot up the back of his head.

'We'd get along a whole lot better if you didn't treat me like I didn't know how to shake piss from the end of my dick. Tonight I picked up two names that connected with Callilou Carter: Cicero Grimes and Luther. Just "Luther". I put the name "Grimes" into the computer at HQ and I'll be goddamned if there isn't a Luther

Grimes on the list. And damn me again if he isn't your elder brother.'

The pain wasn't that bad but there was something degrading in the hand on his neck that sent pulses of rage through his nervous system. Who did this fat bastard think he was? Ignore it. Talk to him.

'I haven't seen Luther in getting on ten years. I don't know where he is and I don't care.'

'Not what you'd call a nice man, your brother. In the army they called him the Tough Bullet. 101st Airborne, US Rangers. Turned down Officer Training School three times. A regular Milt Warden. And as mean a psychopath as ever won the Distinguished Service Cross instead of a state scholarship to the electric chair. Now even a dumb old boy like me can put two and two next to each other even if he can't add them up.'

Jefferson let go of Grimes' neck and sat back into the sofa. The pain disappeared as Grimes rotated his head in a circle but he felt the cop's eyes violating his mind and as he listened to him the pulses of rage got stronger and faster.

'When it comes down to it you're a pretty seedy guy yourself, Doc. Like Artie said, I hear things. People confide in me. I got a real kick out of picturing you lying here in bed, high on pills and booze and sweating like a rajah while flower-child Maggie sat on your face and – what was her name – Eileen? – Jesus – sat on your prick and waggled a dildo around in your ass.'

Jefferson tousled Grimes' hair and grinned. The gesture threw a switch in Grimes' head and he leaned forward and spat full force in Jefferson's face.

Jefferson ignored the spittle scattering his cheeks and made a grab for Grimes' throat. Grimes lunged to his feet and paused to catch his balance. His joints screamed with stiffness. As Jefferson rose from the sofa Grimes raised his foot high and stomped on the policeman's kneecap.

Jefferson fell back onto the sofa, stifling a shout. Elation filled Grimes' mind like smoke. You goddamn bastards.

The shitbird was two paces out of his chair and reaching under the back of his T-shirt when Grimes kicked him in the belly, hooking the toe of his shoe under the shitbird's right ribs and locking his hip, driving the kick into the liver. The shitbird screamed and went down. A .45 automatic fell from his hand. Grimes stood over him and raised his foot to stomp the shitbird's head into the carpet. He'd grind his skull beneath his heel and dance, laughing, in his brains. For an instant he had the sense of someone watching him from inside his own head and nodding with approval. His father. Tears of rage blurred his vision.

'Grimes.'

Jefferson's voice cut through the smoke in Grimes' head and stopped him with his foot poised over shitbird's body. His limbs shook with tension. He lowered the foot and rested it on the shitbird's throat before turning his head. Jefferson had him covered with the magnum.

'You're a violent guy, Doc. Any more fancy tricks with those feet and I'm gonna have to blow one of them off. You want to get out of this deal in one piece you'll have to stop believing you're Sylvester Stallone and start using your head.'

The shitbird made a gargling sound. Grimes reluctantly removed his foot and stepped away. He knew – and Jefferson knew – that he'd fucked up. Jefferson rose from the sofa, wincing as he put weight on his injured knee, and walked over to a straight-backed chair standing against the wall by Grimes' desk. He sat down and leaned one arm on the desk top. He pointed with the gun.

'Back on the sofa. Sit with your legs crossed underneath you.'

Grimes sat down and folded his legs in front of him. He tried to find a comfortable position but with his arms handcuffed behind him it was impossible. His head contained hot liquid. He was a stranger in his own body. He put all his effort into breathing steadily and the liquid started to cool down. He stared at Jefferson without speaking.

After a moment Jefferson said, 'That's better. You haven't asked me what I want yet, why I'm here.'

'I know why you're here and I don't have it. You're wasting your time.'

'Time,' said Jefferson. He massaged his knee absently. 'A category so elusive that neither science nor philosophy has yet determined its nature. You're going to learn a lot about time tonight. How long do you think you were standing against the wall, for instance? Fifteen minutes? An hour? Three hours?'

'A category so elusive,' said Grimes. 'I'll have to take out a subscription to the Police Gazette.' From the corner of his eye he saw the black hood lying on the floor. He turned his head so that he couldn't see it.

'You know, Grimes, I like you. You interest me. Control is what we need. Control of ourselves, control of others. We want power and we'll do without all the rest to get our hands on it.'

'I can't even get the Sanitation Department to haul my garbage away, so don't talk to me about power. I go out of my way to avoid it. Not like you. You've got your fat finger on the prostate gland of every politician in the state.'

'That's a nice thought,' said Jefferson, 'but you're talking politics and you and I are beyond anything as simple as that tonight. I thought you'd understood that. Politics have nothing to do with morality. Politics is wild dogs fighting in the gutter over heaps of rotting meat. Rotting meat stinks. Violence causes terror. I'm a big nasty dog. I can eat my fill whenever I want but it doesn't really satisfy. Maybe I'm looking for a little something extra.'

'I don't follow this bullshit,' said Grimes. 'I don't know what you're talking about.'

'Bullshit is exactly what I'm talking about,' said Jefferson. 'This bullshit.' He waved his hand. 'This cute little fire station's the biggest bull's turd I ever even heard of. You must've spent too much time watching Batman when you were a kiddie. What do you do when a junkie needs some help? Slide down that brass pole in a pair of tights and a stethoscope?'

Jefferson laughed at Grimes' expression and Grimes forced his eyes to the floor. He couldn't trust himself to look at the cop's jeering face without trying to smash it in.

'I'm sorry, Doc. This is a nice place you got. I can see how all those junkie scumbags who pay your wages must feel safe when they get here. Or at least the few you condescend to treat. No time for women or wimps, isn't that right? The Carter woman is the exception that proves the rule. Just being sick isn't enough to get to see the famous Dr Grimes.'

Jefferson appeared to be enjoying himself. Grimes' scalp crawled with loathing. It had taken him a long time to find a niche for himself. A lot of people had tried to talk him into something 'better', offered him jobs, partnerships, encouragement. He'd ignored them all. His work here wasn't prestigious but it was his and he took an inverse pride in its position on the margins. Jefferson's contempt cut deep.

'That about sums up your business, doesn't it, Doc?' said Jefferson. 'Your skills aren't for sale in the usual sense. You treat on the basis of your own personal fancy. Or have I been misinformed?'

Grimes' face felt swollen and numb. He searched for a measured response and failed and the words suddenly fell over each other on their way out as if they'd been waiting to escape for a long time.

'I don't give a shit for beautiful people coking themselves to glory in the executive washroom. They can fuck themselves in as many ways as they can afford to and I'll laugh while they do it. I pick my clients, sure. So does everyone else.'

Grimes stopped in confusion. His lips were contorted. He couldn't move his tongue.

'You pick 'em, alright. Soldiers, cops, ball players, fighters. Cicero Grimes, the tough guys' friend.'

'Fuck off, Captain.'

'Isn't it true, Dr Grimes,' Jefferson dropped his voice an octave, 'that you also treated one Philip Alfonse Romero of Detroit, also known as Michigan Phil?'

Grimes' stomach turned over. 'I didn't know.'

'They call Phil the slot machine. You put in money and out come bodies. Men, women, kids. Phil ain't particular. And you whipped him back into shape.'

'I didn't know.'

'You sorry son of a bitch.'

'Fuck you. I'd treat him again.' He didn't know if that was true or not but at the moment he felt it.

Shitbird rolled over and vomited crunchy peanut butter and grape jelly onto the carpet.

Jefferson sighed. 'I spend so much time with trash,' he said and stood up. 'You should try it. It brings you closer to some greater design. Or at least I hope it does.'

He bent down and grabbed one of shitbird's ankles.

'Don't disappoint me again, Doc. Stay where you are.'

Like a giant child trailing a teddy bear he dragged Artie's whimpering body into the kitchen.

Grimes wanted to hurt Jefferson so badly his teeth ached. He wrenched his hands against the bracelets. The pain calmed him. He had to conserve himself. The time in the bag had eroded his reason. He could feel it. The smoke behind his eyes, the aggression pacing up and down in his chest. The fat bastard had him acting like a beast, goading him with lies and distortions. He had to do better.

Jefferson returned from the kitchen alone. He threw a wet towel over the pool of vomit and settled himself in his chair.

'How's your Daddy these days?' he said.

Here it came again. Grimes swallowed a bitter lump and bit his lip.

'Must be pushing seventy,' said Jefferson. 'Old and grey instead of bad and red. It's an age where having a family he can be proud of must be a real comfort to a man.'

78

Grimes' lip started to bleed.

'George Grimes. He's on the computer too. Technology. Don't you love it? George spent more time in Joliet Prison than he did at home when you were a youngster, didn't he?'

Grimes got a picture in his head of the frayed shirt collar and a kid with a bloody nose. He felt his eyes smarting. Jesus. He had to get a hold of himself.

Jefferson noticed and smiled sympathetically.

'When a poor boy with a commie jailbird for a father goes off and becomes a doctor I can see how he might keep a big chip balanced on his shoulder. If he did then all that country club ambition would turn his stomach. Yessir. If that poor boy wasn't very sophisticated, if he had weird ideas about social justice and the rights of man, it might just stick in his craw to see those overpaid assholes living so high and mighty. Especially when Daddy's had to spend his life washing cars and stacking crates cause he drew five to ten for fracturing a policeman's skull on a picket line. And him with a Silver Star, too, for helping to save democracy.'

Jefferson chuckled.

'You cocksucker.' It was the best he could do.

'Nice vocabulary. Did you learn to talk like that in Chicago while Daddy was making belt buckles or is it something you picked up down here in the ghetto?'

When Grimes didn't answer – and not to answer was a crippling effort – Jefferson shook his head.

'Explain this to me, Doc. You could spend four hours a day dozing in an air-conditioned office while people who don't know any better paid you a hundred grand a year to dole out little coloured pills and tell them why their dicks won't go hard anymore. Instead you live down here in garbage city. Okay, I know your Daddy is an old Red and some guys get off on that working-class-hero shit but you aren't that simple a son of a bitch. So tell me. Why?'

'I like it here,' said Grimes. 'It's cheap. It's quiet. I like the neighbours. You meet a better class of person.'

'Down these mean streets? You're a real romantic. From the ghetto to the country club and back.'

Jefferson leaned forward and pointed out of the window.

'The people out there are scum. They're just as corrupt as the ones you think you've escaped. Worse. The system shits on them from every angle while the richest people on earth live like lords on every side and laugh themselves to sleep at night. And what do your neighbours do about it? Not a goddamn thing. The ones that don't sell themselves to the enemy for the state minimum wage spend their lives poisoning their friends and cutting each other apart. Take a look out of the window. Take a look.'

Grimes unfolded his legs and walked with stiff steps towards the window. He was glad of the chance to stretch himself. He looked outside. The street was stagnant and deserted. He wished his mind were the same.

'They've sold their birthright for a pocketful of dried catshit,' said Jefferson behind him. 'Shit, you actually talk to these people? You go down to Sweetbread's for a beer and slap hands with the niggers and make jive talk? Or are they just another prop to make you feel good about yourself?'

Grimes stood staring through the window and didn't answer. Across the intersection at Sweetbread's Bar a blue neon beer sign glowed. Outside the bar, pointing towards the firehouse, was a red Camaro Z28 with dented body-work. He noticed that someone sat behind the wheel smoking a cigarette.

Grimes needed a smoke himself. He didn't bother to ask for one. His mind was too blurred for him to think about why Jefferson was taking a chainsaw to his life. He'd expected threats and beatings, a remorseless pursuit of Callie's money. He'd been prepared to hurt but this damaged him more. And it made him mad. Jefferson knew his stuff. Even as Grimes recognized the psychological traps the cop set he couldn't help falling into them. Every swell of anger weakened him but the effort required to control it was too great. He turned around, tried to shift the dialogue onto neutral ground.

'Every minute we sit here talking the money's getting farther away.'

'I know the money isn't here. You think I'm shitting my pants to get my hands on it but you're wrong. I will get it, make no mistake, but it's not enough to get me out of bed in the mornings. We both have an opportunity here to learn some things of great importance.'

'Sure, Captain. When I want to know how to kiss a mobster's ass I'll give you a call. Till then you can save the second-rate sociology for the young centurions at the police academy. You're pitching it at just about their level.'

'I'm offering you my hand, Grimes,' said Jefferson. 'Spit on it and you'll be sorry. A man who lives like you do needs advice on how to improve himself.'

Grimes stood with his back to the window. His head told him not to argue but his shoulders were hunched and his wrists were bleeding against the handcuffs. He wanted to ram his head into the wall.

'I need lessons in self-enlightenment from a fat mother-fucker like you like I need bowel cancer. You want to know why I live here?'

He was losing it.

'Okay. It's simple. I like it. I like it because I don't have to see a crowd of swollen, self-satisfied faces when I walk out my front door. I don't have to work with greedy morons with high IQs and no intelligence. I don't have to listen to them talking about the new hot tub or last night's lobster dinner, or smile when I want to vomit on them, or hear their shitty little thoughts on their shitty little lives. I wasted too many years doing that. It's fucking degrading.'

He'd lost now and didn't care.

'I hate their fear and insecurity, their anaemic love lives and hand-me-down dreams and ambitions. The people

81

here are too piss-poor to care. They help to keep the smell of all that shit out of my face.'

Grimes felt himself plummeting into a vortex of malice and contempt, at the centre of which stood himself. The words foamed out with the flecks of saliva spraying from his mouth.

'And you,' he said.

Grimes walked across the room with such ferocity that Jefferson stood up and drew his revolver. They met over the vomit-soaked towel. Jefferson placed the flat of his free hand against Grimes' chest and pushed. Grimes dropped his weight into his feet and leaned forward, craning his head as if he would sink his teeth into Jefferson's throat.

'Fucking copper,' said Grimes. His face trembled. 'Garbage man. Errand boy. You wipe their shit up with your tongue and when a lump of undigested food comes through you lick it clean and eat it and congratulate yourself for hustling a free meal. You poor asshole.'

Grimes smiled in his face.

'I'm nothing. I'm shit. I already know that. That's why you'll never get your teeth into that million-dollar turd. Never.'

He bellowed with pain as Jefferson's forearm smashed into the side of his neck, clubbing him to the ground.

'You goddamn bastard.'

Grimes' voice shuddered in his throat.

'You goddamn bastard.'

Jefferson stood behind Grimes and hooked a hand round his chin, arching him backwards. Thick fingers dug into his face. Jefferson bent his head so close that Grimes could feel the cop's lips against his cheek. When Jefferson spoke the measured tone was gone: his voice was the sound of gasoline being poured on a gagged man bound hand and foot in a deserted warehouse.

'You are dreaming, medicine man, if you think this is as bad as it can get. I make a call, you spend the next six hours being fucked in the ass by niggers and Porto Ricans.

I can wire your cock and balls into a cage with a starving rat. I can . . .'

'Do it, Errand Boy, do it.'

Grimes ground the words out between his teeth.

'You wanna fuck me yourself, you can do that too.'

Jefferson let go of his head and Grimes fell forward, his face landing on the damp towel. The smell was acrid. He could feel Jefferson standing above him, thinking. Grimes grinned, a movement of his face over which he had no control. A thought formed in his head and hung in the air before him before floating away: the fat bastard was worried.

'The quality of mercy is not strained,' said Jefferson.

He punched Grimes in the right kidney and Grimes, thinking stupid thoughts and not expecting it, cried out into the towel.

'It falleth as the gentle rain from heaven.'

When Jefferson's fist hit him a second time Grimes came close to blacking out. A moment later the bag went over his head again and Grimes was dragged, weak-legged and struggling, back to his feet and shoved face-first against the wall.

CHAPTER EIGHT

Joe Gags woke up with a mouth full of gall and wished that he'd never been born. His body felt stiff and cramped and poisoned. He muttered a string of obscenities to himself but found them no more than mildly comforting. His watch read 08:15.

The watch had an alarm that played 'The Yellow Rose Of Texas'. He never used the alarm because he didn't like the tune and he didn't like Texans. He didn't like digital watches either but the one on his wrist had been a freebie and he didn't see the sense of spending good money on a real watch. He had been asleep at the wheel of his Camaro for nearly four hours. He massaged his face and felt his eyes stinging for a moment. He needed to piss. The car was already hot from the sun, and the air inside had the clinging texture of silent farts. He unwedged himself from the corner of the driver's seat and shoved the door open. Even at that hour the air was heavy but it did have some oxygen in it and he filled his lungs with gratitude.

His legs were stiff and he used his hands to help lift them from the car. He stood up and forced himself to groan his way through some stretching exercises. When he felt able to move without pain he walked down the alley behind Sweetbread's Bar and took a piss against a wall. Farther down the alley a body lay on the ground, dressed in rags. Joe watched the piss trickle down a gradient and form a puddle two inches away from the body's face. Probably a drunk. It could have been a corpse but if it was, Joe Gags didn't want to know. He walked back to the street, reflecting that this was one bastard of a way to spend Sunday morning.

After leaving Jefferson last night Gags had returned to his poker game and played like a drunken Indian. He had blown three hundred dollars, including the hundred Jefferson had pushed into his shirt pocket. Three hundred wasn't going to change the rest of his life but it hurt, especially when he could only blame himself. Luck had played no part in his game. He'd just shafted himself, hand after hand, with stupid plays. He'd gone home and taken a few snorts of Kentucky Gentleman but sleep had been impossible. The thought of Jefferson putting the vice-grips on Cicero Grimes had laid like a rock in his belly, just as it had throughout the game. Without any clear idea of what he would achieve, Joe had driven back to keep watch on Grimes' apartment. An hour after arriving he'd fallen asleep.

There was no sign of life at the firehouse across the intersection. Gags walked around the block and found Jefferson's Eldorado in the same spot it had occupied last night. He also checked that Cicero Grimes' car had not moved. They could have used another car – Gags did not know what back up Jefferson was using – but it seemed reasonable to assume that Grimes and Jefferson were still in the building.

Joe Gags was disappointed. Falling asleep in the car had been a genuine error. If Jefferson had blown – with or without Grimes – whilst Gags had been asleep he could have gone home to bed with his conscience clear enough to be bearable. Now he would have to hang around. It was a deep pain in the balls.

He wondered how Grimes was bearing up and thought about how he and Grimes had first gotten to know each other.

For ten years Joe had taught karate in a church hall four blocks from Grimes' home. Teaching karate didn't make him any dough worth talking about but he enjoyed it. Most of the pupils were tough kids looking to get tougher, but the training was severe and they came and went pretty quickly. Maybe one in forty had the discipline and guts needed to reach black belt standard. Grimes had surprised him: a white guy in his late twenties who clearly wasn't a bum or a hardcase and who took everything that was thrown at him without whining and came back week after week, then year after year. And Jesus, the guy turned out to be a fucking doctor.

Joe Gags viewed the medical profession as the most successful organized criminals in the country. Until he met Grimes he'd always found them, to a man, to be the worst kind of fat-assed macho wimps; pampered cock-suckers who shat themselves at the prospect of doing anything more strenuous than posting a bill to a patient. He was bitter. Sure he was. When he'd been on his knees the bastards had cleaned him out of cash then told him there was no more room at the inn. Why he ever got hooked on smack he still didn't know. But when Joe had been convinced that the stuff was going to kill him, Cicero Grimes had saved him and said that the 'Why' didn't matter, so Joe Gags never asked himself anymore.

As he sat in the passenger seat of the car, working his way through a polystyrene container of chicken nuggets in sweetcorn relish and a large coke, he recalled how Grimes had pulled him through. He'd been sitting in Frenette's, wearing Ray Bans to hide his pupils, when Grimes had come in, sat down with his drink, taken one good look at Joe's slack face and flaking skin, and asked him, 'How long have you been taking that shit, Joe?'

The shame and disgust were so intense that Joe wanted to punch Grimes in the throat. With difficulty he said, 'A year, maybe more. Maybe I don't care to remember.'

'You want to talk about it?'

Joe slammed his hand down beside his glass and sent peanuts jumping from the dish on the table.

'Talk, talk, fucking talk. That's all you cocksuckers ever want to do. I need to get off this shit, not talk about how I

*got into it. I seen three pyschiatrists in the last six months.
They squeezed my balls with bullshit questions, handed me
a bunch of bullshit drugs and put me in a group with a
bunch of bullshit yuppie scumbags who were so bored with
all the fucking dough they were making they had to roll it
up and snort shit through it. Jesus.'*

He contorted his voice to mimic his tormentors.

*'We understand the way you feel, Joe. Addiction can
happen to anybody. There's no need to be ashamed.'*

*He spat on the floor and shook his head at himself. Grimes
didn't deserve this shit.*

*'I am ashamed, Grimes.' His voice was quieter now. 'This
shouldn't have happened to a guy like me. I can't accept the
excuses like they can. I need to be punished for it, not told
I'm okay, you're okay. I'm just a working stiff. I act like an
asshole, I expect to be called an asshole, not patted on the
head. Am I making sense?'*

*Grimes nodded. 'You're an asshole, Joe. You listen to too
many Merle Haggard records.'*

*'Funny guy.' He swirled his drink around the bottom of his
glass. 'Look, Grimes, I didn't mean to call you a cocksucker. I
know you ain't like them others.'*

*Grimes waited quietly without interrupting and that
made the hard part easier.*

'Is there any way you can help me?'

*'Forget everything you think you know about being a
junkie, Joe. There's nothing supernatural about heroin. Your
body tells you it can't do without it but it's lying. You can
carry on taking it or you can stop. I can't choose for you.
But if you want to stop I think I can help you.'*

'I'm scared of hurting.'

*'It hurts to stop,' said Grimes. 'More than I can know.
But so does finding your best friend eating your wife's pussy,
or your father telling you he's got cancer, or a million and
one other things. Look around you. Human beings are built
to hurt. That's what they do best. Heroin stops hurting sooner
than a lot of other things.'*

'I'm weak,' said Joe. 'I've tried. A day, two days, then

I'm shovin' my nose back in that powder like a prize hog at a county fair.'

'If you decide to stop, I can take weakness out of the equation,' said Grimes. 'But it means giving up all your freedom to me. The decision to do that is yours but once we start there'll be no going back. You'll have no more choices, no rights at all. Basically you'll be a prisoner under torture. You'll hate me, fear me, despise me. But if I didn't think you were up to it I wouldn't offer to help.'

Joe felt like a sick lemon. He threw back the last of his whiskey. 'I've been keeping this away from official channels. I haven't claimed on the department's insurance cover, been paying those bloodsuckers downtown out of my own pocket. I sure as hell couldn't pay you up front.'

'Take two weeks leave, soon as you can, try not to die in the meantime,' said Grimes. 'You can pay me some other time.'

It was the roughest ride he'd ever taken.

Grimes had rented a hunting lodge out in the back-country and loaded a trailer with equipment and food. They'd left the City on New Year's Eve with Joe trying not to throw his guts up. For ten days Grimes pushed him without mercy. He forced him to run through the woods until vomit spilled down his sweatshirt, to pump out endless reps on the barbell until his tissues roared like flame, to beat on the heavy bag until his arms were too weak to soap himself in the shower. Grimes matched him rep for rep and a kind of fever took hold of them. At night they smoked cigarettes and drank beer, listened to George Jones and Conway Twitty on the tape deck and slept the sleep of the justified.

At first they were too tired to talk much. Joe bit down on his pain and Grimes was just there. Then, as they both got stronger and the rest of the world became unreal, they talked about things they would never have talked about in the City. Their past, their work, their fears. Women. Joe found it weird but comforting. It wasn't

88

until later that he realized that the weird feeling must have had something to do with trust. He never recovered the feeling again, with Grimes or anyone else. But that was life.

He stayed off dope and fell back into his old routine. Grimes gave up his position at the hospital and made a living treating guys with the same kind of problems Joe had had. Grimes could have done a lot better. He took on maybe a dozen clients a year and lived on a quarter of the money he could've made in a downtown practice. When Joe asked him why, Grimes said that at least he didn't have to kiss anyone's ass or have anyone else kiss his and that out on the fringes it was easier not to think too much about what he was doing or why.

Grimes was kind of a strange guy but Joe liked him and felt that he owed him a debt he could never repay. Now Grimes was up to his neck in bad-smelling shit and Joe didn't really want to help him. It was what you might call a moral dilemma. Joe Gags wasn't used to moral dilemmas. His view of the world was simple and effective. There was Us and Them: the Cops and Everyone Else. Sure there was a difference between the street shit – who in a better world would be simply washed away into the sewers or gassed or electrocuted or gotten rid of by whatever means you please as long as it was quick – and your straight citizen. But your straight citizen secretly despised the cops too. He needed the cops; he supported them and paid for them; but he also knew that they had power over him, and face to face with a cop he was scared as anyone else.

Nobody on this earth was without guilt.

That was okay with Joe Gags. His loyalties were straightforward – the department, right or wrong – and he never had any conflict with his conscience. The world was a shit drain and he helped to hose it down. It was dirty work. If he took a little something extra from time to time he saw that as his due. Everyone else in the fucking world was helping themselves to the gravy. Cops deserved more than most – a lot more – but all they ever got was a hard time.

So Cicero Grimes presented a problem. He was the only friend Joe Gags had outside the department. They still trained together. From time to time they sank a bottle of Wild Turkey and talked. They never got as deep as they had out in the backwoods but Grimes had a way of listening, and Joe found it a relief after all the tough talk down at the precinct and the monosyllables he exchanged with Jackie, his wife.

Grimes didn't much talk about himself. He seemed to spend a lot of time thinking – a bad habit which Joe Gags had tried to persuade him to abandon – and was obscurely discontented. Gags was happy to stay on his own track and play poker on Saturday nights and fuck his wife twice a week and a hooker twice a month without ever questioning things too much. He had his ups and downs. He didn't expect life to be a bed of roses so it never occurred to him to ask himself what the hell it was all about. To Joe Gags it was clear that it wasn't about anything at all, and that didn't worry him. But it worried Grimes.

And now Grimes was worrying him. Gags did not know what Jefferson was doing with Grimes but he was sure they were not sitting round the coffee-table playing pinochle. It would've been nice to go in and bust Grimes out but it just wasn't an option.

Jefferson would have taken him out in a second.

Gags wasn't frightened of taking on Jefferson any more than he was frightened of throwing himself under a train or shooting himself in the head. Such actions would've been stupid and useless and fear had nothing to do with it. Bullshit. Fear had everything to do with it. Jefferson was a machine. He had an IQ of 180 and all kinds of fancy education under his belt but he talked and acted like he'd been raised in some deep and dirty gutter in the back of beyond. Sometimes he could be bought, other times not. He had to be loaded but he lived strictly within his salary. No one ever knew exactly where he was coming from. That was part of why he scared people, even the big shots who fooled themselves into thinking he had them to answer to.

The other part was his physical strength. His body absorbed bullets like they were vitamin pills. The last people dumb enough to mix it with him had been four Colombians armed with machetes who'd hit him in the middle of a Sunday afternoon barbecue at his home. He'd disembowelled the first man with a steak knife and hacked a second apart with the machete he took from the first. While the other two thought about making reservations on the next flight back to Bogota, Jefferson reached his gun and shot them both through the head. The first man lived long enough to have his face charred over a bed of burning charcoal briquettes. Before he died he told Jefferson who he was working for. A week later a farmer thirty miles west of the City found the body of little-league coke dealer Wilfredo Gomez half-devoured in one of his hog pens.

The Medical Examiner said that Gomez had still been alive when the hogs had started eating.

Joe Gags felt bad but for the time being Grimes was going to have to hang in there and tough it out alone. If Jefferson brought him out alive Gags would follow them and see if an opportunity to spring Grimes loose developed. It wasn't much of a chance but that was as far as Gags could see himself going. He settled down to wait.

There was an alternative. Whatever Jefferson was doing in there was sure as shit illegal. Gags could have called the police anonymously and had a pair of patrolmen sent around to investigate a disturbance in Grimes' apartment. He could have arranged for a lawyer to be there at the same time. Jefferson wouldn't be arrested or punished – the idea made Gags laugh – but it would get Grimes out of the hole he was in, at least for the time being. Gags thought about it long enough to realize that Jefferson would know in a second who had made the calls. Then he thought about Wilfredo Gomez.

Sorry, Grimes old buddy, he thought. Just can't be done.

CHAPTER NINE

Clarence Jefferson T3 thought of himself as a man who liked to get to the heart of a matter. It hadn't happened yet – ever – but he continued to live in hope.

Weighty words. He paused, chewing slowly on a mouthful of wholewheat hotcakes, and considered their meaning. 'Heart' for instance. As in broken? Empty? Bleeding? Of gold? Of stone? Of darkness? The conceit pleased him. Yes, in that lonely inner region of stress and strife you could always count on darkness. He shovelled another forkful of carbohydrate into his mouth and looked across the room at Grimes.

The doctor was slumped forward with his face and shoulder supporting his weight against the wall. Above his head hung a photograph of Warren Oates. The first interrogation session had given Jefferson a frisson of excitement as he'd realized that he hadn't been mistaken in hoping for something out of the ordinary. Interrogation was developing into dialogue. That excited him because dialogue was rare. With the likes of Cleveland Carter and Joe Gags he merely communicated – an exchange of information and little more. With Grimes he saw the opportunity to forge a mutual language of feeling and maybe – just maybe – provide the groundwork for a moment of meeting.

Jefferson finished his breakfast and carried the plate into the kitchen. He poured himself a second cup of coffee, took it through into the living-room and settled down in his chair again.

He reflected that sometimes, in the utter loneliness of

his work, he wanted to scream out loud. Only by keeping moving, moving forward like a boxer's doubled fist, by trampling underfoot, by accumulating power, could he keep the screams at bay. He knew the risks involved in making a commitment to Grimes. The mutual language they shared was violence – the language of history and of nations, of the cradle and the grave, of kings and desperate men. Jefferson was fluent.

As far as he could see – and he'd looked hard – violence bled from every pore of the world's filthy sweating hide. To escape into comforting fantasies of love and fulfilment and justice seemed to him an appalling lie, but no one really seemed to want to know about that or why it might be so. Jefferson sought the why. Not the why of science or politics or psychology – he'd been through that and come out feeling cheated – but the living why, the state of feeling and knowledge that resonated in the blood and could only be approached through a moment of meeting between two naked souls. Perhaps that moment was insanity – or death – but if so, then he welcomed either over the void that filled his chest.

That Grimes spoke the language too was evident from the clues scattered thickly about his life. The family – George and Luther Grimes – the self-imposed isolation, the martial arts, the failed flight into medicine, the shit on the walls, the obvious guilt and self-loathing that had poured out when Jefferson had pushed the right buttons – these facts told the beginning of a story – like . . . RED . . . DUST . . . FIRE . . . TWILIGHT . . . BONES . . . that Jefferson felt and understood. Together, together and yet alone, they would dissolve and then recreate the rest of the story and in the space between them the meaning would arise.

For a moment Jefferson felt a shifting in his entrails, of fear and pity, of the fear *of* pity. PITY . . . FEAR . . . PAIN . . . Pain awaited them both, for in the struggle Jefferson would have to risk as much as he might gain. He set his coffee cup down. On the floor beside him was a cardboard box full of old letters, a fragmentary diary, dog-eared notebooks. They belonged to Grimes and provided a commentary on his inner life. Bit by bit, feeling his way by observation and instinct, Jefferson would reintroduce Grimes to his own past and either crack his heart in pieces or give him the tools to build something better.

If he failed he'd console himself with the cash. He thought about that. He didn't need the money. It wouldn't buy him anything that he wanted. But somehow there was a principle involved and now that he was aware of the money's existence he felt obliged to take it. Maybe he was trapped by his own reputation; but there'd be time to think about that later. Right now he had work to do.

The first notebook Jefferson had read, from when Grimes was in his early twenties, was full of the stuff you'd expect from a young punk who wanted to kick ass but found himself stuck in a library instead. Nietzsche, Burroughs, Whitman, Blake. Jefferson, with satisfaction, had recognized a lot of it from his own youth. Now he picked up another book from the pile and opened it. On the inside of the front cover were written the words of another captain: Ahab himself.

'How can the prisoner reach outside except by thrusting through the walls?'

A thrill ran through Jefferson's body and he smiled grimly. How indeed? He looked across at Grimes for a moment, at the stubborn frame that still refused to fall, and wondered what walls were pressing in on him within the confines of the black cloth bag.

Jefferson sipped his coffee and settled down to read.

CHAPTER TEN

Sometimes – like the mornings when he woke at 4am and couldn't get back to sleep, or when one too many Wild Turkeys tipped him into melancholy – it seemed to George Grimes that he'd worked his whole damned life for nothing but the pain that held it together. He blinked hard and raised his hands to rub his eyes. The movement made his joints crack and he groaned. His head throbbed in the palms of his hands and his mouth was dry. A couple of blocks away church bells were ringing and he looked at the clock on the wall. Christ. He hadn't slept until after nine in years.

But then it wasn't so often he sat up alone until almost dawn, downing half a bottle of whiskey to try and still the motion of the grinding wheel turning endlessly inside his head. Just as well. He'd fallen asleep in the armchair and now his legs were numb and he couldn't move them. He shuffled his body around and the blood-flow returned painfully to his buttocks and legs. When the pins and needles eventually wore off he raised himself from the chair with his arms and slowly stood up. His feet hurt and he noticed that his ankles had swollen up some and were bulging against the edges of his shoes. The sight reminded him of how old and worthless he was and made it more difficult to justify getting up at all. Habit and pride won out and he moved across the room.

The room was stiflingly hot and he felt sticky and unwashed. When he looked in the mirror he saw a damp patch on his shirt where he had drooled during his drunken sleep. He shook his head and walked through to the bathroom and stripped his clothes off. He took a long shower and a close shave. By the time he returned to the parlour he'd changed into a fresh set of clothes, drunk a quart of ice water and he felt a little more human.

The fried chicken dinner he'd prepared for him and Gene still lay congealed on the table and one by one he scraped the dishes of food – of cob corn and sweet potatoes and butter squash – into the trash can and stacked the dishes in the kitchen sink. He was sixty-nine years old and he guessed that none of it really mattered much anymore except to him – and who gave a damn about a stupid old man and the regrets heaped around him like piles of ancient dust? The madness in the blood flowed from one generation to the next and no one knew how to stop it.

'Well, now you're alone, old man, and better off that way.'

George Grimes flinched as he ran water into the sink. Gene hadn't ought to have talked to him that way; but he couldn't really blame him. He hadn't been much of a father to the boy. Or to Luther either for that matter. Now one would kill the other and likely as not he'd never see either of them again. An age-old sense of impotence and despair welled up inside him and turned into a deep and melancholic rage. He wanted to pound the dirty dishes to pieces and keep on pounding until his fists were bloodied to the bone. He gripped the edge of the sink for a moment then turned off the water and went through to the bedroom to find the keys to his car.

He hadn't meant to sound like he was telling Gene what to do but sometimes it was hard for a father to remember that his son wasn't ten years old anymore. He'd always been hard on the boys but then they'd been hard times. He'd had to show them how to survive, how to take one in the belly without going down and then come back with ten, twenty punches in return. Maybe he should've mixed a bit of sugar into the brew, showed them how much they meant to him. Maybes, buts and should've. Pisswater, bullshit and balls.

He scraped a handful of change and some paper money into his hand from the bedside table and put it in his pants. The change jingled in his pocket and he suddenly remembered his own father, biting and kicking as he was dragged away by the B Specials to die of pneumonia in one of their stinking gaols. Perhaps he'd brought the bad blood over from Ulster, when he himself was just a kid, cowering with his mother in the hold of that damned ship. True or not, none of that made any difference now; but maybe he could make a difference. Maybe it wasn't too late to undo some of the wrong. He picked up the car keys and went out onto the street, locking the front door behind him. He had to try.

He couldn't let them break his heart without putting up a fight.

CHAPTER ELEVEN

'Tell me about it,' said Callie. Her voice was clear. But why had she said it?

'Why did you say that?' said Grimes.

His voice was muffled by the cloth. The cloth was a second skin on his face and the skin was diseased – itching, soggy, peeling – and forever his. A cockney voice in his head sang: *Our orders was to break you, And of course we went and did.* He wasn't sure where he was. His limbs were tubes of mush. He could barely feel them. His mouth was as dry as brick. *For God's sake fetch the water . . .*

Callie sat straddling his hips and fucked him slowly, letting saliva fall from her mouth onto his chest. The saliva ran down the grooves between his ribs and soaked into the sofa. While she moved on top of him she reached behind her with her right hand and found his balls and rubbed them in the moisture leaking from her cunt.

Grimes said 'Fuck me.'

The second skin still muffled his voice. No one had ever fucked him like this before. Except Jefferson. He giggled into the bag. She'd fucked him without a break for two days, used his body like it was something she'd bought and paid for. Odd feeling, man. What you might call a mixed feeling. Jesus. Let her. He was ready to do anything she wanted. Anything at all. She was the wagonmaster. She'd turned it all round. He loved her.

'I love her.'

What did that mean? He'd probably never know; unless Jefferson could tell him; or Luther. After all, she fucked Luther too. Oh yes. Maybe she was fucking him right now, while he, Grimes, was sweating his sanity away into Jefferson's black bag so she could hang onto life, liberty and the pursuit of happiness. He'd asked her about that – about fucking. That was how all this had started. He'd come inside her, painfully, and she'd sucked her lips and smiled to herself and then he'd asked her.

'You fuck your friend like this too?'

Callie ran her hands down over her belly and thighs and onto Grimes' flanks. 'What friend?' she said.

'The man you helped rob the bank.'

Jealousy gave Grimes a tight feeling below his navel that increased the intensity of his longing. On balance he liked it.

'You called him Luther. When I asked "Luther who?" you said he'd kill you if he knew.'

'I told you about that?' This time anxiety broke through in her voice.

'You don't remember waking up last night,' said Grimes.

'I'd forgotten about it,' she said. 'It was horrible.'

'Yeah, you had a bad time,' said Grimes.

He looked at her for a few seconds and continued.

'I found you fighting the sheets and crying out in your sleep. You were soaking with sweat. Increased dreaming is common after cocaine withdrawal. Nightmares can be bad, especially if you're already paranoid. In the nightmare your man Luther was threatening to kill you and you were trying to convince him that you loved him. Seems he didn't believe you. I let you talk. The story was garbled but enough detail came out to make sense. You were still talking when you fell back to sleep.'

Suddenly Grimes didn't want her so close to him anymore.

'I need a cigarette,' he said.

He slid out from underneath her and stood up.

'You want a beer?'

Callie nodded and he brought two bottles of Carta Blanca from the icebox. When he came back Callie was wrapped in a white bathtowel that set off her tan. She was smoking a Marlboro. Grimes sat in the armchair and lit a Pall Mall.

'You needn't worry,' he said. 'Everything you say here is in confidence. What you did in the past, what you do when you leave, none of that is my business.'

But he wanted it to be his business. All of it.

'You want to talk about it, that's fine. You don't want to talk, that's fine too.'

'There's a lot of money involved,' she said.

Grimes concealed his relief. 'A million dollars is the figure you mentioned.'

'Some people might figure that knowing about it would entitle them to a piece.'

'I couldn't give a fuck for the money, but I can't prove it. You might look around this place, though. If I was hungry for the good life I could do a lot better.'

There was a long pause while Callie thought things over and drank her beer.

Finally Grimes said, 'Sometimes all kinds of things become clearer if you talk about them. Keeping a secret like that must have taken some effort. I can see how a line of coke might've made the stress easier to deal with.'

'Tell me about it,' said Callie. 'Jesus. Sometimes it got to me worse than others. You know? Thinking about getting caught, trying to figure out a way to get my end of the money without getting killed, wondering whether I should split right away or wait until the heat died down. Plus at home I'm still having to live like Anita Bryant, except when Cleve feels like ejaculating down the leg of his pants. The coke helped me feel confident enough to do what I knew was best. I also had to deal with the gang.'

'How many?'

'Four. Luther brought them in from out of state. They were as cool as ice until we'd finished the job. Then they turned into a bunch of paranoids, least that's what I called them at the time. Funny, huh? It was my idea to sit on the money for six months before splitting it up. Luther saw the potential in that but the guys didn't like it. They were no cream puffs but they were scared of Luther. If they made any complaints he'd roll his eyes and froth a little and leave his finger marks on one of their throats, and they'd do whatever he said. Afterwards, when we were alone together, he'd laugh about it and make out he had just turned the psycho act on to keep them down, but it always looked pretty real to me. Once or twice, when things weren't going his way in the sack, he turned on me too.'

As Grimes listened to her talking he felt a deep sense of dread stir in his belly. He'd felt it the night before when she'd first used the name, but he'd ignored it. A name meant nothing. There were enough Luthers in the state to start another Reformation. But Grimes could feel those hands on his throat. He'd seen what they could do: as a child and a teenager in the street gangs in Chicago; as a helpless asshole in Nicaragua. His fist tightened on the beer bottle in his hand.

'Tell me what he looks like,' he said.

'Handsome,' said Callie. 'Or maybe horny's a better word. Yeah. He made me feel horny as hell. That's how I met him. My car broke down one time and he was a mechanic in the garage I went to for repairs. Tall, muscle-y but slim, long black hair brushed straight back from his forehead and tied in a pony-tail.'

The jealousy squeezing his guts got tighter. Perversely, Grimes still wanted the feeling. It hurt but he wanted it. He could see the hard lean torso and the long hair, could see Callie going down on him and enjoying it. His balls tingled and his cock became erect again. Echoes of the primal scene. He dragged hard on his cigarette and let her go on.

'He had a widow's peak like yours. In fact he looks like you except his face is leaner and his nose is bigger and sharper. And his eyes are brown, nearly black. Eyes that look all the way through you sometimes like you're not there. You got to understand that I hadn't had any real sex at all since I married Cleveland. I took the car back the next evening and invited him out. We fucked each other the same night, bent over the hood of the car in the parking lot of Cleve's church. Hey, I'm not embarrassing you with all this, am I? You look uncomfortable.'

102

Grimes became aware of the muscles tightening in his face. He tried to relax but couldn't. A plexus of nameless and primitive emotions enmeshed his throat and made it difficult to speak. The erection hurt him. He took a swallow of beer and said, 'Did he ever talk about his past?'

'Not much. He said he had no family, never been married, bummed around a lot in Mexico, that kind of thing.'

'Did he ever talk about Angola?'

'The state penitentiary? He spent two years in there after he got into a fight with three sailors . . .'

'And left one with nothing below the neck except memories,' finished Grimes.

'You know him then.'

'He's got a tattoo on his right shoulder. A screaming eagle in red and blue. 101st Airborne.'

That's Luther. He didn't tell me he knew you personally. Or maybe he did, I wasn't taking much notice of what he said by then. I really thought he was taking me to be tortured by the Mafia and the police. It feels weird, thinking about it now.'

'He wouldn't have told you that he knew me,' said Grimes. 'What's his full name? Luther who?'

'Logan.'

'Logan.' Nice joke. Gun crazy. Johnny Guitar. He remembered Luther taking him to see it; and a whole bunch of other westerns too. The pain of nostalgia pressed on his chest.

He said, 'How close are you and Luther? Do you love him? You going to go away with him, settle down maybe?'

'Jesus, no,' said Callie. 'He's too unstable. I like him, but not that much. The problem is he's completely crazy about me.'

She licked her lips and gave Grimes a hard look.

'I don't have a hundred-thousand-dollar education like you but I know who I am. There's a kind of woman that tough-guys types fall for in a bad way. Ever since I was a teenager guys have been fighting over me and telling me they were in love before they even knew my second name. For a time it made me feel good. Then I realized that none of

them knew who I was or even gave much of a shit. I was just a sexy picture from one of their motorcycle mags, someone to look cute while they posed on their hogs and swapped tough talk.'

Grimes smiled. 'How do you reconcile all this hill-billy feminism with hunting Luther's cock like it was an endangered species?'

'Listen, big shot. You don't know. It would have been real easy to end up married to one of those jerk-offs back home. Like all my schoolfriends did, like my sister. Guys have such big dreams when they're young. They're all going to be heroes. Ten years later they're living in front of the TV with a six-pack by the chair, working on their pot bellies and waiting to die. Like Dad. Dad was a bullying scumbag who thought he was a good husband because he bought Mama sexy underwear three sizes too small for Christmas. I left home the day after my sixteenth birthday and didn't go back until after he died. Mama made excuses for him all her life. He broke wind in her face for thirty years and she never once stuck up for herself, or any of us either. I didn't know why then and I don't know now, I just knew it would never happen to me. I've been fucked a thousand ways from sundown but no one's ever touched me unless I had my own good reasons for letting them. Including you and Luther.'

'I'm sorry,' said Grimes. 'I shouldn't have cracked wise. I just wonder how things are going to work out between you and him.'

'Luther will do anything I ask him to but he's unstable. If he knew I planned to leave him after the split I think he'd kill me. That's not your paranoid drug psychosis either. He'd kill me before he'd let me leave him.'

'What are you going to do about it?' said Grimes.

'I wish I knew.'

'And the money. What's going to happen to all that money?'

'I don't know.'

'I don't believe you,' said Grimes.

104

She looked uncomfortable and lit another cigarette while Grimes waited.

'Okay, so we don't want to split the money six ways. Luther reckons he can kill all four of them, grease them he says. I believe him.'

'I'd believe him too; but I still don't believe you. I like you, Callie. I could spend time with you. And you're also the toughest cookie I've met in a long time, which is great. I reckon the minute it suits you you're going to put two or three bullets through the back of Luther's head.'

'You're crazy.'

'I don't think so. If I'm right, and I'm not crazy, there's a possibility we can help each other out,' said Grimes.

'What do you mean?' said Callie.

Grimes felt nauseous as he said it, but he said it anyway; and meant it: 'Luther's real name is Grimes, like mine. He's my brother.'

He paused. It was harder than he'd imagined.

'I want to kill him too.'

The boy's stomach churned and his teeth ached and he felt both elated and terrified at the same time.

Grimes couldn't make out the boy's face; couldn't see his eyes; but he had no doubt who the boy was.

His stomach churned. His teeth ached.

'Listen to me! I've had about a bellyfull of this reconciliation talk. That's just a fancy word the ass-kissers in this union use for selling us out. Those fat-bellied bastards pay themselves good wages. All they ever do is tell us to get back to work. They drink at the same country clubs as the bosses so what the hell can you expect? Talk solves nothing. The bosses understand that real well. They do their negotiating with hired guns and axe handles. I say it's time we negotiated back!'

There was a rumble from the crowd of sixty or so men and George Grimes grinned. The boy felt power emanating from him, as if George Grimes could stretch out a hand and destroy the city of Chicago with a thunderbolt. He wore a white vest stained with sweat and blood, and bib overalls. Cannonball shoulders built from hauling meat carcasses glistened in a hard bright sun. Beyond the crowd of wildcat strikers stood three ranks of policemen holding nightsticks. Behind the police were half a dozen men in double-breasted suits and snap-brimmed hats. Their hard beefy faces were swollen with hatred. George Grimes pointed a walnut-knuckled hand at the suits.

'There are the guilty men, boys! They're packing guns under those coats. You can bet your ass they weren't packing guns on Iwo Jima. We did their killing for them. Now they stomp on our balls with iron boots and expect us to be grateful just because they got a smile on their face while they do it.'

He swung a clenched fist in the air.

'I say fuck them and fuck them good!'

'Yeah!' He had the crowd boiling. Some of the men were rolling their shoulders and pounding their fists into their hands, looking behind them at the police.

The boy's teeth ached. His stomach churned. He came out from behind the barrel at back of the loading dock and climbed on top to get a better look.

In the distance two more suited men arrived and joined the first group. An envelope exchanged hands and four of the men passed through the police lines and began to make their way through the crowd in a wedge.

'Well listen, hey listen! This fight ain't about dough. It's about freedom. Our freedom. Those cops ain't our people. They're mercenaries. They won't help you. And neither will the politicians or the law or the goddamned union until WE take it all back. If we don't fight now we'll be stomped on for the rest of our lives . . .'

The men in suits had mounted the loading platform and one of them was waving a sheaf of papers at George Grimes and trying to make himself heard.

' . . . And to start with,' went on Grimes, 'we're going to take these bastard gangsters and open their assholes wide.'

106

George Grimes fell on the company agents like a starving lion on raw meat. Swinging his hips and shoulders into huge, crude, unblockable punches, lashing out with his workboots, butting and biting and wrenching, he ruptured their soft gunmen's bodies and toppled them from the platform like swill.

The yard was in chaos as the police moved in, clubs swinging and whistles blowing. Bloody-faced bodies began to litter the ground. A squad of officers worked their way towards the loading dock and George Grimes. A shot sounded out and a bullet sang from a wall above Grimes' head. He turned and noticed the boy and the joy of anarchy vanished from his face.

Seeing the angry face, the boy felt really scared.

George Grimes ran over and grabbed him down from the barrel.

'Gene, what are you doing here?' Grimes looked panic-stricken. 'Look your Dad's in trouble and maybe he won't be around for a while to look after you. Now you get away from here. Look out for Luther for me while I'm gone. Now go.'

The boy staggered backwards as George Grimes shoved him away and turned to meet the rush of policemen. The boy started to run, into the passage through the abattoir, but looked over his shoulder in time to see the blue uniforms swarm over his father. For a moment he couldn't see him, then a uniform reeled back, fell to his knees and crawled away, screaming and pouring gore before collapsing onto his face. Then a second. A third. Nightsticks rose and fell, rose and fell. Under the threshing arms a terrible creature still swung and grabbed and tore, but every blow of every club was striking home. The boy could hear the rhythm of wood and boot on skull and ribs and backbone. With sudden exaltation – that sense of escape that comes with moments of extreme desperation – the boy ran forward.

And threw himself into the storm of clubs.

Shovels of earth flopped onto his face, blinding him,

silencing his little-boy cries, clogging his mouth and nostrils. He struggled against the weight of the dirt but knew it was in vain. Worms moved over his skin, cool and moist.

'I'm a dead man,' he mumbled.

He was a cadaver embalmed with darkness. At least the bag was no longer on his head. The peace of the grave changed to panic as he found himself pursued by rats through a labyrinth of sewers. He waded knee-deep through a morass of black faeces, his legs screaming at the effort, the stench scorching his lungs. He weakened, and his pace became slower and slower until he toppled forward and the rats swarmed over him, nibbling at his testicles. Fluorescent lights flickered and flared. He was no longer lying on a river of excrement but on a bed, the sheet fragrant with the secretions of sex. Callie lay across his belly and murmuring, licked his cock. He felt his cock becoming hard. The door to the room crashed open and hit the wall. Luther Grimes stood on the threshold, naked, a bloody towel clasped to his groin and a sixteen-inch Bowie knife in his hand.

'She cut my balls off,' he said. 'I want my prick back.'

Grimes sat bolt upright and shuddered. The mattress, the sheets, his legs and body were covered in steaming slime and Callie had disappeared. He struggled free of the bed and ran to the window. He threw it wide and jumped out. He dropped through the air, blissfully free, falling forever. He landed in a pair of huge arms and looked up into Jefferson's eyes. The eyes were gentle and sad. So sad. He put his head against Jefferson's chest and wept.

The images seethed in his head. Memory and fantasy. He could no longer distinguish between them. He loved her. Luther loved her. Jealousy flooded his mouth, sour and hot, and he knew that sooner rather than later she would leave them both, but how? And who was 'she'? He swallowed. Luther was his brother, his hero, his mentor. Luther raised him and Luther loved him. And he loved Luther. He knew he did. And feared him, and his viciousness and strength. Kill the cocksucker and enjoy it.

Luther stood over a dead woman. Another dead woman. So many. Behind him a young girl looked on silently. But the woman had blue-black hair and Callie's was yellow. Then Luther died as Grimes locked his forearms about his neck and broke the cervical vertebrae. So he was dead already then. Grief scraped its nails down his cheeks and Grimes wept.

Another fantasy, another memory would replace the last before he could make sense of them. He saw the face of the chief resident in surgery, his pimpled skin swelling from behind a green face-mask, eyes bulging above the sterile paper like ambitious piles, fetid breath issuing perverse instructions, lies for hire, poison, the words lashing Grimes' heart with steel wires. Grimes tore the mask off and found the face of his professor in psychiatry, smiling with immeasurable sympathy, nodding with endless patience, listening with limitless understanding. Grimes pointed his finger at him and the face warped with outrage and maggots fell from its mouth. Sweet Jesus, sweet Jesus. Time and imagination, thought and sensation, reality and hallucination were fusing into a single delirium. The categories that normally structured the world for him no longer existed. The seals between the different parts of his mind were leaking, allowing infinite stores of memory and dream and emotion to swirl together like disastrous chemicals.

During brief periods of lucidity he realized that he was probably becoming psychotic. At such moments every cell in his body screamed for a fucking break, and white noise hissed through his ears in a dense jet. If he concentrated and dissected the different sources of ache and pain and itch and numbness flooding into his brain he could identify the pressure of earphones against his skull. He recalled Jefferson placing them on his head and the noise starting: a grinding uneven hiss with a regular cycle. After a few minutes he recognized it as the sound of a hi-fi needle scraping in the blank grooves at the end of a record. Then the recollection and the pressure and the noise would disappear and he could hear children's voices chanting in Spanish, echoing from hollow walls, and feel the stomp of soldiers' footsteps and the heat and crackle of flames and the shudder of exploding shells. He cried out for a clamp, a bag of saline, more morphine. But no one could hear him.

Sad. Unbearably sad.

Grimes started to cry again.

CHAPTER TWELVE

When a man lived deep in the bayou country he got used to not hearing much in the way of human sounds. Day and night the noise of the swamp – of wind and branch and slow-moving water, of insects and birds and small mammals – was so constant that it became silence. Any sound made by human hand, or the work of human hand, rose like a column of smoke through the dense green leaves. So although the noise was far away and he couldn't say exactly what it was, Luther Grimes heard it at once and knew he had an unexpected visitor on his hands.

He was lying naked on his bed. The old trapper's cabin he'd made his base for the past three months was a primitive mildewed hole. There was no power, no telephone, no running water. He had to eat a lot of canned food, and the mosquitoes bit his ass when he went to take a shit. But hardly anyone knew the place existed, the nearest cop was forty miles away and besides, he'd endured a lot worse.

When the noise outside disturbed him he was masturbating. This was his habit on most days when he didn't see Callie and today in particular he didn't want sexual tension adding its weight to the other stresses on his mind. Quickly but without hurry he swung his legs from the bed and put on a pair of jeans. On his feet he pulled a pair of boots and wrapped and tied the laces around each ankle without taking the time to thread them through the eyelets in the leather. From the crate by his bed he picked up a Ruger Blackhawk .41 Mag and as he walked to a chest of drawers at the end of the room he checked the loads in the gun. From the top drawer he took money, a passport and some keys and put them in his pockets. On his way to the door he grabbed a tiger-striped combat jacket from the back of a chair and threw it over one shoulder.

Because of the freshening wind it was cooler outside than in the cabin, but the heat was so damp that any movement at all started him sweating. The inside of his arms slid against his flanks as he walked. The intrusive sound was obvious now: a car engine moving slowly along the narrow track that wound from the parish road two miles to the east. The cabin was set in a small clearing surrounded by cypress trees and palmettoes that were gradually reclaiming the space for themselves. Luther cocked the Ruger and slid into the bush. Fleshy leaves draped themselves over his shoulders. He stood without motion, breathing silently. From here he could observe the track and the clearing and if need be could reach the station wagon he had parked at the rear of the cabin without being seen.

When he recognized the old Ford pick-up truck he lowered the hammer of the revolver, stuck the gun in the back of his jeans and stepped out from the trees. He winced internally. Today was a bad time for his father to come calling; but there was no way Luther would tell him so. As Luther walked up to the truck, shrugging his arms into the combat jacket, his father shut off the engine and climbed out from behind the wheel. George Grimes had a grey tinge to his skin and desperation in his eyes.

Luther kept the worry he felt from his voice and said, 'Dad. Good to see you.'

'Luther,' said his father and they shook hands, short and hard. 'How you doin'?'

'Pretty good,' said Luther. 'Busy as hell but good.'

He took his father's arm and walked him towards the cabin.

'I got a project just about to pay off for me. If it goes the way I planned I'll be leaving the country for a while.'

They paused at the cabin door.

'Oh?' said his father. 'A long while?'

'Yeah,' said Luther. 'I may not be coming back.'

His father suddenly looked old. Luther had never thought of George Grimes as being old before. He'd had wrinkles and grey hair for years, but that wasn't old. Old was a look in the eyes that said you'd given up the fight and were ready to be grateful for whatever scraps they left for you. Old was people nodding and smiling while you spoke without listening to a goddamn word you said. George Grimes was just about the only person Luther ever did listen to. Seeing him like this – slowed up and hunched in and nervous – made Luther feel bad. It made him think that maybe he should've done more to look after him.

'Hey, you look kind of tired,' he said. 'Come and set yourself down. I can't offer you a cold beer but I'll make coffee, if you like.'

George Grimes shook his head.

'If it's all the same to you I'd rather walk. Don't often get the chance to see the country.'

'Okay. We'll go down to the water. Watch your step as you go.'

As they made their way through the trees and the muggy heat they swapped small-talk, about each other's health and the heavy weather coming up from the Gulf, and about the bastards George Grimes worked for at the warehouse and how they were pushing him to take a cut in pay because there were a hundred and one illegal Latinos begging to do his job for thirty per cent less.

Luther let George do most of the talking, partly because he felt his father needed it, partly because he never spoke to his father about anything that really mattered. He admired and respected George Grimes, his toughness and his pride, and he never lied to him, but he'd always kept his deeper thoughts and feelings to himself. If that was something he ought to have felt sad about he didn't, not anymore. So as they walked, Luther listened but his mind strayed elsewhere – to Callie and the split and what they'd do in Mexico. When they reached the edge of the bayou his father turned round and asked him if he'd heard from Gene.

'So that's why you're here,' said Luther.

George Grimes broke a branch from a bush and hunkered down on his heels, plucking the leaves off one by one. Luther couldn't see his face.

'I think he knows where you are,' said George Grimes.

'He tell you that?' said Luther.

'No, not exactly. He came to see me last night. We had a fight, you know how it goes sometimes with me and him. He said some things.'

George Grimes shrugged and kept his face turned away and hunched down into his chest. The branch in his hands shook and a tremor ran across his broad square shoulders. Only once before – a long time ago – had Luther witnessed his father crying. His guts squirmed and he didn't know what to do. He clenched his fists and looked out across the wilderness, searching the trees rising from the shallow eddying water for an answer. A low swamp hum more implacable than silence drifted back through the warm green haze. With a conscious effort Luther reached out to take his father's arm and raise him up.

Before he could touch him his father turned and said, 'Promise me you won't hurt him, Luther.'

His voice was faint and rough as if his throat was scorched with smoke, and his eyes were smudged with the colour of broken veins.

It's too late for that, Luther wanted to say, I already hurt him and there's no way to make it right because that's the way the world is. But he said, instead, 'I wouldn't. You know I wouldn't.'

'I don't know any such thing.' George Grimes stood up, throwing the stripped branch into the river. 'Why should I know? You neither one of you tell me a goddamn thing. Gene's a good man. I gave him a lousy start – Jesus Christ, I've thrashed myself for that for thirty years – but somehow he made something out of it, something great and fine . . .'

I'm the 'somehow' thought Luther, I'm the fucking 'somehow', and you still don't see that, you blind old bastard. The bitterness swelled against the confines of the vessel he'd built inside himself to contain it. While you were cooling your stupid Irish heels in Joliet prison I was putting him through school and protecting his ass from all that shit on the street, where you left us. Me, Luther Nobody. I held the centre. I had the balls. Now you want me to do it again. Well fuck you . . . The pressure peaked and the vessel held and Luther kept silent as his father went on.

'Now look at him. He's dumped his life into a garbage-bag of whores and cops and goddamned drug-addicts. Why? Why?'

'The world you know's gone under, Dad, long time back. You wouldn't drop it so they left you behind. I live in the backstreets, where there isn't too much light and where most folk don't want to go. I never felt comfortable anywhere else. But Eugene's staked himself out across the border between them, between my world and theirs. Maybe he's afraid to know where he really belongs.'

His father wasn't listening. 'Why is there bad blood between you two?'

'I can't tell you.'

'I have a right to know.'

'No,' said Luther. 'You don't. I did him wrong. A double wrong.' He thought about it. 'A triple wrong. He's got the right to feel whatever he feels and more. I got no defence. But if he won't tell you, I can't. It's his story, not mine.'

George Grimes' shoulders sagged and he looked out across the water as Luther had done, as if he were trying to see beyond the horizon of his own hurt and find out what to do for the best.

'You once told me,' said Luther, 'that as long as I took

the consequences like a man and didn't crawl, you'd never be ashamed of me, no matter what badness I did.'

His father's gaze remained fixed on a vanishing point deep within the hum of the swamp. 'Yes,' he replied. 'That's what I told you.'

The wind was getting up and for a second Luther almost felt cool. He took his father's arm and his father turned towards him. They held each other's eyes for a while until it became too painful and Luther looked away.

'Let's go back,' he said.

They returned along the trail together in silence and when they got to the cabin Luther offered his father some coffee again and again his father refused.

'I'd best head on back. You got things to do.'

'Yes,' said Luther.

They walked over to the Ford pick-up and George Grimes climbed into the driver's seat and sat with the door open. For a moment he seemed to struggle with himself.

'I never thought Gene was better than you,' he said, abruptly.

Luther saw that it was hard for him and kept quiet.

'Just because he went to college and became a doctor and all I wasn't more proud of him than you. When you came back from Vietnam holding yourself like a man I was never prouder. It made me feel we had something we shared because, like I said to Gene, you and me trod the same bloody turf for our country.'

'You never said that to me,' said Luther, and then was sorry because of the guilt and despair that swam into his father's face.

'I didn't think I needed to. There's some things that men should understand between each other without having to paint a picture. Isn't that so?'

Luther swallowed thickly. 'You're right, Dad. There was no need to paint a picture.'

Luther had had enough and wanted to be alone. He badly wanted a Lucky too but they were over in the cabin.

116

'Listen,' he said, 'you should get back now. You don't want to get caught out on the highway when this storm hits. You never can tell how vicious they're gonna be.'

George Grimes nodded resignedly and Luther closed the truck door. They shook hands through the open window and George held on to Luther's hand after the shake stopped.

'Promise me,' he said.

Luther squeezed his hand. 'I give you my word.'

George Grimes gave his head a small shake, his eyes swimming and his lips pressed together. Then, without either of them speaking again and keeping his eyes on the windshield, George Grimes started the engine and drove away down the track.

Luther went back to the cabin, grimacing at the dim foulness of the air inside, and poured himself a glass of Jack Daniels and lit a cigarette. He tossed the revolver onto the bed and lay down.

Staring up at the low ceiling, he suddenly felt older than his father, older than the swamp outside. The caper with Callie – the robbery and the plan tonight to double-cross the others and keep the cash for themselves – was meant to be his last go round. He'd reached that age in his life when he didn't want to have to spend time wondering what came next, and this last year he'd almost come to believe it – to believe in her, to believe that he could finally back off.

'Back off to what?' he said, to the ceiling.

There was too much unfinished business, but he was sick of being the strong one, the one who always had to take charge. That was the story of his life. When his father had been carted off to Joliet for attempted murder during some nothing strike that nobody wanted except Mr George Grimes, Luther had been fourteen years old and brother Eugene eight. Luther had moved in with a woman, a painter over twice his age named Sylvia who thought he was a cute eighteen. They'd kept Eugene out of the hands of the authorities for six years until George had come home and fucked everything up again by taking Eugene away. Luther, knowing that the day he lost his temper with his father he would kill him, had left a note for Sylvia and enlisted in the army for a nine-year stretch.

In the discipline of the army he'd found an enemy worthy of the wildness in his heart. Anything so juvenile as to try bucking the system never crossed his mind. He ate the system, made it his. He consumed the discipline like fuel. He never bitched, never hesitated, never flinched. He kept all the disobedience in his eyes where his instructors and NCOs would read it and pick up the glove and try to break him. They never did. And between the moulds of their brutality and his own internal anarchism Luther turned himself into that rare being, the superb soldier.

Or, as his buddy Beckett had been fond of putting it, the controlled psychopath in search of death.

Through Airborne training and US Rangers school he saw the weak fall out and himself get stronger. On weekend furloughs, just to find out, he would drop into bars where fat, bearded would-be hardcases wearing 'Hell's Angels MC' on their jackets would pick on him, because of his haircut, in pairs of threes or fives. The odds never made that much difference. Then the war came and he didn't need that shit anymore; because they sent him to Vietnam.

Afterwards he despised deeply anyone who suggested that the war had turned him crazy; so much so that if he wasn't feeling good he would deliberately prove their point by smashing two or three of their stupid bones. The war broke a lot of guys, but that wasn't surprising, and Luther never felt a flicker of contempt for any of them. His own men, teenagers mostly, looked to him for strength and support and found it, always, whether they broke or not. He led them with distinction and Top Sergeant Luther Grimes came out of the war as he went in – himself, only more so. Two million dead they said. Just a number. Especially to the shit-guzzling dogs who kept it going and the liberal jerk-off scumbags who spat on his men when they came home. Well at least some of them weren't just numbers to me, he thought, Americans and Vietnamese. He'd seen their suffering faces, he'd felt the liquid heat of their blood. And he'd known, from early on, that they couldn't win and that he'd never find his own direction home.

The monologue of memories in his head was winding him up tighter than was good for him. He lit another Lucky and blew out the first lungful with disgust. It had all gone sour, the war, the army, and him with it. Corrupted, degraded and smeared with the shit they all deserved. His last tour he couldn't bear to lead another frightened bunch of under-trained, under-equipped boys into the butcher's yard and had volunteered for long-range reconnaissance. In Saigon he'd found out how a man with his skills could make a lot of dollars if he didn't mind selling his soul, and by that point Luther Grimes wasn't sure that he had one.

The rest was shit, all of it, he knew, and had brought him little enough but a truck-load of grief, a million bucks and a desperate love for a woman who, likely as not, was fucking his brother right now and getting set to betray him. No, the war hadn't changed him much.

Luther Grimes lay on his back, sweating and smoking in the stagnant room, and tried to work out what to do next.

CHAPTER THIRTEEN

When Grimes collapsed for the third time in an hour Jefferson took the earphones from the doctor's head and switched off the hi-fi. Swearing at the pain in his injured knee he squatted down, picked Grimes up in his arms and carried him over to the sofa.

The black suit that Grimes wore was saturated with sweat. When Jefferson peeled the bag off his head Grimes wrinkled his eyelids to the light but that was the only response he made. Jefferson tugged his bottom lip. When he'd clubbed Grimes to the ground earlier on he'd hit him harder than he should have done. Introducing physical violence into this method of torture was of dubious value. The method created appalling mental stress. Physically it produced constant pain in every joint and muscle without damaging the vital organs. An optimum level of tension had to be maintained and too much brute force could upset the balance. He had seen men escape from the stress into lunacy or hysterical mutism.

Jefferson had no use for either a lunatic or a mute.

He had studied the technique as developed by the British Army in Northern Ireland. The experience of the British during a series of counter-insurgency campaigns in Malaya, Kenya, Cyprus and Aden was that physical torture was unreliable as a means of generating useful information, though it had the handy fringe benefit of terrifying the population at large. This had been Jefferson's experience too. A lot of punks would cave in if you gave them a nasty look or a few slaps. But some men could be beaten all night long without giving satisfaction.

120

State of mind and temperament were more important than physical toughness.

Certain personalities thrived on defiance; pain seemed to fuel their resistance. For others punishment was escape, penance, redemption, abdication from responsibility. Guilt and self-disgust could soak up a great deal of torture, but sensory deprivation worked on different registers in the mind. Jefferson had found it useful, but the technique undoubtedly left marks. It changed people. You had to use it with intelligence and respect. Grimes had withstood over eight hours of punishment without asking for anything. It wasn't a record, but it was impressive.

Jefferson took the handcuffs from one of Grimes' wrists and stripped off his jacket and shirt. Grimes was heavy and muscular. The definition of the muscles was blurred by some subcutaneous fat but his body looked surprisingly hard and functional. The skin of his torso was several shades paler than that of his face and forearms.

Jefferson had the sudden desire to touch Grimes' flesh, to hold him close. He was not sexually aroused. No way. His desire was more complex than lust. Lust was something to excrete into women, preferably whores. No, he wanted to close the distance. He had to get beyond Grimes' hatred and aggression. Without really knowing it he'd been waiting years for an opportunity like this and now it was desperately important: Grimes had to be made to understand him. At least one man had to understand him. He might never get another chance. If he could break through the violence in Grimes he would succeed. That was why he could not let him go. That was why he had to continue to punish him.

He handcuffed Grimes' hands in front of his body so that he could remain on his back, and then rubbed his body down with a bath towel. Grimes grunted and shifted but did not wake up. Jefferson wrapped the towel around Grimes' shoulders and went into the kitchen. Earlier on he had found a packet of vanilla tea in a cupboard. He boiled water and made a pot of the tea and carried it through into the living-room.

He sat down beside Grimes and rubbed a knuckle into his breast bone. After a few seconds Grimes stirred and tried to push Jefferson's hand away. Jefferson persisted.

Grimes said, 'Fuck,' and opened his eyes.

Jefferson offered him a cup of tea and said, 'Drink it.'

Grimes shuffled himself up into a sitting position, bent forward and sniffed at the liquid in the cup with suspicion. Jefferson drank a mouthful of tea and held the cup out again.

'Vanilla tea. No poisons, no drugs,' he said.

Grimes took the cup in both hands and drank the tea slowly, rolling each mouthful around his swollen tongue before swallowing. When the cup was empty Jefferson refilled it then went and sat in his armchair. Grimes emptied the cup again. As Grimes drank Jefferson watched him marshalling his resources, overcoming the demands of body and mind for sleep, rest, oblivion. Grimes put the cup down on the floor and massaged his face and, as best he could, stretched his torso and shoulders. When he'd finished he relaxed back on the sofa. His face was as close to alert as he was going to get this side of twelve hours' sleep.

'Where's the shitbird?' said Grimes.

'You mean Artie Mann,' said Jefferson. 'He's probably sleeping in your bed. I gave him permission to take time out for a fix. Heroin.' Jefferson shrugged. 'Artie's not a lot of help but he has the advantage of being expendable. I don't expect him to live long enough to die from AIDS.'

The sun was shining through the window and there was light traffic on the street. Sunday morning coming down.

'You want some food?' said Jefferson.

'Is that breakfast or lunch?' said Grimes.

'You want to eat or not?'

Grimes shook his head. 'I wouldn't refuse a cigarette though.'

Jefferson got out of his chair and found the red pack on the table. He shook one out and put it between Grimes' lips. He read the slogan from the crest on the front of the pack and smiled.

' "Wherever Particular People Congregate". That's nice.'

He lit a match and held it out to the cigarette in Grimes' mouth. 'Those things are sure to kill you,' he said and sat down in the armchair.

Grimes exhaled with relief. 'Fuck you.'

Grimes dragged again on the cigarette and settled back onto the sofa. He lay staring at the smoke above his head and for a few moments seemed to have forgotten about Jefferson, but then he sat up.

'Let me guess what's next. Just when I start to relax you take the cigarette off me, punch me in the belly till your fists get sore, then put the hood back on my head. Okay.'

He flicked the Pall Mall at Jefferson and stood up. As he stood up his legs wobbled and the bath towel fell from his shoulders.

'Let's get to it, then, fat man. Just spare me any more bullshit.'

Jefferson did not move from his seat, but bent over to pick up the burning cigarette which had landed on the carpet at his feet. Grimes was swaying and his eyes darted about as if he expected more people to enter the room and start doing bad things to him. Jefferson found the spectacle painful.

'I admire intelligence more than courage,' he said. 'Sit down before you fall over. Have another smoke. Let's try to talk for a few moments.'

Jefferson tossed the cigarettes and matches over onto the sofa and watched Grimes come to some realization of the shape he was in. Grimes lit another cigarette and sank back onto the sofa. He lay looking at the ceiling, dragging on the cigarette too hard so that a red cone half an inch long glowed at the tip.

'What are you thinking about?' said Jefferson.

Grimes shook his head. When he answered his voice was calm. It was the first time Jefferson had heard it express anything other than defiance or fear.

'Nothing you'd be interested in. I was just remembering a picnic Callie and I took out by the lake, and how cool the water looked through the trees.'

'By the banks of the old Pontchartrain. Are you in love with her, as they say, or just hooked on her pussy? Or can't you tell the difference?'

Grimes did not take his eyes off the ceiling. ' "I don't know" is the answer to the first question. As to the difference, I'm not sure. I like her. Lots. We made love, had sex, fucked each other, whatever you like to call it. I said I'd help her get her money. I started to love her, but she's right, I don't know who she is and it's crazy. Maybe when this is over I'll take another look and see what happens.'

'What is this "love"?' said Jefferson. 'Teach me.'

'The kind I'm talking about is like having that goddamn bag on your head, only no one can take it off for you. It's dependency, need, helplessness, anxiety, deceit. It's a fucking disaster. One minute you can leap tall buildings in a single bound. The next you want to pull your own teeth out, push your face through a concrete wall, hang yourself from a meat-hook. Jesus. I don't know what I'm talking about. Do you?'

'Maybe,' said Jefferson.

He broke his gaze away from Grimes'.

'I have needs. I don't like that but I've learned to live with it. Women relieve the needs. I resent the dependence but I accept it. I never met a woman could tell me anything I couldn't learn from a cheap magazine. I fuck them, as I like to call it. Sure. I've had five at a time. I've had them piss and shit on me while they swallowed my come.'

'How you choose to degrade yourself doesn't interest me,' said Grimes.

'Wrong, Doc. They're the ones who're degraded, not me. Like you say, it's my choice. Their choice is between doing what I say and not eating. As for romantic love, it's just a bunch of chemicals swilling around the brain that makes people realize they spend most of their lives in a fucking coma. They act like fools for a while then go back to sleep.'

'What kind of cheer-leaders did you date?'

'Cheer-leaders don't date fat boys. I did without and was happy to do so. When I got married I chose a woman I could despise without her getting too far up my nostrils. Eleanor is moderately, but only moderately, intelligent and attractive. She's socially successful, widely admired, and of a good family. She's patriotic, pious, faithful and charitable. She believes that if people like her do nice things for each other, the world will become a better place. She's the type of wife any politician would be delighted to drag around in front of the herd. Naturally she's also bigoted, hypocritical, terrified of anything she doesn't understand and hasn't had an original thought of her own in forty years. So whenever I have doubts or start to get ideas about retiring to the sun, I think about Eleanor. The disgust she inspires always convinces me that I should carry on the good work.'

'I didn't realize you were an idealist,' said Grimes.

'I'm a much misunderstood man, Grimes. I was hoping you might show a little more insight than most.'

'Insight? I've been beaten, suffocated, and scared shitless. I've had a white noise piped into my ears until I was fucking hallucinating. Your junkie shitbird's thrown up on my carpet and I have to sit here while you take a long and smelly piss on my life. And you expect insight. Maybe even sympathy. God damn if I don't admire your gall.'

Grimes laughed. There was a crazed edge to the laughter. He sat up and looked at Jefferson more closely and the laughter faded.

'Maybe you have got more on your mind than getting that money into your pocket.'

The realization seemed to frighten him, and Jefferson was glad. He didn't like being laughed at. At one time a lot of people had laughed at him. Now no one dared and he was no longer used to it.

'Don't taunt me, sonny,' he said. 'You're putting on a real tough front and I'm impressed, I really am. But I know that your guts are crawling at the thought of going back in that bag.'

'Okay,' said Grimes. 'You asked if we could talk so I'll be frank. I'd like to shoot you in the balls with your own pistol and sing you a lullaby while you bled to death, but I can't. And I don't want to spend any more time with my head inside your bag. So, okay. I don't mind flattering you for a while. I can see how hanging out with the likes of Artie might limit your normal means of communication to breaking people's bones. So I appreciate how you might want to use real words, real thoughts, real ideas for a change.'

Grimes' voice was rising again.

'But if you want some kind of dialogue here you're gonna have to be nice to me. I don't know what time it is, what day it is. I'm having trouble putting sentences together. I'm not even sure if this conversation really exists or if I'm still standing against the fucking wall imagining it. If I hadn't been brought up to believe that big boys don't cry I'd be weeping my fucking eyes out right now. So you wanna talk, I'll listen, but don't expect me to make like Carl Rogers.'

Jefferson paused for five seconds and said: 'Who's Carl Rogers?'

The pause worked. Grimes came down.

'A guy. He thought that deep down inside everybody wanted to be loved by as many people as possible. I don't think you and he would have much to say to each other.'

'Not like you and me, huh?'

Grimes said, 'I've met bad guys before, visiting the prisons. Serial killers. Rapists. None of them knew what the fuck they were doing, not really. They weren't insane. They'd just taken the dream to its limits in the best way they knew how. You know better. If greed isn't reason enough, why act like a war criminal?'

'There's a war alright but the crimes aren't mine. The world isn't a fuck-hole because of guys like me. The people are to blame. We, the people. The decent hard-working, tax-paying, have-you-hugged-your-kids-today people. They're the guilty men. And women.'

'You sound as if you care,' said Grimes.

'What the fuck do you think this is all about?'

'You want to save the world. Sure. Give me a gun and I'll help you.'

Jefferson leaned forward. 'It's very simple,' he said. 'The people must be told that they are shit. Remember that. The people must be told that they are shit. The images must be broken. They can't be allowed to go on feeling good about themselves. They're living filth. My job is to make them realize that.'

'Your job is to get a hard-on every time you kick someone's face in.'

'I know who I am,' said Jefferson. 'I know where I live. You think it isn't hard? You think it makes me feel good?'

'You love it.'

'I show people what they are. I never did anything to anyone that wasn't a reflection of their own life. If they don't sleep so good at night that's not my doing. I eat shit every day and believe me it tastes bad. But before I go I'll let loose a fart that will blow through this state like poison gas. It won't change very much but it'll be something. For me it's enough.'

'What's next?' said Grimes. 'The "Checkers" speech?'

Jefferson didn't laugh.

'I shook his hand once, you know, the President. When they flew us back from Nam he met us at the airport. I enjoyed dropping thirty million dollars' worth of high-ex on Charlie, but the homecoming, Jesus. Flags and bunting, marching bands, crowds of puling relatives – a complete fucking nightmare . . .'

Jefferson paused. He'd never told this story before. Talking about it felt strange.

Grimes said, 'Go on.'

'He gave me some kind of medal. I dumped it in a garbage-can and spent the next twenty-four hours in a motel room with a .45 on the table in front of me. It wasn't the war that bothered me, none of that guilt-for-what-we'd-done shit. And it wasn't money either. Money was running out of my mother's asshole and she was dying to take a shit on me. But when I pictured my life dribbling away over thirty spineless years, all I wanted to do was die. Two years in a gook POW camp never took me that low. I survived there because I realized that they didn't care whether I lived or died. I don't mean the gooks – I mean folks back home, my family, my buddies. Trouble was I cared about them. I needed a connection that wasn't there and, I knew then, never had been. Bad City. Lying in the dark in six inches of stinking water I cut the need out. I escaped from the city and I've never been back. I watched friends suffer and die without pity. I listened to my own body scream and ignored it. I lived because I was alive and for no other reason at all.'

As Jefferson spoke he felt an intense pressure building up in his thorax. Anger, malice, deep, deep hurt. He wanted to smash something; break, stomp, trample; to cause someone, somewhere some pain. To pay all those fuckers back. The pressure got worse as he realized that the debt could never be paid. His fists coiled and uncoiled in his lap, the knuckles changing from pink to white and back again.

Grimes said 'Tell me what happened.'

For an instant Jefferson lay gaping and gutted and he almost fell for it. That was how badly he wanted to talk. But Grimes blew it. The fake concern – of course it was fake – the low, reassuring voice, the careful absence of threat, the bogus promise of friendship. Psychiatrist tricks, tricks he used himself. Some gland in his brain went into spasm. All his goddamn life. Always and everywhere

128

someone was trying to take him down. Always and every-where there was someone trying to tell him he wasn't good enough, he was wrong, he was just another fat fuck who wasn't worth the price of admission. He lurched abruptly from his chair, walked across the room and punched Grimes in the groin. Grimes doubled over and gagged soundlessly into the upholstery of the sofa.

'When are you people gonna learn?'

Jefferson was shouting for the first time.

'Twenty-four hours a day there's a hundred thousand cocksuckers trying to take it all away from me. Twenty-four hours a day I gotta teach 'em all over again that no one – nobody – tells Clarence Jefferson what to do. Why is that, Mr know-it-all Doctor Grimes? Mr fucking smart-guy? Tell me.'

He took Grimes in a head-lock and started to choke him slowly.

'What's it all about, Alfie?'

Jefferson felt his own face swelling with blood.

'Who's been sleeping in my bed?'

His voice soared with unrestrained rage.

'How fucking blue can you get?'

'Jesus, Cap, you're gonna kill him.'

Jefferson let go of Grimes and turned round. Artie Mann stood in the doorway holding his .45 in his right hand and his belly with his left. He looked sick and weak and his face was grey. The gun waved about in his hand like a blind man's cane.

Jefferson said, 'Put the gun down, asshole.'

Artie tucked the gun into the rear of his jeans. Jefferson walked over and jabbed his fist into Artie's bruised liver. Artie screamed and went down on his knees. After he got some breath back his bewilderment was pathetic.

'Oh fucking God, what was that for?'

Jefferson grabbed Artie's upper lip between finger and thumb and lifted him to his feet. Artie squealed all the way.

'Because I told you before: don't call me "Cap". And don't ask stupid questions.'

Jefferson turned round and picked up the black bag from the table. His head was spinning. For a moment there he'd lost it. How? Grimes was sitting with his head between his knees. Jefferson took a step towards him.

Grimes' speed took him by surprise: he should have been too weak to move like that. Before Jefferson could react, Grimes had lunged from the sofa and butted him in the nose. Grimes moved from the legs and waist, his spine held rigid so that his skull was the tip of a two-hundred-pound battering-ram. Jefferson felt his face cave in like a collapsing beer can. He roared a spray of bloody saliva but didn't allow the pain to cloud his mind. He slid backwards with Grimes' weight against his chest, one hand clawing at Grimes' face, gouging for the eyes. He grunted again as Grimes smashed an elbow into his left ribs and he felt more of his bones breaking.

They both tried to knee each other at the same time and their legs crashed together. Grimes' momentum was spent. Jefferson shoved him backwards and followed through with a feint to the head but Grimes read the feint and ignored it and kicked Jefferson with his shin, hitting him again in the left ribs. Once more Jefferson rode a surge of breathless pain and fired another hook at Grimes' head, this time a real punch. Grimes blocked it with his arms, unable to throw a quick counter because of the handcuffs. Jefferson ducked low, grabbed Grimes' ankle and heaved, stepping backwards and crashing him down onto his back. Holding the leg and continuing the same move Jefferson wrenched him over onto his belly. Grimes' arms were trapped beneath him. Jefferson stood astride him, grabbed his other leg and took him into a Boston Crab. Jefferson's knee crunched with pain and he lost his balance. If he fell he'd shatter the doctor's spine. He grunted and swayed. He recovered his balance. Then he applied controlled pressure until Grimes was bellowing a torrent of words from which Jefferson could only pick up snatched phrases.

'Kill me, cocksucker . . . Finish it now.'

Jefferson released the hold and stood up. Grimes writhed softly on the floor, talking mainly to himself. Jefferson cut off the obscenities by pulling the black bag over Grimes' head. He stood up and backed away from the prone figure. He breathed in shallow gasps, the pain in his ribs paralysing his respiratory muscles. His mouth was filled with blood. He was shaken. This wasn't right, goddamn it. He forced himself to be calm. The situation was under control. Grimes lay still on the floor but Jefferson knew he was conscious.

Splattering blood down the front of his shirt, Jefferson yelled out.

'Artie!'

He choked the word off as his chest seized up with pain. He hadn't been hurt this badly in a long time.

'Artie!'

'I'm still here, Captain.'

Jesus, he'd forgotten. He had to regain his grip. He grabbed a straight-backed chair from by the wall and dragged it over to where Artie stood. Artie cringed away from him.

'Sit here,' said Jefferson. Don't go any closer to him than this. If he starts to get up off the floor you call me. Don't try to tackle him and don't shoot him. I'm going to clean up.'

Jefferson grabbed Artie's cheek and squeezed hard using plenty of fingernail.

'You remember all that?'

Artie stood on tiptoe to relieve the stretch on his face.

'Sure, Captain.'

Jefferson gave him a shove, let go and went into the bathroom. He stripped off his shirt. The act caused him considerable pain. He ran his fingers over his side, prodding his ribs, and reckoned that two of them were cracked or at least badly bruised. He would have to avoid any

131

more close combat. Over the next few hours he would stiffen up and slow down and he could not rely on his body to move with the efficiency he was used to.

He looked at his face in the mirror. His nose was deformed and swelling by the second, his upper lip was cut and blood still dripped from his chin. But it looked and felt worse than it was. His vision was clear, there were no cuts near the eyes, and his jaw had not been damaged. He did not feel concussed. He cleaned himself up with firm, accurate movements as if he were working on someone else and ignoring the pain he caused. He found a packet of gauze swabs and unfolded them and tore them into long strips and packed them into each nostril with the handle of a toothbrush. The result was ugly but effective. The cut on his lip did not require attention. He rinsed his mouth with Listerine and waited until his eyes stopped watering. It took him two minutes to work his shirt back on.

Apart from the pain and having to breathe through his mouth he felt okay. Looking at himself in the mirror he realized what a relief it had been to lean on Artie and speak to him like he was a bucket of shit. Like putting on an old pair of shoes. He'd strayed too far from the straight and narrow way he set himself so many years before. Drop this other shit right now. Stick with the money. But the money was second prize in a game-show that suddenly disgusted him, and he wanted something extra. He wanted it. The pressure in his head started to rise again but this wasn't the time. He pushed the thoughts away and found a bottle of dihydrocodeine in the bathroom cabinet. He swallowed two tablets and put the rest in his pocket.

He also found a bottle of pharmaceutical grade dexamphetamine sulphate. Handy. He swallowed two of those too and walked back into the living-room rattling the bottle of pills in his hand.

CHAPTER FOURTEEN

Callie looked at Luther Grimes, sprawled out on the double bed with the tarnished brass frame, and tried not to ask herself what she really wanted.

Luther's legs were tangled in the sheets, and muted sunlight from the open window fell across his stomach. His hair was loose, the way she liked it, and tangled about on the pillow. It was late afternoon and through the leaves and branches of the trees outside a fresh wind was building up its strength.

Luther stretched his arms and the sunlight set off the shallow grooves between his stomach muscles. Closer up it glistened from hundreds of tiny sweat droplets not much bigger than the pores in his skin – the kind of sweat you work up from lying in a humid room without doing much of anything at all. His trunk was more deeply tanned than his legs, and around his crotch and buttocks there was a band of skin that was almost white.

Callie decided that she liked the band of white skin. Luther's cock was sleek with saliva and semen and lay heavily against one of his thighs. Callie liked that too, and the bitter taste lingering in the back of her throat. She lay beside him rubbing circles in the sweat with her forefinger and wondering why he turned her on so. Luther wasn't a thoughtful lover; he just took what he wanted when he wanted it and if she didn't like it that was too bad. Strange thing was that, despite her better instincts, she usually wanted it too.

Maybe that was because, even at the best of times, even

when he was playful and gentle, there was something in his eyes that made her feel scared.

Luther took his hand from the nape of her neck and reached for a pack of Luckies on the floor.

'It took me a long time to learn to appreciate a blow-job.'

He stuck a Lucky in his mouth and lit it with a Zippo. The Zippo was decorated with the screaming eagle of the 101st Airborne. The same design was tattooed on the skin over his right shoulder.

'I mean being given one.'

His arm, holding the cigarette, dangled over the edge of the bed. The smoke curled straight upwards until it caught the breeze from the window and was dispersed across the room.

'Fact is, I couldn't handle them at all until I joined the forces and started giving head myself.'

The thought of Luther going down on one of his fellow troopers gave Callie an ache deep down in her belly. She licked Luther's sweat from her fingers then put her hand between her legs. Her cunt was wet. She gathered some of the wetness on her fingers and coated Luther's lips with it.

'You never told me you liked men too,' she said.

'It was a long time ago,' said Luther. 'There were three of us who were real good buddies, me and Beckett and Johansen, and we used to fuck and suck each other whenever we got the chance.'

'Was that because you were cut off from women?' said Callie. She slipped one of her legs between his and rubbed her cunt against his thigh.

'No,' he said. 'We did it because it felt good and we were friends and because we wanted to. The fact that we would've earned a vacation in military prison if we'd been caught added extra excitement. I used to have palpitations for an hour and a half before meeting them. It was a nice high.'

A wistful expression came across his face. Callie couldn't remember seeing him look that way before.

'It was the best of times and the worst of times,' he said. 'That's what Beckett used to say. Always had his nose in a book. But maybe he was too smart. He said from the start that the reason we were fighting Charlie was so that a bunch of stubby-dicked greedheads back home could make themselves a shitstorm of money from our blood. I never saw it that way. I understood about the greedheads, sure, and the sacks of shit that ran the war from Washington and Saigon, but that didn't bother me. Knowing that you've done what you think is right is all that counts. Other people can tell you you're wrong or that you were a sucker but they don't know what they're talking about. They haven't had that feeling.'

Luther shook his head. There was anger and regret in his voice.

'Beckett enlisted for the adventure. High adventure. He got it all right.'

He flicked ash from his cigarette into a half-empty coffee cup on the floor.

'He's sitting in a wheelchair somewhere in Montana writing Westerns. A great guy. I still love him.'

He finished his cigarette in silence. Callie kept on rubbing his chest. The cabin was just one big room, out in the bayou country west of the city. The nearest paved road was two miles away. The swamps outside smelled bad and the mosquitoes drove her crazy, but inside the cabin she felt good. The cabin reassured her that she had done the right thing in coming here instead of sweating it out alone in the hotel.

The night before she'd stayed up late, unable to sleep for wondering what had happened to Grimes and how she was going to get out of the city. When sleep had finally come it had been disturbed by bad dreams in which she was pursued and captured by the cops. In the dreams she kept waiting for Cicero Grimes to come and help her out; but he never did, and she woke up late, feeling lousy. The thought of spending the day alone waiting to get arrested had made her feel worse still. So, taking her chances on the road, she'd hired a car and driven out to Luther's cabin with the suitcase of money on the seat behind her.

As she'd headed west on US 90 the DJ on the car-radio had told his listeners to buckle themselves in for the worst storm of the year so far. Then he'd played Bessie Smith singing 'Backwater Blues'.

When she'd arrived at the cabin she'd half-expected Luther to get mad at her for deviating from the arrangements they'd made, but he'd been quiet and distant, almost sad. She'd distracted him with a flattering display of interest in his cock and now that the soothing effect of the blow-job was working on his nerves she felt more relaxed herself. No way could she tell him that his brother – and maybe the cop Jefferson too – knew when and where the split was taking place. She didn't know for sure how Luther would react to that news, but most likely he'd go completely mega-apeshit and that would not be good.

She'd had enough of apeshit men. Cleveland Carter. Cicero Grimes. Luther. Maybe there was something wrong with her. Every man she'd ever known had been choked with frustration in one way or another, even if it was buried deep. They always yearned for that little something extra without ever quite knowing what it was.

Callie knew what she wanted. That afternoon on the highway she'd still had the option of disappearing alone. It would have been easy to run away from what lay ahead, but she knew that she'd never be able to relax knowing that so many people were still alive and after her money: Luther, the four men in the gang, Jefferson. Maybe Grimes too, though she didn't think so. She'd been preparing herself for months, she'd played it through in her mind. None of them really took her seriously, not even the doctor, and he tried harder than most. They'd admit she had the brains but never the nerve to take them on on their terms. Well tonight she would wrap the whole business in one neat package and shove it up their collective ass. Then she could spend some time finding out who she really was instead of working out what someone else wanted her to be. She looked up from Luther's stomach as he tugged her hair.

He said, 'Did I ever tell you how my Ma died?'

Callie wondered why he was talking so much. It was out of character.

She said, 'No, you didn't.'

'When Pa came home from the Pacific he brought back a chestful of campaign ribbons, half a dozen shrapnel wounds and a taste for telling people what to do. I was about five years old, I guess. After he'd been home a week I asked my Ma when he was going to go away again. Me and Ma had had a good war. She worked and I ran wild. We looked after each other pretty good. Then this guy rolls up I've hardly ever seen who's spent the last four years kicking ass in a serious fashion and enjoying every minute of it. Ma didn't like being pushed around. She wouldn't give up her job and she didn't give a good goddamn about what Pa had done on Okinawa. I don't remember exactly what they used to fight about but they fought a lot.'

Luther looked at her for a second to see if she was listening.

'I think Pa enjoyed it – a more argumentative son of a bitch was never born – but Ma hated it. She'd hold her own but it got her down worse and worse and I guess she grew to hate him. This went on for years. Ma lost her job. Not enough work for the GIs coming home. Pa said damn right, she said bullshit. Pa was what they called a radical, as red as you please and proud of it – I never have understood why because he's no fool – but he was a man's man, you know, and he never knew how to treat women. One night – I must have been nine or ten – I heard them shouting and fighting, heard Pa hit her. Then things were quiet for a while. I was just falling asleep when I heard this big bang that nearly shook me out of bed, and then Pa started screaming, over and over. Since then I've heard a lot of people crying out in pain – all kinds of pain – but I never heard a sound like that again.'

Luther's face was twisted. For once his eyes had lost their scariness. Callie put her hand on his lips.

'Luther, honey, I don't think I want to hear any more.'

Luther brushed her hand away. 'I opened the door to their bedroom. Pa was lying naked on the bed, rigid, covered in blood and slime, screaming for Jesus to help him. Ma was naked too but she was dead. She'd blown the back of her head off with Pa's Army .45 while she was going down on him.'

'Oh Jesus,' Callie said.

'My kid brother came in behind me. I dragged him away. At the time I didn't know that's what she'd been doing. Later, when I grew some hairs on my balls and found out about women I put the picture together for myself.'

'I wish you hadn't told me,' said Callie. It had made her feel a wave of sympathy for him that she didn't need. And for Grimes too. It was the first time Luther had ever mentioned him. She hoped that didn't mean something.

Luther cupped her head in his hand and ran his fingers through her hair.

'Don't feel bad about it. It was thirty-odd years ago. Shit,' he said. 'Maybe I got some idea why she did it. Sometimes you just have to do a thing, you have to go with it, even when you know it isn't right. I used to think that the only way to be free was to always do what you wanted, to live on your impulses, without ever looking ahead or behind. That way you have nothing to fear and no one can have power over you. But sooner or later you want to do something that isn't right, and you don't know why but you want it so bad you don't care what it costs or who you hurt. You just have to do it.'

His grip on her hair had tightened as he spoke.

'You know what I mean?'

'No,' said Callie, 'I don't think I do.'

She wondered what he was getting at. No way could he know about her and Grimes. No way. Her hair was hurting but she didn't complain. Luther searched her face with something like desperation in his eyes and then bent over her. When he kissed her on the lips she could taste and smell her own juices.

'I'm glad you don't,' he said. 'It's a bad place to have been. I love you like hell, you know that?'

Callie felt his hands hold her tight and there was an edge to his voice that made her believe him. Normally he was Maximum Joe Cool. My name's Luther Grimes: I don't bleed. A spasm of doubt took hold of her and she wished she were somewhere else. All she wanted out of this deal was the money. All of it. No guys unless she wanted them. No need to spread her legs to get ahead. All she had to do was squeeze a trigger. Easy.

Now, lying in Luther's arms, feeling his body against hers, strong and salty and warm, the idea of firing bullets into him in a few hours' time was obscene. She'd seen plenty of things, but never a killing. Except in the movies. She had a feeling it wasn't going to be that simple.

'Why are we going to kill all those men tonight?' said Callie.

'Because you don't want to divvy the pot six ways. You want that we should keep it all to ourselves.'

'Isn't that what you want too?'

'I just want you.'

Again there was that urgency that she didn't remember hearing before.

'Anything else is a bonus,' he said.

Luther took her by the waist and rolled her over onto her side and pulled her backwards towards him until she felt her buttocks nestling in his crotch. His penis was erect. She took his hand and slid it between her thighs. A moment later she was wet again and she pushed his hand away and reached between her legs and took hold of his cock. Its tip was moist and slippery with the remnants of

139

his last ejaculation and she spent a moment rubbing the tips of her fingers over the slick surface. His mouth was close to her ear and as she guided him inside her from behind he said 'fuck' and then 'Jesus'.

Luther wrapped one hand in her hair and the other around her breast and she could feel his teeth grating against her shoulder blade. She arched her back and let him pull himself in and out of her with long slow strokes. At the end of each stroke, just as she felt his balls brush against the top of her thighs, he shunted his cock forward for a final grunting inch which made her gasp. She reached down and rubbed her clitoris with the middle finger of her right hand. Luther moaned like men weren't supposed to moan and she felt herself starting to come. She thought about fucking the two brothers, each behind the other's back, and it turned her on more. She reached out to grab and squeeze the tarnished tubes of the bedstead and matched the noise he was making with her own.

Luther pleaded in her ear: 'Don't leave me.'

When he said it she realized that if things went like she'd planned this would be Luther's last fuck.

Her horniness vanished and guilt and sadness took its place. She wished to God he didn't make her feel this way because he was a bastard and she feared him. But as they moved against each other in the thick stormy air and she forgot about the goddamned money and the plans she'd made for the future, she wept into the sweat-damp pillow and made a second wish: that she could stay there always and forever, fucking Luther Grimes in the earth and wood room, and never have to think about death.

CHAPTER FIFTEEN

Cicero Grimes slept but did not rest.

When he'd first turned in he'd been restless, unable to escape from the deadly rhythm of his thoughts. Luther and Callie. Callie and Luther. He was sick with longing. Christ, he didn't even know who she was. A stranger who robbed banks and wanted to kill her boyfriend. Two packs of Pall Malls had failed to shift her from his mind and his body felt sick and poisoned. He'd hardly eaten all day. Food tasted like sawdust and did nothing to fill the hollow place in his guts.

He didn't know, now, whether he was going for Luther because he wanted to or because it was what she wanted. The scale of his need humiliated him for he knew it had little to do with her and everything to do with the hole in himself he'd spent a lifetime trying to fill. Medicine, women, exile, revenge. One thing was certain: he was going all the way. He would do anything to have her, to take her. Yes. To take her away from that bastard he would kill with his bare hands.

She lay between cool sheets in the room next door. The memory of a dozen hours before, of the desperate, guilt-crazed fucking on the table and floor and sofa, had afflicted him in fevered outbreaks of lust and fantasy throughout the day. While she slept, exhausted, he had masturbated twice without pleasure or relief. Jesus wept. He felt like pulling his teeth out. In his mind's eye he saw her biting Luther's nipples as she fucked him on a sweat-stained mattress in the swamps. The thought salted his lust with jealousy. It was absurd. He should have been beyond this. People paid him in US dollars for advice on their feelings, their behaviour. His own diagnosis was simple: he was out of his fucking mind. Ludicrous visions of a future with Callie rode through his imagination: country idylls, a home, children. Then other, darker visions of the dream crumbling into conflict and misunderstanding, resentment and despair. Eventually, gratefully, he lost consciousness.

An hour later he half-surfaced to see Callie standing in the doorway to his room, her body outlined through the shirt she wore by a light in the corridor behind her. He tried to sit up but his body weighed a thousand pounds. He could not move his limbs. She pulled the shirt over her head and dropped it on the floor then walked over to the bed and pulled the sheet aside and stood staring down at him. The insides of her thighs slid in his sweat as she straddled him without speaking and parted the lips of her cunt with her left hand. With her right she took hold of his cock and guided his glans inside her. Still he could not move. His muscles hung on his bones as if they were made of dough. She leaned forward and grabbed two handfuls of his flesh, one by his waist, the other from his shoulder, and heaved him towards her as she slid down onto him and then let him fall back. And then again. And again. And he thought: Out of the cradle endlessly rocking.

The mattress sagged as Luther climbed onto the bed and knelt behind Callie, astride Grimes' legs. Grimes almost came as Callie turned and kissed Luther over her shoulder with fierce lunges of her head. Strands of damp hair clung to her throat. She yielded to the pressure of a hand against her back and bent forward, and Grimes felt her breath on his face and then her teeth on his jaw, grating on the bone. He looked at Luther's face and found it lovely, frightening, a collection of shifting shadows and lean angles that gleamed in the light from the corridor. His hair, long and oiled, shone in the same dim light. Grimes could not see his eyes. Luther placed his hands on Callie's hips to hold them still and bent his head forward until his face hung over her buttocks. He let a rope of saliva fall from his lips into the

142

cleft between them. His right hand shifted from her hip and moved in a slow circular motion beyond Grimes' vision while Grimes felt her breathing in short, thick pants against his neck. She tensed and moaned into his shoulder and then relaxed and moaned again. Grimes wanted to join them in voicing his pleasure as he felt the pressure of Luther's penis against his own through the rear wall of her vagina. But still he was helpless – out of the cradle – and could not move.

Grimes closed his eyes. The harmony of movement enveloped him like the rolling of the ocean. His ears were filled with human sounds, mingled and liquid. Luther and Callie. He loved them both. He felt Luther stiffen and shudder as he came into Callie's rectum. A moment later Grimes came too, in a long slow roll that felt like a wave of the same ocean running over an empty beach. Callie cried out and arched her back.

When Grimes opened his eyes to look at her she was no longer Callie. Her hair was black, as black as Luther's. Her skin was olive instead of tanned and her face was that of a girl, a teenager at most, a Latin face, beautiful.

Grimes recognized the face and cried out. His entrails turned to lava. His muscles strained but still he could not move. He cried out again and woke up.

'Easy, Doctor, Easy.'

His shoulders shook in spasms. Bright light burned orange-black through his eyelids. Two hands gripped his upper arms and held them steady. The pressure of the hands calmed him. He kept his eyes screwed shut as the hands helped him to his feet and across a few stumbling paces to set him down on the sofa. He brought his own hands to his face and dug at his eyes with his fingertips. His fingers became wet. His shoulders shook with sobs and his face felt grotesquely contorted as grief stretched him on its rack. He wanted to stay there. He wanted never to stop. He felt the sting across his cheek a micro-second before the sound of the slap reached his ears.

'You're losing it, Grimes. Put it back together. Look at me.'

'He fucked her,' said Grimes.

'What are you talking about?'

'He fucked all of us.'

He felt as if he were talking underwater. As soon as the words left his mouth they disappeared like bubbles and he couldn't remember what he'd said. The presence beside him disappeared and Grimes lay down on his side, on the pillow of his arms, and tried to find oblivion. He was drifting away into a liquid sleep when the hands sat him up again.

'Open your eyes.'

A pause.

'Open your eyes.'

A slap.

Grimes opened his eyes. Jefferson held out a glass of cranberry juice. His face was monstrously swollen. Dried blood was encrusted around the rims of his nostrils and fibres of rusty gauze poked out of his nose. Grimes stared at him without taking the glass. Jefferson supported Grimes' head and held the glass to his lips.

'You're dehydrated. Drink it,' said Jefferson.

The juice was tart and cold. Grimes shivered as he swallowed it down. The coldness lingered in his belly and gullet after Jefferson took the glass away. Grimes was still naked to the waist. Jefferson refilled the glass and this time Grimes sat up and took it in cupped hands. The bracelets round his wrists clinked together. Before Grimes could ask, Jefferson put a Pall Mall between his lips and lit it for him and Grimes sat smoking and taking sips of juice.

'Take these,' said Jefferson.

Grimes took a handful of pills from Jefferson's palm and swallowed them, washing them down with juice. He did not care what they were. At last his mind felt numb and he was grateful. As soon as the pills disappeared down his throat he forgot about them. Jefferson topped up his glass a third time and limped away.

Grimes finished the juice and smoked in silence, staring at the picture of Warren Oates on the wall. Warren looked in bad shape. After a moment Grimes heard Jefferson lever himself out of the chair and move about behind him with muted grunts of effort. Grimes burnt his fingers on the cigarette butt and dropped it to the floor. He watched the butt burn a short, shallow trench in the carpet. The odour of burning wool came and went. Jefferson sat down in the armchair.

The room filled with sounds which in their calm and beauty seemed other-worldly, as if they did not belong in the universe which Grimes now inhabited. J.S. Bach. Solo violin. Grimes felt the precious numbness receding. He gritted his teeth to stop his face from trembling as the music stirred emotions for which he had no name. Tears ran down his cheeks and fell onto his chest. In the past the music had been a sphere in which to float, beyond time and space and conflict. Now, no matter how hard he tried, he could not get inside the sphere. The music seemed to last a long time.

When it stopped Jefferson said 'Is it good, friend?'

Grimes turned to look at him. Jefferson had an old notebook open on his lap. Grimes responded without having to think.

> 'It is bitter, bitter,' he answered.
> 'But I like it.
> Because it is bitter.
> And because it is my heart.'

Jefferson closed the book and placed it on the floor beside him and picked up a sheaf of papers. All the papers were creased where they had been folded in four. He looked at the first sheet and started to read.

Dear Eugene,
I wish you would write back to me sometime. It's hard to keep busy in here and lots of times I start to

thinking of you and it sometimes drives me crazy trying to figure out what is going on in your head. Dad told me you won't talk about me any more but he told me he can see it still eating you away inside, like cancer, he said. He said you had it all wrong and that you'd think he'd know better than to act like a stupid bastard like me. That is, you would know better, Eugene, than to act like him.

'I know what I did was a bad thing. But it was more like a crazy thing than a bad thing, you know what I am like, sometimes I can't stop myself, but I know that's no excuse. Jesus I've told you that enough times. I could still cut my dick off every time I think about it. Like I keep telling you I did take care of her good, Anna I mean. I didn't just leave her. She was a sweet thing, I guess she still is. I know that don't make much difference to you. And it won't bring Dolores back and I know how much you loved her.

'Lots of times I thought about finding you. It would have been easy enough, you were leaving tracks all over Central America trying to find me. But I knew you'd try to kill me and I couldn't take the chance. I know I did an evil thing but I still want to live, I can't help that, and if you tried to kill me I might have to kill you, and I don't want that to happen, that's why I've always run from you. Maybe if you came to see me where you wouldn't be able to try you would feel different now. Hell, it was a long time ago. A man shouldn't carry that hate around with him for so long, especially for his brother. I am not a doctor like you are but I know that it can't be good for you and I am not worth it.

'Come and see me sometime, please, I still love you you know and I think it would help you get over it because I don't think you are scum like I am. Your loving brother,

Luther.'

Jefferson put the letter on his lap. 'That one was from

the State Penitentiary at Angola,' he said. 'You want to hear another?'

Grimes hadn't believed that he had the energy for any more grief but the letter reached him. 'You rotten bastard,' he said.

Somewhere in the distance, behind the weariness, a sense of pressure was building up inside his chest. The dense smoke in his head was thinning out. His thoughts were gathering momentum like the first movements of a freight-train making its way out of the yard. He flexed his fingers into fists and then relaxed them.

'Is that why you were drawn into this shitpool? Because you want to kill your brother?'

Jefferson looked amused.

'Revenge and love. I've been spending too much time with deadbeats like Artie. You're more of a dreamer than I thought if you plan on taking the Tough Bullet single-handed.'

'So I'm more of a dreamer than you thought.' His voice was tired.

'Revenge achieves nothing. I would've thought you'd be above it.'

'You'd have thought wrong,' said Grimes. 'You can't know.'

'I know it'll take more than a black belt to take your brother out. His army records are interesting. They were pretty sure he was dealing heroin in Nam but they could never prove it; and he was a major league gook killer so who knows how hard they tried? The Tough Bullet? Sure. Asking him to bring in a sack of gook ears was like sending down to the 7-eleven for a six-pack and a bag of Twinkies.'

Jefferson paused before running another blade between Grimes' bleeding shoulder blades.

'He paid your tuition through college, didn't he?'

Grimes flinched. 'He helped with my loans. He said it came out of his pay-cheque.'

'Pay-cheque? Luther's pay-cheque wouldn't have paid for the whores and sour mash he got through on his weekends in Saigon. The money he sent the University of Chicago Medical School came from selling white powder to the troops. And when he left the army he carried on the good work. All those years at college. Tens of thousands of dollars. You never paid him back for all those trips he made south of the border, did you?'

'No. I never paid him back.'

Grimes felt the last of his pride drain away.

'I tried but he told me my money was no good to him.'

'You knew he was running narcotics.'

'I chose not to know. I never asked. I wanted to be a surgeon, I wanted to make a contribution.' His voice twisted with irony. 'I wanted to do something that might be of some use to somebody.'

'That's a high ideal,' said Jefferson.

For once there was no sarcasm in his voice.

'How come you ended up shovelling shit in Louisiana?'

'I got fired from the programme. I told a bunch of patients they didn't really need the surgery my boss recommended for them.'

'I heard that story from a little bird. Even at second hand it smelled like a heap of pious bullshit. The little bird believed it, but then most folks don't count on their friends telling a bunch of lies to make themselves look good.'

Grimes said, 'Joey Gags.'

It became clearer how Jefferson had been able to take him apart so accurately. There was a foul taste in his mouth.

Jefferson smiled. 'You shouldn't think too badly of Joe. He was very reluctant to talk about you. I had to remind him of his obligations as a husband and father. Joe's no coward but he's no asshole either. Maybe you could learn from him in that respect. You aren't leaving this room until I get what I want. You can leave while you still know how to order a beer and tie your own shoelaces, or you can leave in a strait-jacket and spend a few months on tranquillizers eating babyfood with a plastic spoon.'

Jefferson leaned forward.

'I got other friends in psychiatry besides you. I'll put you in a nice place in the country. Lots of friendly niggers in white shirts and pants who'd love to take care of a handsome boy like you. They'll keep you so doped under you won't even be able to keep count of the number of times a day they fuck you in the ass. If you're real lucky maybe you'll get a three-minute visit once a month from some asshole with a stethoscope. He'll listen to what those nice nigger nurses have got to say and they'll tell him: "He sure ain't getting any better, Doc." And the Doc will take a look at this poor fucker with food spilled down the front of his shirt and his pecker hanging out of his flies and a bad smell drifting around him because his anal sphincter's as slack as an old whore's quim and he'll say: "How are you today, Dr Grimes?" And you'll open your mouth and drool for him and scratch your head and he'll say: "You're right, gentlemen. We'll have to increase his medication again." You get the picture, Grimes?'

'I believe you,' said Grimes. 'You've been there.'

Every cell in his body, every fibre, wanted to shut down and be done with it. He felt both frenetic and exhausted at the same time. Sitting in his chair like a pagan idol, Jefferson looked as fresh as ever. Power oozed from him. You could see it in puddles around his feet. He looked ready to play for another twelve hours.

Grimes said, 'What do you want?'

'Trust,' said Jefferson. 'Tell me the truth and the trust will come with it. Tell me why you dropped out of the surgery programme.'

Grimes' mouth was dry. He lit a cigarette. The tobacco tasted foul and hurt his chest but he had to smoke. He inhaled deeply and pulled his face.

'It's true I fought with the director of the division, just like I said, but that was my way of getting out with dignity. I couldn't take the pressure. I despised the people I worked for and that made it impossible. I couldn't learn

149

the way they set it up but their way was the only means available to mastering the craft.'

Grimes blew out a long lungful of smoke.

'Sometimes I tell myself I could've made it if I'd wanted to; that I quit because making it wasn't important enough, not because it was beyond me. Most times I know better.'

'That's all?' said Jefferson.

'That's all,' said Grimes.

There was a pause.

'Joe Gags said you spent some time in Nicaragua digging bullets out of peons. You wanna talk about that, too?'

'No,' said Grimes.

'He said you married some woman down there, a beaner.'

'Shut your mouth.'

'He didn't know a whole lot about it, though. Said she got killed in the war and you lost your stomach for it and came home.'

Jefferson jerked his thumb at the papers on the floor.

'Your brother's letters talk about a woman called Dolores. A beaner name. And they talk about Central America too. All kinds of money to be made under Somoza. Lots of opportunity for a man with Luther's background. And he keeps apologizing for Dolores being dead. Sets a man's imagination to working. What happened?'

'I didn't tell Joe, or anyone else. I won't tell you.'

Grimes was breathing too quickly. His shoulders were hunched with tension and the dryness in his mouth was getting worse.

'I've got to know, Grimes. Why does a man like you end up in a heap of shit like this?'

Grimes started to light a fresh cigarette from the butt in his hand and realized he was speeding. He only ever smoked at this rate when he was speeding. The dry mouth, the pressure in his chest.

'You fat fuck,' he said. 'You gave me speed in the juice.'

150

'You took the tablets straight from my hand, dumb-ass, half an hour ago when you were blubbering into your hands like a ham actor.'

'Scumbag.'

Grimes started to get up from the sofa. He stopped as Jefferson drew his revolver and pointed it at Grimes' feet.

'Sit down. I already let you get away with too much physical stuff. You come any closer than you are now I'll shoot you in the ankle.'

Grimes sat down and bit his knuckle.

Jefferson raised his voice, 'Artie! In here. Now.'

Artie appeared from the bedroom. He still looked sick. Jefferson kept his pistol aimed at Grimes.

'Give me your gun.' said Jefferson.

Artie handed over his .45 and Jefferson held it in his left hand.

'Now, Artie,' he said, 'I want you to kneel down over there, undo Dr Grimes' pants and put your dirty little hand on his pecker.'

'Jesus, Captain. You know I ain't no fucking faggot. In the penitentiary, okay, them motherfuckin' nigger cock-suckers didn't give me no choice, but God, I didn't enjoy that shit, I swear.'

'You think you got a choice here either?' said Jefferson. 'Do it.'

Grimes kept still and held Jefferson's gaze as Artie Mann came over and knelt down between his knees. With clumsy movements Artie unbuttoned and unzipped Grimes' pants. Grimes felt Artie's hand, clammy against his belly. His skin crawled.

'You care much what happens to this shitbird?' said Grimes.

Jefferson replied: 'I don't care at all.'

Artie Mann screamed and gagged as Grimes grabbed him by the throat with his handcuffed hands and hoisted him upwards. He butted Artie in the face once, twice, three times, each time bellowing with rage and release. He felt high. He felt good. He felt very good. He mashed Artie's face into a bowl of stinking offal then dug his thumbs in above the Adam's apple, lifting Artie's tongue back to block the larynx. He used just enough pressure to seal off the airway so that Artie would have time to think about what was happening and wouldn't die too quickly from a cardiac arrest. Artie tried to prise Grimes' fingers loose but he didn't know how. And he didn't have the strength to match Grimes, his own fingers were like his arms and body: thin and etiolated and weak. As he started to die he thrashed pitifully between Grimes' legs and Grimes had to grip him hard with his knees. Blood vessels started to burst in the whites of Artie's eyes. The skin of his eyelids was speckled with tiny red dots. The thrashing movements started to fade.

'Nobody ever loved Artie, either,' shouted Jefferson. 'Ain't that why we are what we are?'

Grimes looked up with an obscenity on his lips and stopped dead.

Jefferson was standing behind Artie with a mirror held in front of his chest and in the reflection Grimes saw the eyes he dared not meet in dreams. A face with blood and mucus smeared across the forehead stared back. The lips were drawn back. And from a pair of pale blue eyes – so pale they were almost grey – burned a white-hot flame of pure violence.

He stopped strangling Artie and let his arms fall. He relaxed the grip his legs had on Artie's body. Artie fell forward against Grimes and slid downwards, smearing his chest and belly with blood. He stopped, unconscious, with his face resting in Grimes' crotch.

Grimes turned away from the mirror, choking with revulsion. He grabbed Artie's arm and lowered him backwards – gently, gently – to the floor. He held his thumb to Artie's neck and found the carotid pulse. The pulse was rapid but strong. With jagged, clumsy movements he tried to wipe the blood from Artie's face then stopped, looking for something to use as a cloth.

'Ugly, isn't it?' said Jefferson. 'A face that you've

smashed in with your own hands is the ugliest thing in the world. Take a good look.'

'I have to fix him up,' said Grimes.

'Take your hands off him.'

'You've got to let me fix him up,' said Grimes.

'I said leave him alone.' Jefferson's voice was savage.

When Grimes started to tear a piece from Artie's T-shirt Jefferson kicked him in the chest. The kick lifted Grimes back onto the sofa. He lay there wheezing. Jefferson grabbed Artie by the arms and dragged him over to the wall. He propped the body up against the wall facing Grimes and stepped back. Artie looked like someone playing a bit-part in a zombie movie.

'Artie stays there, where you can see him good,' said Jefferson. 'You try to touch him I'll blow his right arm off.'

'You're insane.' Grimes could not breathe without pain. 'You would have let me kill him.'

'Anytime you feel like it, Doctor, there he sits. You've been talking about killing folks as if there wasn't much to it. Truth is, you're right. I thought you'd appreciate a chance to find that out.'

Artie opened his eyes and made a croaking sound. He pawed gently at his throat and tried to speak. His voice was painful and faint and he had to try several times before he could make himself heard.

'You gotta get me to a hospital.'

'Take yourself into the bathroom and clean yourself up,' said Jefferson. 'You look like a meat counter.'

'You said this would be an easy way to make a couple of bills, Captain. I never counted on getting fucked over like this.'

He sounded as if he'd been drinking bleach.

'Let me give him a hand,' said Grimes.

Artie cringed against the wall.

'You stay where you are,' said Jefferson to Grimes, 'and keep whatever guilt you got to yourself.'

He turned to Artie. 'Get your scrawny ass up off the floor.'

Jefferson walked over to Artie and dragged him brutally to his feet. He shoved him towards the door and then came over to sit on the sofa beside Grimes.

'It's not too late, Grimes. You think I like doing this to you? It sickens me. You try just a little harder and we can work this out together. What do you say?'

Grimes closed his eyes. He felt as if all the pain of his life was lining his insides in one big open wound. Jefferson had torn off all the scabs; except one: the one only Grimes could tear open, for himself. He realized, after what he'd done to Artie, that he could hold on, now, indefinitely. The fat cop could hammer on him for the rest of the week and he could take it. He was tougher than the rest. Maybe he was the only one who'd ever cared about that, but now he knew. It was a matter of choice. Let Jefferson keep going and maybe kill him or drive him insane; or open that last wound and do what he should've done a long time ago: find Luther and tell him it was all right, it was over.

He was tired, and insanity and death looked like the easier options. He opened his eyes and looked at Jefferson, for once catching the cop with an unguarded expression, a strange shining expression of childlike hope. Grimes knew how lonely he felt and suddenly pitied him. He made up his mind.

'What do you want to know?' he said, knowing the answer.

'Tell me why you want to kill Luther.'

'Okay,' said Grimes. 'I'll tell you.'

CHAPTER SIXTEEN

As the Doc smoked and rambled it became clear to Jefferson that he had a special gift for seeking out cruel and unusual punishments. Jefferson himself, with his black bag and meaty fists, would never hurt him so much, that was for sure.

Grimes tried to keep his story short and to the point but the drugs sometimes made him wander and Jefferson had to bring him back. And there were the classic effects of the sensory deprivation: difficulty in organizing his thoughts, confusion, blank periods when he appeared to be far away – perhaps seeing people and hearing voices out of the past – and outbursts of intense and primitive emotion. At such moments Jefferson, with a chill of doubt, glimpsed the immense rage and destructive power that Grimes contained and suppressed within him. Grimes' devotion to medicine as an unconscious counterbalance to his violence made sense. Gently, inexorably, Jefferson pushed him on.

By the time he quit the surgery programme in Chicago, Grimes was only a year away from full board certification as a general surgeon. Against the odds he'd won himself a first-class seat on the gravy train, and a lifelong licence to steal was virtually sitting in his back pocket.

Did it make him feel good?

'I felt like I was wearing a pair of pants soiled with another man's turds.'

Grimes left it all behind, making sure by the manner of his leaving that they would never take him back, and ran, heading south.

155

'Six months after I left Chicago I was in Mexico City trying to figure out why nothing in the world mattered enough anymore for me to want to do anything about it. My life was running through my hands like water. I had the blues and I had them bad. There was no reason for it that I could see but nothing I could read, nothing I could think, nobody I could talk to, could give me a single good reason for wanting to get out of the pit I was in.'

Down Mexico way Grimes didn't prove himself the world's greatest at winning friends and influencing people. Isolated and rotting in a one-night cheap hotel he was just another gringo loser shitting green chilli peppers and waiting for nothing. Then he received a letter from Luther . . .

Callie grunted gently as Luther withdrew behind her and rolled over onto his back. She stretched her neck and shoulders and wrapped her arms about herself. Feeling distant she turned on her side and closed her eyes.

'How did you get along with Dr Grimes?' said Luther.

The question was unexpected. Callie didn't feel so distant anymore. It was time to take care of business. She kept her face half-buried in the pillow and her voice natural.

'We got along fine. He's a nice enough guy. Square but nice. And he seems to know his business.'

'Is he happy?'

'Happy? I don't know. These guys don't show their personal feelings to their clients, you know? It's not professional. He didn't say anything about himself and I didn't ask. I don't know why he works out of that crummy dump though. He could do a lot better.'

'Sure he could but he never will.'

She heard Luther light a cigarette.

'You wanna know why?'

Yes, she did. Grimes had refused to tell her the why and she was curious. On the other hand she didn't want to talk to Luther about it in case she let something slip and ended up face-down in the swamp.

She said, 'Sure, honey, but maybe later, huh? When we don't have so much else on our minds.'

'There is nothing else on my mind. He's my kid brother, Eugene. Named after Eugene Debs for Chrissake.'

Callie rolled over and stared at him, hoping she looked like she'd just heard something new.

'Why didn't you tell me he was your brother?'

'It wasn't necessary and anyhow you were way out of your tree.' He shook his head. 'I gutted some people real bad in my time but nothing like the way I gutted Gene.'

He looked at her and she thought, he knows. She squirmed inside. He doesn't know. She was just being over-anxious. Even so she wanted to shut the subject down.

'You've never said a word about your family before,' she said. 'Tonight I'm getting an autobiography.'

'So what?'

Luther leaned towards her and Callie pulled her head back from the anger in his voice and face.

'Maybe I got a bad feeling about what's gonna happen tonight, like maybe I'll get shot. Maybe I need to clear my mind, I don't know, like a confession or something. You say you love me . . .'

He paused as if the phrase were a death threat.

' . . . so sit and listen. You think I could tell you if I wasn't fucking crazy about you? No one else has ever heard any of this shit.'

'I'm sorry,' said Callie.

She was scared. She tentatively stroked his face and Luther twisted his head away, his features stony. She persisted and after a moment he submitted and lay back on the pillows, staring at the roof while she caressed him.

'Nobody ever loved and trusted me like you do,' she said. 'Or like I do you.'

Luther gave a cynical grunt and she faltered before going on.

'I'm just uptight about tonight. Tell me whatever you like.'

After a sullen pause Luther said, 'I was in Nicaragua, helping to fight the Reds . . .'

Luther was based in Managua, teaching Somoza's gangsters how to fight a guerilla war and making a little extra on the side from dealing weapons and narcotics. It seemed that Luther really believed the old-time bullshit about the red sandwich and the hordes of Commie peons waiting to invade Texas. Grimes – his own politics at that time a naive ragbag of secondhand liberal do-goodism – followed him down to Nicaragua and, unexpectedly, found a convincing illusion of contentment.

The illusion, not surprisingly to Jefferson's mind, was stimulated by the well-oiled mucus membranes found inside a woman's pants. In explanation Grimes produced a line of sub-Hemingway drivel about the sense of hope he'd found amongst the people and their belief that life was worth fighting for. Good for them and maybe so: but Jefferson could smell cock and cunt before Grimes even mentioned the woman's name.

Dolores Roca. There was something real between us. She was strong, intelligent, courageous. And she had a fantastic cunt.'

'You got any pictures of her?'

'No. I used to but I burnt them. Now I only see her face in bad dreams . . .'

'I introduced them,' said Luther. 'I'd been balling her on and off for a coupla months. She was educated – in California I think – and rich. Her family made a shitload after the Second World War helping United Fruit to scalp the peasants. Or 'the People' as she liked to call them. You know the type. Revolution was a game, excitement, intrigue, a way of working off some guilt about her papa's money. And a chance to mix with tough-looking guys with big peckers and plenty of hair on their balls.'

158

'Like you.'

'Yeah, like me. I was working out a cocaine-for-weapons deal with the Sandinistas. I hated their red guts – still do – but a guy has to take care of business and by then it was clear that born-again Jimmy fuckhead up in the White House wasn't going to give Somoza the tools he needed to win the war. Dolly – she didn't like me calling her that but she put up with it – hung around the fringes of the group I was dealing with. Getting her into the sack was as easy as shelling peas. Or maybe that's looking at it the wrong way round. I cut a real romantic figure after all. Like maybe Gary Cooper in "Vera Cruz". No, Burt Lancaster. Yeah, most definitely Burt. Gene was on his way from Mexico City in one of his what-the-fuck-does-it-all-mean? moods. He'd dumped everything I'd given him into the trash-can. They fell for each other right away. I guess he was a romantic figure, too. We never told Gene we'd been lovers.'

'You stopped seeing her then?'

'More or less. We still made it together now and again, when Eugene was up-country doing his surgery shit with the rebels, but I usually had better things to do. They got real serious about each other and then Dolly produced a fourteen-year-old daughter I didn't even know existed. She was called Anna . . .'

The Roca woman had been married off at sixteen to sweeten some wheezing politician who'd helped the family get even richer than they already were. It wasn't a happy union. She stayed around long enough to see their only child, Anna, out of diapers and then made tracks for the States. She smoked pot and dropped acid and got herself a degree in politics from Stanford, and when she ran out of jewellery to sell she came back home and threw herself back on her family and the shrivelled dick of her obese and aging husband. By the time Grimes met her she was comfortably and happily widowed, dabbling with the Sandinistas and looking for love.

Grimes fell right down the hole between her legs.

'*I'd found something that felt real and it seemed to have a future. One night I cut a slug out of a friend of hers who'd been shot by the police. The work grew from there. I helped a few more people in Managua then started making trips up-country where a lot more people were getting hurt. Sometimes she came with me, other times she stayed behind with Anna. The three of us started living together. A sweeter-looking child than Anna you never saw, but she was quiet and withdrawn. Luther was around and that made me feel good because we'd been apart for so many years. Anna liked him better than she did me. He'd make her laugh and take her out on his motorcycle. I was happy. Christ I deserved to be happy. I worked for it. I put my whole fucking heart into it.*'

Grimes' fists clenched and Jefferson felt a lurch of sympathy. Uncertainly he put a hand on Grimes' arm. He didn't want him to stop now.

'*We got married . . .*'

'Dolly spent the night before her wedding in my bed, squealing with delight while I fucked her ass and dug my fingers around in her cunt.'

'Luther, Jesus. Who you think you're talking to?'

Luther's face was blotchy red and swollen and squirmed with dark feelings that Callie didn't want to know about.

'Shut your cheap goddamn mouth and listen to what I got to say.'

Luther paused and rubbed his forehead with the back of his fist.

'That was the last time we fucked each other. Being actually married made some kind of weird difference to her. Some kind of Catholic nuttiness, I guess. She and Eugene settled in together and seemed real happy. Maybe I was jealous and didn't know it. Maybe Eugene pissed me off with his good-guy heroics. Whatever the reason, the little girl was a real heartbreaker.'

'You mean the daughter?' said Callie.

160

'Anna, yeah. She didn't have much time for Eugene, or Dolly either for that matter. She liked me a whole lot better. I showed her a thing or two . . .'

One morning Grimes and Dolores headed out of the city during one of the last big government operations against the rebels. They were turned back at a roadblock and went on home. When they got there Dolores walked into their bedroom and found Luther and Anna fucking each other breathless on the nuptial couch.

'Dolly went completely fucking ape. Tried to stab me with a pair of scissors. I caught her arm. I just wanted to control the situation. But she grabbed my balls and tried to tear them off, the bitch. I just reacted to the pain . . .'

Grimes walked into the room in time to see Luther smash his elbow across Dolores' throat.
'By the time I reached her her heart had stopped and she wasn't breathing anymore.'
Grimes banged on her chest with the base of his fist and got a pulse back but he couldn't get any air into her lungs. Whether it was laryngeal spasm or just severe tissue damage he couldn't know, but she was heaving for oxygen and not getting any. The scissors on the floor were too blunt to cut a hole in her trachea. Time trickled away. The instruments he needed were in the trunk of the car outside. He turned to Luther. Luther had his pants back on.
'His eyes were the original pissholes in the snow . . .'

Luther had turned his back towards Callie. She was curled up with her arms crossed over her chest and was no longer touching him. When she swallowed her mouth was dry.
'Go on,' she said.
'Fuck. Gene threw a bunch of keys at me and told me to get his medical bag from the car. His actions were cool, I'll give him that, but there was mortal fear in his eyes.

No anger, no hate – too soon for that I guess – just fear. I took the keys and ran outside. I swear I meant to go back but Anna followed me outside. It was fucking weird. She pulled me away from the trunk and said "I want to go away from here."

'I could hear Gene shouting for me from the window up above and in my mind's eye I could see him pumping Dolly's chest and blowing down her throat, like I'd seen desperate medics do it time after time in Nam, trying to force life in where life wouldn't go. Maybe it was because I'd never seen that shit work, but I knew Dolly wasn't going to make it. What was done was done.

'So I said to Anna "Why not?" And we fired up the car and left . . .'

Grimes stopped to regain control of his voice. He had Jefferson's fist clasped between his fingers and his nails gouged strips of skin from the back of the cop's hand.

'*He didn't even leave my bag behind. Just left me standing in the street, staring at his dust and screaming. I felt like my hair was on fire.*'

Grimes ran back inside the house and found a decent knife. When he got back to Dolores she was seriously dead.

'*She hadn't taken a breath in over five minutes and her face was congested and speckled with haemorrhages. I don't know. Every fucking day I don't know. Maybe if I'd tried I could have got her breathing again. And maybe she'd have lived and I'd be sitting around Managua right now dandling her children on my knee . . .*'

Grimes looked at him with calm, haunted eyes and Jefferson felt another unexpected emotion: respect. He should've felt contempt because a man who let himself suffer like this was weak and a fool; but he felt respect and, again, the shimmer of doubt, as if he were wondering, without letting himself admit it, whether maybe Grimes wasn't stronger than him after all. Grimes went on.

' . . . But I didn't try and so here I am, sitting around with you instead . . .'

'That was the last time I saw him. A dusty shape in the rearview mirror, shaking his fists in the air.'

Luther sighed and got up from the bed and fetched a fresh bottle of Jack Daniels from a drawer in his chest. He broke the seal, took a long pull and sat down on the bed again. He offered the bottle to Callie. She refused. If she took a drink at all it would have to be a big one and to deal with psychobilly Grimes II she wanted a clear head. Luther smoked another cigarette.

'He looked for me but he never really had a chance. He made a fool of himself all over Central America, and Colombia too. Spent all his money bribing the right people for the wrong reasons and vice versa. I let people know that I didn't want him to find me but I didn't want him killed. There was a moment towards the end, in Medellin, when . . .'

Luther stopped, looking into nowhere, remembering. He kept the memory to himself and shook his head.

'Anyhow he never found me. He stuck with it for too long before he found the sense to quit and I guess by then his head was maybe fucked up forever. But shit, that was his fault, not mine . . .'

Grimes' determination and money lasted ten months.

'*I was still in love with Dolores and had this debt that I didn't know how to pay. I wanted to find Anna and take care of her. Revenge came later, when I finally understood I'd never be able to pay the debt at all. After a year I tried, one day, to remember what Dolores looked like and how it had felt to be with her and I couldn't. Then I realized that I couldn't have cared less. There was no love left, no obligation. Just a handful of bitter seeds. I came back home and took up psychiatry. If I wanted to find out the why of it all I never did; just memorized a new set of lies.*'

Grimes let go of Jefferson's hand.

'How long did you stay with Anna?' said Callie.

'A year, more or less. I figure she loved me, for a while at least.'

'And you loved her.'

Luther stared at her. 'Yes.'

'Where is she now?'

Luther pulled on his bottle and, as he took it away from his lips, gasped at the strength of the liquor and showed her his teeth.

'She's married to a cocaine millionaire in Medellin. Clean air, good mountains. I miss it. We should go visit her sometime.'

Callie wondered briefly if he was kidding. While she debated inside her head what to do next she smiled absently at Luther and said, 'Sure. I'd like that . . .'

'It's time to go.'

The statement took Jefferson by surprise. Grimes stood up from the sofa and stretched. His face was flat, as if his mind was made up and he wasn't going to question it anymore.

'You hear me?'

Jefferson said, 'Time to go where?'

Grimes closed his eyes. 'I'll take you to the money.'

His voice sounded metallic, as if he'd said something he didn't quite believe.

'Again,' said Jefferson.

'I'll take you to where Luther and his pals are going to split the cash. Tonight. But we'd better move soon. We don't have much time . . .'

Luther stood up from the bed and pulled on a pair of black workpants and a navy-blue T-shirt. He was still looking at her with baleful eyes through the hair hanging over his face and she still couldn't shake the feeling that he knew.

Her instincts told her that whether he knew or not she still had him by the balls. Men were like that. Men were strong and ran the show but if you had the nerve to be stronger they'd cave in, every one of them, every time. Not too many women had worked that out and most of those that did didn't have the strength of character to use it. Callie had no pity for them. On the whole women begged for every kicking they got and then lay around bleating for sympathy. Not her. She could be more man than any of them. Even Luther Grimes.

She said, 'When is it time to get rich?'

'You rest for a while, if you need to,' said Luther. 'I've got some things to do.'

He picked up a digital watch from the crate he used as a bedside table.

'We leave in an hour . . .'

Pleasure, yes indeed. Excitement. Jefferson almost rubbed his hands together. Pleasure, excitement and hullabaloo. And one way or another he would be certain of profit. The money had hooked him into this affair and putting it in his pocket would be sweet enough, but he wanted more and now it actually seemed possible: he might get Cicero Grimes too.

'I want a shower,' said Grimes. 'And a clean shirt and suit. I want bacon for breakfast. I want as many cigarettes as I need. Otherwise we stay here until it's all over.'

Jefferson spread his hands, palms upwards.

'Whatever you say, Grimes.'

He smiled.

'After all, you're the doctor.'

CHAPTER SEVENTEEN

Callie woke up feeling heavy. Her head was full of haze and fuzz and the bottom half of the sheet was twisted around her waist Her legs were bare. She sat up wondering what had awoken her and uncertain of where she was. The light from the window was dim and the air in the room felt like warm glue. She put a pillow behind her back, brushed her hair out of her face and looked across the room.

Luther was sitting at the big old oak table with his back to her. His hair was tied back with black elastic. From a sheath on his belt the hilt of a long knife stuck up towards his left elbow. The table was covered with weapons. Outside it was dusk and a gas lamp provided a pale yellow light. Next to the lamp stood a shot glass half full of whiskey, and two grenades.

In his left hand Luther held a long-barrelled revolver with its cylinder open. Two rows of bullets stood on the table. As she watched, Luther took the bullets one by one between his right thumb and forefinger and slid them into the chambers with a lingering movement that had the quality of a caress. When he had exhausted the first row of bullets he snapped the cylinder shut and held the gun close to his left ear. With his left thumb he cocked and lowered the hammer six times, listening carefully to the uniform clicking of the moving parts. She could tell that he found the sounds pleasing. He pushed the revolver into an oiled holster and laid it on the table. One by one he fed the second row of shells into a speed loader and set the speed loader beside the revolver. He paused to drink from the glass of whiskey.

Callie got out of bed and wrapped the sheet around her shoulders. Luther turned his head to watch her as she stood up.

'You'd best get ready,' he said. 'It'll soon be time.'

She walked over and stood behind him and ran her fingers through his hair. She was still thinking about the girl down in Columbia and touching him took a conscious effort. Luther showed his appreciation by twisting his head away from her hand.

'Save the lovey-dovey stuff till later.'

He picked up a modified double-barrelled shotgun from the table. The stock had been cut away down to the pistol grip and the barrels were sawn off so short that when Luther broke the gun open and loaded it, the cardboard tips of the cartridges poked out of the ends of the barrels by an eighth of an inch. Luther snapped the gun shut with two hands and held it up for her inspection.

'Scary, huh?' he said. 'Double-ought bucks. It's not too reliable for killing 'cause you can't be sure where the load is going to go, but that's why it works.' He tapped the shotgun shells with a fingertip. 'Staring down the ends of these fuckers would scare the shit out of a bronze statue of General Patton.' He put the gun down. 'This is for you.'

He picked a second sawn-off shotgun from the table. The barrels of this one were much longer, about fourteen inches, and it had a full stock. The twin barrels were over-and-under.

'We've been through it before and we'll go through it again in the car,' said Luther. 'This will give you a shot pattern of about three inches at the range you'll be shooting at so you can't just point it anywhere. Point it at his belly and give him both barrels, one at a time. Aim each shot. Shoot from the shoulder like we practised, not from the hip. When it's empty, drop it on the floor and cover me with your Browning. Make sure you got a shell jacked in the chamber before you go in. Leave the hammer cocked and the safety on until you pull it from your pants.

I look like I need some back up, you start shooting. Remember to pick your targets and use at least two shots for each man.'

'My stomach keeps turning over,' said Callie.

Luther made a big effort. He took her hand and squeezed it. 'Keep your head and everything will go just the way you want. You get dressed now.'

He stood up and went over to the two suitcases that Callie had left by the door when she arrived. One of them was a black Samsonite. He laid the Samsonite flat on the floor and squatted down before it. The catches wouldn't open when he tried them.

'Give me the key,' he said.

Callie dug around inside her purse and handed it to him. This was a bad moment. She smiled at him.

'You know this will be the first time I set eyes on this cash since the robbery. That gave me a kick, you keeping this hidden in the church right under your old man's nose.' He unlocked the catches. 'That was smart, locking the suitcase. I once saw Sterling Hayden lose two million bucks in an airport 'cause he didn't lock his suitcase. You should've seen his face.' He lifted the lid and looked at the bills stacked to the brim inside.

Callie didn't ask who Sterling Hayden was. Luther seemed to know criminals all over the continent. She went to stand behind him and put her hands on his shoulders. 'Didn't you ever worry that I might disappear with it?' she said.

'Not really,' said Luther.

'Why not? It wouldn't have been difficult,' she said.

'No,' said Luther. He closed the suitcase and locked it and put the key in his hip pocket. 'But staying alive to spend it. That might have been more of a problem.' His voice was matter-of-fact.

Callie shivered. 'I'd better get dressed,' she said.

'Yes,' said Luther. 'You do that.'

*

In the centre of the floor Artie had made a heap of Grimes' books and hi-fi records and journals, his magazines and clothes, and the cardboard box full of old letters. Grimes stood smoking a Pall Mall. His face was stiff with the effort of controlling himself. He hadn't spoken for half an hour while he'd showered, changed and eaten. That wasn't easy for a man whose brain cells were swimming in amphetamine. Jefferson wondered how many brain cells Grimes had lost in the past eighteen hours. At least some of them would never be the same again.

Artie came back from the car with a can and began spilling gasoline over the pile on the floor. His weasel face was bright with pleasure. Jefferson watched him with disgust.

After a moment Jefferson said, 'That's enough. Go back to the car.'

'Gee, Captain, I was hoping you'd let me torch it.'

'Do as I say,' said Jefferson.

'Can't I even watch?' said Artie.

Jefferson stared at him.

Artie said, 'Shit,' under his breath and left with the can.

Jefferson glanced at his watch. It was twenty-four hours since Cleveland Carter's call had interrupted his workout. He turned to Grimes. 'Why don't you do the honours, Grimes? Set the past behind you. You gonna come in with me you can do without all this memorabilia cluttering your mind. Burn it.'

Grimes didn't hesitate. He walked over to the pile of kindling and threw his cigarette into the middle. The paper and gasoline exploded into flames as he turned away.

When Grimes stomped back towards him Jefferson braced himself for an assault. But Grimes walked past him to the doorway where he stopped and turned around.

'Let's go kill those cocksuckers.'

Joe Gags was sitting behind the steering wheel of his Camaro thinking about the size of his dick. He knew it wasn't the biggest dick in Louisiana but shit, it wasn't the

169

smallest either – at least he hoped not – and it did its job and he'd never had cause to complain about it. Neither had his wife, Jackie, though they never talked about sex – except for that time he'd given her a dose of gonorrhoea while she was pregnant with Sal.

Jesus that had been a pain in the balls. Still, you lived and you learned. He'd learned to wear a condom after that – they weren't so bad, after all – and he'd never had the clap again or any other kind of VD either. It sure made a man think. If he hadn't given her the clap he might never have worn a rubber and maybe by now he'd be lying in a fucking plastic bubble with his hair and teeth falling out and his skin peeling off and all his fucking buddies too scared to speak to him or shake his hand in case they caught AIDS too. That shit was bad news. As he'd tried to explain to Jackie, every cloud had a silver lining. But she'd been hard to convince.

He'd started thinking about his dick while checking his revolver for the umpteenth time that day. It was a Smith and Wesson .38 Special with a four-inch barrel. A good solid work gun: quiet to look at and maybe old-fashioned now, but it was a serious weapon. If you slapped a couple of .38s into a man's belly he might not fly through a plate-glass window but he'd sure as hell say uncle. And you didn't have to worry about the slugs going through two or three walls and blowing the brains out of some poor asshole sitting drinking beer and watching a Star Trek re-run in another apartment. These days everyone was crazy about Magnum loads and wanted to walk around with four or five pounds of metal dragging their pants down. Joe didn't understand it. Maybe they all watched too many goddamn movies. Maybe it had something to do with the size of their dicks, he'd thought. Maybe all those movie stars had small dicks, too.

He stopped thinking about guns and dicks when the door to Grimes' apartment opened and a scrawny white guy wearing a blood-stained T-shirt with 'FUCK IRAN' printed on the front stepped out into the street. The man had bits of sticking plaster over the bridge of his nose and around his eyes. The plaster looked as if it had been applied by someone having an epileptic fit. He had three-time loser written all over him. Gags knew that Jefferson used such creeps all the time. They had a terrific mortality rate.

Joe Gags pulled his baseball cap low over his forehead and slid down in his seat to watch. The creep disappeared down the street on foot, pausing to push a thick envelope into a mailbox. Joe waited. Eight minutes later the creep pulled up outside Grimes' door in Jefferson's Eldorado, got out of the car and opened the trunk. He took out a can of gas, shut the trunk lid and went back into the building.

Three minutes later he returned to the car, put the can back in the trunk and sat in the driving seat. Soon after that Grimes came out onto the street. His hands were handcuffed in front of him and he was wearing a black linen suit with a white shirt, open at the neck. His shoulders had the lifeless sag of serious exhaustion and when he walked he held his elbows to his ribs and took short steps as if he were in pain. But, hell, he was sure enough alive and in one piece and he was still holding his head up high. Joe saw him glance at the Camaro and look away. He couldn't tell if Grimes had recognized him or not.

Jefferson appeared behind Grimes. His face was twice its normal size and he was limping. Joe smiled to himself. Good for you, Grimes. Jefferson said something to Grimes and opened the rear door of the Eldorado. Grimes climbed in. Jefferson scanned the street, registered then ignored the Camaro, and got into the car beside Grimes. The Eldorado pulled away from the kerb.

Joe Gags sat up straight and paused with his hand on the ignition key. He was scared but excited. He could tail them. That at least was something he knew how to handle. He could also go home and have a beer and laugh at the clothes the cops in Miami Vice were wearing this week.

But he'd been hanging around all day and he needed to do something. He could always back off again if things got too hot.

He started the engine and drove around the corner. As he passed the firehouse he saw flames leaping about behind the first-floor windows.

He had to admit it. Jefferson sure knew how to apply the testicle clamps to a guy's personality.

Grimes sat in the back of the Eldorado and smoked in silence.

As they left the sprawl of the City behind them the evening redness in the west dripped its colour across the clouds and threatened a bloody finish to the day. Far ahead of them lay the swamplands, dark green now but slowly turning to black. Lightning marked out the horizon and minutes later a low rumble, more a feeling in the chest than a sound, rolled through the air heading north.

Even Jefferson, sitting on the seat beside him, was strangely quiet.

Grimes knew that his head would go out of its way to let him down. He couldn't predict the effects of the psychic trauma and the drugs that he'd taken, but neither could he let them give him an excuse. What he did now would let him know who he was; who he always had been. No more speculation.

This was his last go round.

CHAPTER EIGHTEEN

Luther Grimes turned the station-wagon into the driveway leading up to the camelback farmhouse and turned off the engine. The farmyard was thickly overgrown, and cypress trees and live oaks rustled in the wind. Fresh tyre tracks marked the vegetation of the drive and outside the house, a hundred yards ahead, he could see two cars pointing towards him. The front door of the house was closed and in a window to the right a light was burning. Apart from the sounds of the wind gusting through the trees the place was quiet. Luther sensed the imminent violence of the storm; its power excited him. This was a good time to do it.

In the preceding weeks Luther had taken time to get to know the farm well. Not the lay-out of the rooms and the hidey holes amongst the buildings out back – that was the work of minutes – but the gut feel of the place, the spirit in the soil and the trees and the air. If a man could tune in, like an animal, he could sense the things that shouldn't be there. The best game hunters learned that. If you didn't learn it before going on long range patrol you died real early.

Twenty years before, moving through the jungle at a British slow march, putting his foot down like he was walking on rice paper and didn't want to tear it, stopping every ten yards to look, smell, listen, feel, Luther had learned how to sense when something wasn't right. Small sounds mostly, but other things too that were hard to explain, holes in the sounds that shouldn't have been there, disturbances you couldn't measure with any machine.

So he sat in the station-wagon with the windows open, relaxing himself, focusing, filtering out the movement and noise in the wind and the trees until he knew that all four of them were inside the house and could almost hear their stomachs churning and smell the moisture leaking from their assholes.

From their point of view it made sense to be inside. They could handle themselves all right, but they knew Luther's record and no way were they fools enough to try to take him in the open. A man who'd spent three tours greasing VC on their own killing floor wasn't going to get himself zapped by four beer-guts from the city. But inside the house they would figure they could make it work, especially Mickey, the mean little cocksucker. There was an outside chance they'd play it straight and make the split without crossing him. But it didn't really matter squat: whichever way they played it they were going to die.

And maybe him too. He wondered what was going through Callie's mind. She was hidden out back of the farmhouse, probably making her way inside right now, alone in the dark with four killers. She had guts all right and he admired that plenty in a man or a woman, but especially in a woman because he'd hardly ever known any like that. It was funny but if she did have the balls to go against him it would only raise his reckoning of her even higher, make him want her even more.

He turned the engine over and drove up the track to the house and stopped with the headlights flooding the front door. Nothing happened. As if the bastards hadn't been watching him for five minutes. Luther blew on the car horn and got out, hauling the Samsonite suitcase full of money behind him. The suitcase was heavy in his left hand. He left the car lights on and leaned his hip against the fender. The front door opened.

A slight man in his fifties with a short, salty beard

and gold-rimmed spectacles came out onto the stoop. Leonard, the electronics man. He was dressed in a summer-weight suit and carried a flashlight in his right hand. His left hand was empty but his coat was unbuttoned and there was a bulge under his right armpit. His face looked tight and shiny and when he smiled he looked strained.

Luther said, 'How're you doin', Dutch, you miserable old fart. I do believe that's the first time I ever seen you smile.'

Leonard forced out a nervous laugh. 'I've got a lot to smile about, Luther. We all have. We've been waiting a long time for this.'

'Who's that you got sneakin' in the dark behind you?' said Luther. 'Parker? Come out, you fat bastard, where we can all see you.'

Parker was a big guy who fancied himself as something of a jock. Liked to lift weights and go jogging, that kind of shit. But he liked whipped-cream biscuits and too many beers with lunch and he never had been able to get rid of his gut. He ambled out onto the stoop, trying to look cool. Who knows, thought Luther, maybe he feels cool. Parker was wearing slacks and a denim jacket and like Leonard carried a flashlight. His free hand rested on his right hip, casual like, close to where he carried his gun in a holster in his back pocket.

By now Luther could sense the other two, Mickey and MacDonald, shifting around in the parlour behind the dirty panes of glass in the window to his right. Cute. Come on in, Luther buddy. Two guns in front and two behind and man that was all she wrote. It was as good a set up as any and it was simple.

Parker pointed his finger at the suitcase and said, 'What's in the bag, Luther?'

Luther pushed himself away from the car and held the case up for a moment. 'It's the head of Alfredo Garcia, man.'

No one laughed and Luther lowered the case.

175

'You want to see it here? Or inside?' he said.

He knew the answer but wanted to let them think they were calling the shots.

Parker said, 'Bring the bag inside.'

Luther climbed the stoop and Parker went back inside the house. Leonard stepped sideways to let Luther past and Luther handed him the case. Leonard hesitated, unwilling to fill both his hands. Luther turned the stare on him and Leonard cringed behind his glasses.

'Take it,' said Luther.

Leonard took it and Luther walked into the hallway. At the far end Parker stood jerking his thumb at the closed parlour door.

'The party's in here,' he said.

'Great,' said Luther and smiled blandly at him in the light of the electric torch.

'*Laissez les bons temps rouler.*'

CHAPTER NINETEEN

The narrow hallway was choked with bodies and smells.

This wasn't real.

The smoke of explosives and burning wood scorched her throat.

Tell me it's not real.

Her ears rang from the shock of gunfire and the blast of the grenade.

She had to get out of there.

She started to move and found herself paralysed.

From beyond the flames spilling around the splintered angles of the doorway came a convulsive scream and a short burst of callous laughter. The concussion to her eardrums made the sounds seem far away, but not far enough. The laughter belonged to Luther, enjoying his moment of power. If she didn't move now she'd lose everything she'd worked for. She tried again. Her arms and legs remained flaccid and useless.

Pain and breathlessness constricted her chest. It felt like a heart-attack but she knew better: it was simple sphincter-loosening terror. She felt hot moisture leaking from her anus and trickling down between her buttocks. She dropped suddenly to her hands and knees. Dark slime slithered beneath her fingers and she cringed. The butt of the pistol tucked into her jeans gouged her belly. A few feet from her face lay the corpse of the man she'd killed with the shotgun. She didn't even remember his name. A gust of foul air from his gaping abdomen entered her nostrils and her stomach heaved. She retched a thin drool of gastric secretions into the slime on the floor.

From the room to her left came a gunshot, loud and flat.

With the sound of the shot movement returned to her muscles. She sat back on her heels and pulled out the automatic. By concentrating on the black metal of the gun, by squeezing its realness between her fingers, she was able to block out the nightmare around her and control her fear. She flicked off the safety catch and stood up.

Over the crackle of the fire she heard Luther say, 'Trying to take me with these three clowns for back-up was pure fucking fantasy. You should have known better, Mickey.'

She took a deep breath and held it and peered through the doorway. Fanned high by the draught from the broken windows, the fire was burning in half a dozen different spots, including the roof. The flames provided the only light. Luther, a lean silhouette with a gun in either fist, was standing over a mutilated body. The body squirmed on broken limbs and made small mewling sounds that might have been words. Luther kicked the body in the head and the mewling stopped. Then he pointed a revolver with his left hand and fired once into the broken figure at his feet.

Luther shouted over his shoulder, 'We done it, babe.' He laughed again, this time in triumph. 'We done it good.'

Callie raised the Browning with both hands and pumped three bullets into his back.

Luther's reflexes were fantastic. Between getting hit by the second and third shots, as the slugs were driving him into the floor, he twisted in mid-fall and fired both barrels of the sawn-off shotgun towards the door.

Callie screamed and staggered backwards. She was hit. *She was hit.*

Her heels struck something big and limp and immovable and she went down on her ass. As soon as she landed she was struggling, twisting, frantic to get away. She escaped from the dead man under her legs and crawled for the front door, waiting for cold hands to take her throat from behind and squeeze. Four feet; six feet; ten. She passed a fallen flashlight on the floor, crawling faster, not wanting to stop moving even in order to stand up. The hands never came. She reached the black Samsonite.

The case had been dropped by the front door by the first man Luther had gunned. The top of the case was sticky. Callie leaned on it and hauled herself to her feet. She was dimly aware that her leg was throbbing. The automatic was clutched in her right fist. She swapped it to her left and picked up the case. She'd forgotten how heavy it was, and the handle was slick with blood. The case slipped from her grip and fell. Jesus Christ. Still no hands from behind. She didn't dare turn around. She didn't dare go back to make sure. She grabbed the handle again and squeezed frantically as she heaved it into the air. The screen door was jammed open by the second body. Callie stepped over it and staggered out onto the porch.

After the stench and confinement of the farmhouse, the open air calmed her. She took some deep breaths. The wind was strong and tried to drag the suitcase from her hand. She stuck the Browning into her jeans and, carrying the suitcase in both arms against her thighs, limped over to the station-wagon. The driver's door already hung open and she threw the case in and pushed it across onto the passenger seat. As she climbed behind the wheel she knocked her head.

'Shit.'

She slammed the door. The key was in the ignition where Luther had left it. She started the engine and reversed in a tight circle. Too tight. The rear fender scraped against the Chrysler parked next door. Fuck it. She changed gear and powered the car down the dirt track towards the road. She glanced in the rearview mirror. No one appeared on the porch. Unconsciously she scrubbed the palm of her hand on her thigh and jumped with pain. She looked down. The right leg of her jeans was soaked with blood. More blood speckled her shirt.

She stopped the car where the track met the blacktop and banged the heels of her palms against the steering wheel.

The bastard had wounded her and she didn't know where to go.

CHAPTER TWENTY

As Joe Gags tailed Jefferson's car through the traffic heading west on US 90 he realized that for the first time in his life he felt like a hero.

He was scared all right. With a three-hundred-pound shit-hammer like the Captain poised over his balls, who wouldn't be? But Joe had been scared before without feeling this way. The thought of self-sacrifice usually made him sick. And he didn't have a cleft chin. But he'd been shot at without soiling his pants and, when working undercover, he'd carried a wire into conversations with the kind of guys who showed gold teeth when they smiled and met failed business associates in abattoirs: the kind who drowned the children of stool-pigeons in the Mississippi River and pissed in the water as the current carried their bodies away. Joe even had a few decorations to hang on his shirt.

None of it had ever given him this tightness in the chest or this bubbling sensation in his head. It made him wonder if, after all, he was more than just another dumb asshole working for the man and trying to make believe it was the best way to look out for number one.

He felt like Brad Dexter riding back into the village shouting 'Hold on, Chris, I'll get you outa there!' He'd been waiting to feel like that ever since he'd seen Brad's horse go down at the Biloxi Regal in 1963.

Maybe that was why he was looking out for Grimes.

The question had been bothering him all day. Between fast food breaks and accidental naps and trips to the alleyway to piss he had tried hard to figure out exactly what his end was on this deal and he'd come up with zilch. He owed Grimes something, sure, but then the fat man was right: not enough to risk his life and livelihood. Pride? Jefferson had stung him, making him bend over in Sweetbread's like that, but he'd swallowed worse without sprouting wings: that was what life was all about. That was the shit in the shit sandwich. No, the more he'd thought about it the more reasons he'd come up with for going back home – and the more he'd felt that he had no choice but to go on. The old line about a man's gotta do what a man's gotta do kept running through his mind. If anybody at the station house had said anything like that he'd have snorted with laughter along with all the other guys. But there it was: that was the way he felt.

He just had to face up to it: his mind was fucked up real bad.

Gags turned his attention back to the road as Jefferson's Eldorado worked its way over into the slow lane and took the next exit. Gags followed its tail through the gathering darkness. The sky overhead was obscured by clouds moving inland before the wind. Joe had lived around the Delta all his life. He could feel the presence of a storm in his water and this was going to be a big one. That motherfucker was just waiting for the right moment to move off the ropes. When it did it would whip the shit out of the whole damned state.

Ten miles further on Gags found himself heading south towards the Gulf on an old parish road, alone with the car in front. If he remembered correctly, the strip of pitted blacktop led to absolutely fucking nowhere: a small town way back in the swamps with maybe two hundred strange people living in it, then more swamp and the sea. Maybe Jefferson had a quiet stretch of water in mind for Grimes to go to sleep in.

Jefferson's car passed straight through the town without stopping. The town was battened down for the storm. There wasn't much of the United States left in front of them any more. It was time to make a move.

Gags overtook the Eldorado in front without turning his face towards it. He made the manoeuvre as noisy and aggressive as he could, pumping up the revs and squealing the tyres so that he would pass for some drunken hick crazy on his way home to beat up on the wife and open another jug. In the rearview mirror he saw the three-time loser giving him the finger from behind the steering wheel. Gags pulled a good way ahead, so that the lights behind him were out of sight as often as not, and waited for an intersection. When a dirt road heading east showed up he slowed down and cut his lights, front and rear. He stayed on the blacktop. The lights of Jefferson's car disappeared less often. In the darkness Gags was confident that he was invisible to the car behind and hoped that they would read him as having turned off on the dirt road. Without headlights and with the moon and stars hidden behind the clouds he needed all his concentration to avoid running into the ditch. He hoped they hadn't far to go. Ten minutes passed before he noticed a glow through a bunch of trees up ahead. He speeded up. The glow became brighter and turned into a building on fire. Something was going down. Gags didn't believe in coincidence. If Jefferson was driving down some hayseed road and somewhere on that road a building was on fire then the two events were connected. He wasn't here just to dump Grimes in the swamps after all.

Gags stopped his car with the engine running at the bottom of a dirt track running west from the road. The track was lined with trees and bushes and grown over with weeds and grass and other shit. At the top of the track, one hundred yards from the road, was a house in flames. The house was derelict, an old camelback, and must have been built before the Second World War, or maybe even the First. There were fresh tyre tracks in the grass of the driveway. In front of the house, the flames reflecting from their paintwork, were two cars, both four-door Fords. He couldn't tell for sure if anyone was in the cars but he didn't think so. The wind was gusting so hard from the south that the flames were burning horizontally from the end of the house. So far the fire had only taken hold of the northern half of the building and the mouldy wood was putting up a fight. Apart from the flames and the dancing branches of the trees Joe couldn't see anything moving.

He put the car in gear and turned into the driveway and drove towards the house. Halfway up the track he pulled off to the left and steered the car through a clump of bushes and weeds between two trees. The bushes sprang up behind him as the car rolled over them. He cut the engine and got out of the car with his .38 in his hand. He moved cautiously towards the house, keeping behind the line of trees and undergrowth that ran parallel to the driveway. The wind was something else. It came screaming into his left ear and almost sucked his baseball cap from his head. The sweat in his armpits became chill and he shivered.

The noise of the leaves and branches churning against each other was raucous. The Buddy Rich Big Band could have been working its way through the Duke Ellington song book ten feet to his right and he wouldn't have heard a fucking thing. He probably wouldn't have seen the bastards either. He started to get anxious. This was jungle fucking warfare, man. He was a city boy, neon lights and bad air. He didn't understand the country. He didn't even go hunting or fishing. He spent his vacations in Nevada for Chrissakes, sitting at a table playing poker and looking out for lonely women. Jesus. The pistol in his hand was a comfort.

He got closer to the house and hunkered down beside a tree. He had to hold onto the trunk with his left hand to balance himself against the gale. The front door of the house was wide open. He wasn't sure but in the light of the fire he thought he could see a body huddled in the hallway. There were windows to either side of the door. The north window was smashed apart, its frame splintered as if by an explosion, and flames leapt around inside the room.

A body with one arm missing was draped face down over the window ledge.

Gags tried to reassure himself with the thought of Jefferson. The fat man would be here soon. Stinking bastard though he was he would know how to handle things. He always did. Gags decided to sit tight and await developments. He still had the option of ducking out if he needed it.

Upwind, just behind his head, he heard a sequence of crisp clicks as machined metal parts moved over each other. In his mind's eye he saw a fluted cylinder revolving and a hammer rising above a cartridge. His bowels lurched beneath him.

He didn't feel so much like Brad Dexter anymore.

'You know what that sound is, boy?'

The voice was raised above the wind but it wasn't unfriendly. Somehow it was as menacing as any voice Joe Gags had ever heard. His mouth was dry. He tried to keep his muscles relaxed. Movement was more difficult if you were tense. He tried to work out exactly where the voice was coming from. He did not answer the question.

'I'll tell you,' said the voice. 'It's the sound of your fart hole opening.'

Precisely on cue, and not without a flicker of pride, Joe Gags released a long bubbly fart into the wind. Jesus fucking Christ. He didn't deserve this.

He really didn't deserve it.

CHAPTER TWENTY-ONE

When the Camaro roared past them Jefferson snorted and said 'Pitiful.' Apart from occasionally telling Artie to keep his mouth shut it was the first time he'd spoken since leaving the City.

Artie Mann said, 'All them bastards from the swamps are crazy.'

He jerked a raised middle finger at the vanishing car.

'White lightning and fucking your own sisters and daughters'll do that to you every time. Maybe even your own mama too. Jesus.'

Jefferson stretched himself in the seat and seemed to shrug off whatever thoughts he'd been absorbed in.

'You're using some advanced concepts there, Artie boy,' said Jefferson. 'Maybe we've underestimated you. But that was no bastard from the swamps. More like a jerk-off from the city. He's been behind us all the way. What do you say, Doc?'

Grimes did not answer. For all he cared, the Camaro could have been driven by Jethro Clampett and the Beverly Hillbillies. During the drive towards the Gulf his mind had swung on a pendulum from psychic numbness through flashes of confidence to morbid preoccupation and back. Death had left its imprint on him and now its stink clung to the interior of the car the way an old woman's sweat lingers in the creases beneath her breasts. It took him back to the side rooms where he'd helped the terminally ill to suffer a little longer with tubes and chemicals and machines. There you could only smell death if you got beyond the technology and the ritual and placed your hands on the stale, flat flesh. But in Jefferson's car it condensed on the inside of the windshield.

'So,' Grimes said to Jefferson, 'we're all going to die.'

Jefferson shook his head.

'I'll take care of you, Doc. Now that we're partners you travel under my protection. Anybody who wants to get to you has to go through me and that can't be done.'

On impulse Grimes punched the back of the empty seat in front of him. He held his fists palm-down as far apart as the handcuffs would let him and punched the hardboard of the seat-back with the first two knuckles of each hand.

Artie Mann flinched as the blow shook him and said, 'Shit, man?'

Grimes hit the seat again and grunted. It felt good. The punches grew in power and the grunts in volume, now a punch every second: one-Mississippi, two-Mississippi. His knuckles were capped with calluses from workouts on the heavy bag. He could keep this up all night long. All night long.

Jefferson shoved the barrel of his Magnum into Grimes' ribs.

'Cool it, Grimes. This is no time to turn apeshit on me.'

Grimes ignored him. The seats in front shuddered again. Artie hunched forward over the wheel, whining obscenities. No one took any notice. Jefferson holstered his gun. He leaned over and grabbed the lapels of Grimes' jacket and wedged his elbows between Grimes' forearms. Grimes struggled but the handcuffs were against him and Jefferson was stronger.

'I guess I didn't make myself clear,' said Jefferson. 'You are here to kneel, boy.'

Grimes said, 'You'd better look again.'

Jefferson wrenched his elbows down and Grimes felt his arms jar savagely against the shoulder sockets.

'You're mine! What I want to happen happens.'

For a second it was almost a tantrum, then Jefferson calmed himself.

'You're taking me to the cash, just like I told you to. Your brother and his buddies and your whore girlfriend'll soon be fly-meat, but I told you, that's only the beginning.'

Grimes relaxed his arms and fists and Jefferson let go of the lapels and sat back.

'You're green,' said Jefferson, 'and you've wasted years trying to help people you should've left to suffer or die. But you'll make it, with my help. You got knowledge and skills that I don't have, and vice versa. Together we can do some things. All you need is the right attitude and we'll crush them like beetles. I've seen the rage that's eating your insides. It's been there all your life. Whatever this brother of yours did, that don't explain it. Killing him won't take it away.'

'Listen.' Grimes ground his teeth until his face ached. 'I've got a great idea. Why don't you mind your own fucking business and let me out of the car?'

'Face it, Grimes, this is the world. Bad City. You were born there. I was born there. It's a world designed by scumbags. Only they can be happy in it. It's their machine, not ours. You and I got a chance to sabotage the fucking thing – unless you cripple yourself with pity. Or love. Then you're trapped in the city with the scumbags queuing round the block to kick your ass. For men like you and me – for the few – there's only one way out. Strength; discipline; will. Let me show you.'

Jefferson leaned forwards, his eyes gleaming with the fanatic passion of his thoughts, and Grimes said:

'Oh the blest eyes, the happy hearts,
That know, that see the guiding thread so fine,
Along the mighty labyrinth.'

Jefferson paused for a moment, holding Grimes' gaze, then said, 'That somebody I should know?'

'Walt Whitman,' said Grimes.

'Yeah,' said Jefferson. 'Your cute little notebooks. You burnt them, remember? Forget that old faggot. The only poetry you can make people listen to is the sound of their own pain and fear.'

'I learned a poem once,' said Artie Mann.

Jefferson stared at the back of Artie's head and Grimes could see him debating whether or not to beat the ex-con down.

'Let's hear it then,' said Jefferson.

He looked back at Grimes.

'Show the Doctor here that he isn't the only one who can whip out a smart quotation when he needs to.'

Artie Mann cleared his throat and said,

> 'There was a girl named Betty Box
> Who gave a thousand men the pox,
> But though she's dead she's not forgotten,
> They dig her up and fuck her rotten.'

As he finished Artie started laughing.

'Shut up,' said Jefferson. 'There's something happening up ahead. Slow down.'

As Artie eased back on the gas Grimes looked through the fly-specked windshield. Beyond a row of trees he saw the farmhouse he'd visited the night before. The building was on fire and the trees, bending over in the wind, were outlined by the glow.

'That's it,' he said. 'We're too late.'

'Maybe,' said Jefferson. 'Artie, what happened to that Camaro?'

'It turned off onto a dirt road a few miles back, outside the town. I told you, a swamp rat.'

'Did you see it make the turn?' said Jefferson.

'Well, not exactly,' said Artie. 'He slowed up some and his lights disappeared and then I saw the turn off. I ain't seen him since. He must've made the turn.'

'No,' said Jefferson.

He rubbed his chin on the first knuckle of his right thumb.

'While we were talking comparative literature he tailed us from in front with his lights off. He's probably in there right now playing cowboys and Indians, muddying the water for us.'

'Who are we talking about?' said Grimes.

'My little bird. Your conscience-stricken buddy, Joe Gags. He followed us from the city. Damn. There's no point busting in there now. Artie, there's the driveway to the house. Pull over this side of it. We wait and see.'

The car stopped and sat with the engine idling. Grimes looked at the burning house but could see no sign of life. Luther could be in there, wounded or dead. Callie too. He put his hands on the door handle.

'Sit still, fool,' said Jefferson. 'You'll get your brains blown out.'

'Then I won't know much about it,' said Grimes. 'Thanks for the ride, fat man.'

Grimes jerked the door open and started to climb out. Jefferson grabbed him by the shoulder and Grimes rammed an elbow into his face. There was a crunching sound as the damage Jefferson had sustained to his sinuses was extended. He cried out and fell back across the seats.

As Grimes left the car he stumbled to one knee. The wind was immense. He stood up straight and felt his jacket fluttering against his hips. From the open rear door, the words whipping past his head, he heard Jefferson shouting.

'It takes two to make it, Grimes! You need me.'

Grimes turned his back on Jefferson's words and started running up the driveway towards the fire. His legs felt stiff and clumsy. No one shot him down. He passed two empty cars and reached the porch. Flames billowed about the walls and roof to his right. Their heat scared his cheek.

He took several deep breaths to blow off carbon dioxide from his lungs and climbed up onto the stoop. A surge of bile rose into his throat as his shoes slid in a pool of black jelly. At his feet the light of flames illuminated the slack features of a man crumpled into the floor, jamming the screen door open. A pair of gold-rimmed spectacles with one lens broken hung across the dead man's face from his right ear. The black jelly was matted in two thick clots on his chest. Grimes did not recognize him.

He stepped across the corpse into a physical mass of intense heat and walked down the hallway. At the far end was a burning doorway and a second man lying spread-eagled on his back. Coils of shredded entrails were heaped upon the floor between his legs. Globules of hot fat glistened on the surface of the coils and here and there a length of bowel shifted and swelled as the gas inside expanded with the heat.

Grimes did not recognize this man either.

He felt his lips moving. Maybe screaming or praying – he didn't know which. Maybe he was laughing. The wind and the fire roared in his head like Jefferson's white noise. Dizzied by nausea and smoke, he bent across the second body and leaned his hands against the wall, then jerked them back again as the wood blistered his palms. Flakes of melted paint stuck to his skin. The pain steadied his nerves. He took a breath of superheated air and walked through the doorway into the burning room.

The hairs on the back of his hands shrivelled down to his skin as the heat caught them. He clasped his hands over his nose and mouth and held his breath. The far wall was almost burnt through; above it the ceiling timbers raged. In the middle of the floor, surrounded by fragments of burning wood, was another corpse, this one with multiple shrapnel wounds to the chest and abdomen and a bullet hole through its left eye. The corpse had no face but Grimes knew from its build that it couldn't be Luther.

The hair on Grimes' head was crinkling against his skull now and he could feel his face swelling. A fourth man hung face down out of the window. His pants had melted and run down his blistered legs in dirty globs. A soft lump of congealed blood protruded from between his buttocks like an obscene turd.

Flaming timber fell from the roof. Grimes could no longer hold his breath. Scrubbing his hair with both hands he stumbled from the room, hurdled the two bodies in the hall and ran outside into the yard. He landed badly from the porch steps and tripped. The wind took him down. He rolled over on the ground and lay there rubbing his hands and skull against the grass to cool them. His clothes and hair were smoking. He rose to his hands and knees and looked up at the man hanging from the window. One of his arms had been torn off and a tangle of frayed tendons and blood vessels bulged from the vacant socket. The fourth man wasn't Luther either.

No Luther. No Callie.

Grimes clambered to his feet. His head felt as if it were packed with wholewheat flour. Something struck him on the vault of his skull and detonated with exquisite coolness against his scorched flesh. A second bomb hit him and a third, and then a great squall of rain swept over him and sheet lightning lit up the night. As the sky went dark again a clap of thunder crashed with such violence that he almost fell back to his knees.

'Grimes! You fucking ass-ho-le!'

After the thunder Jefferson's voice did not sound so impressive.

Grimes started to turn around and stopped halfway through the movement. Propped against a tree on the other side of the drive, his legs spread out in front of him to stop him toppling over, was Joe Gags. He was wearing a baseball cap and his head was twisted so that his chin was wedged behind his left shoulder. The eccentric position was made possible by the wide gash gaping through the muscles running down the right-hand side of his neck. The baseball cap was dripping with rain and the former contents of Joe's carotid artery.

Grimes pointed stupidly at the body and looked at Jefferson. The policeman was an obscure blob in the

192

curtain of rain, moving through the trees with Artie, twenty yards away from the house. The lightning flashed again and was followed by a double explosion.

Jefferson turned into a bundle of bloody rags and hurtled from sight.

The thunder pealed, louder than before. Grimes began running towards Jefferson. His shoes squelched with water. He stopped as a bedraggled figure stumbled from the trees and turned twice in a circle, his arms cartwheeling around in the air. Artie Mann stopped as he caught sight of Grimes and Grimes thought he could hear him blubbering in panic above the wind and rain. Artie stretched out his arms and ran towards Grimes as if Grimes would embrace and protect him. Lightning reflected from the sticking plaster on the plunging, gasping face. Grimes unconsciously raised his arms.

Through the chaos of thunder and rain two crisp gunshots slammed and Artie left the ground. He landed lengthwise at Grimes' feet like a bucket of swill thrown into a gutter. The bullets had ripped his scrawny chest apart as if it were a wicker basket.

There was a long pause.

Grimes dropped to his knees and sat back on his heels. He lifted his face and closed his eyes and felt the rain running down his cheeks. Makes the streams and rivers as muddy as can be. He asked himself what he wanted to be on his mind as he died. Something beautiful, something he liked at least. He tried to generate a mental image of something beautiful. Nothing happened. A landscape, a sweet phrase, a face. Nothing came. A few notes of music, the memory of lips against his skin, his father's voice. Again, nothing. Nothing real; just suggestions bereft of feeling. His mind was a parched soil gaping with cracks. His imagination had drained away through the cracks and now the cracks laughed, without mirth or pleasure. This was what he'd worked for and now it was his to cherish.

What a waste.

CHAPTER TWENTY-TWO

'Hello, Eugene.'

Grimes opened his eyes. Luther stood five feet in front of him squinting against the rain. Strands of hair had escaped from his pony-tail and were plastered against his cheek. He wore a tiger-striped combat jacket over a dark T-shirt. In one hand he held a long-barrelled revolver; in the other a stump of shotgun. He pushed the shotgun into a pocket of his jacket.

Grimes said, 'Hello, Luther. How are you doing?'

Luther shrugged one shoulder.

'I've felt better.'

He nodded his head at the bodies bleeding in the rain.

'Were these two comedians with you?'

'I guess they were,' said Grimes.

Luther pointed to the ground at Grimes' feet.

'Lie down on your belly.'

Grimes felt no fear; just a need to explain.

He didn't move. He said, 'I came here to kill you.'

'I don't think so,' said Luther.

In the poor light Luther's face was cut by deep lines. Grimes looked into his eyes and the eyes hurt him bad enough to die. Grimes opened his mouth but it was too dark and too late and he'd run out of words and run out of time.

Grimes said, 'I'm sorry.'

It was the best he could do.

'It don't much matter anymore,' said Luther. 'Lie down.'

Grimes lay down with his handcuffed arms stretched in

front of him. He spread his hands apart and dug his fingertips into the soil. The leaves of grass were cool to his burnt palms. He pushed his face into the soft ground and inhaled the sweet smell. He'd never felt this close to the earth before. It was a shame. He'd spent too long on concrete. Too late again. Too late to talk; too late to touch the Earth mother; too late for stupid, maudlin thoughts. He braced himself.

The blast of Luther's revolver deafened him. He jerked his head away as red hot pin-pricks stung his scalp. The tension in the bracelets at his wrists slackened. When he looked up at his hands the chain links of the handcuffs had been broken apart by the bullet. He stared at the broken ends of the chain without moving.

'What's the matter?' said Luther. 'You got your pecker stuck in a hole or something?'

Grimes pushed his chest up from the ground and stood up. He wiped his hands gently on the legs of his pants. He felt awkward.

'Thanks,' he said.

Luther flicked his hair from his face with a jerk of his head and smiled without enjoyment.

'You thought I was going to ice you while you were face down on the ground. Jesus. Give a dog a bad fucking name.'

'I'm sorry,' said Grimes again.

'Stop apologizing,' said Luther. 'No one I know ever taught you that.'

'I can't think straight,' said Grimes.

'Excuses too. Don't you remember nothing?'

Grimes stepped towards Luther with his hand held out. Luther backed off a step. His right arm tensed but he did not raise his revolver.

'I just wanted to touch you,' said Grimes.

He felt foolish, then angry at himself for feeling foolish, then angry at Luther for knowing better than him.

'Sure,' said Luther. 'Later. First let's get out of this shithole.'

He nodded towards Joe Gags.

'God, guns and guts over there left a Camaro behind that he don't need any more. Can you drive?'

'Yes.'

Grimes looked at Joe's body.

'He was a friend.'

'Yeah, well we didn't have time to talk about that. Let's go.'

When Luther walked away into the trees Grimes saw that he was limping. Grimes fell in beside him and said, 'You're wounded.'

'She put three nine-millimetre slugs in me,' said Luther. 'I'm trying to look on the bright side. If they were .45s I'd be dead.'

He looked at Grimes.

'Then maybe you'd be dead too.'

'Where are you hit?' said Grimes.

'I took one in the ass and two in the back. They'll hang my picture in the Fools' Hall of Fame for this one. Me and Fred McMurray, huh? Shit. I don't know how bad it is. I'm not bleeding much. Not on the outside anyway.'

They reached the Camaro and Luther leaned his left arm on the roof and his head on his arm.

Without looking up he said, 'Does she love you, Gene? Did she turn me over for you or was it just for the dough?'

Grimes put his hand on the back of Luther's neck. The skin was cold and flat.

'She doesn't love me,' said Grimes. 'Or you. She figured you'd go crazy if she left you. You could say when she shot you, she was just trying to spare your feelings.'

'She made me happy,' said Luther. 'For a while, anyhow.'

'Then you've come out ahead of the rest of us,' said Grimes.

'I guess.'

'Why did you send her to me?'

'She was out of her fucking skull. I thought she was going to die.'

196

'You must have figured there was a chance I'd find you.'

Luther raised his face from his arm and looked at Grimes.

'Maybe I did. I been waiting to see you for a long time.'

Grimes opened the car door. As Luther got in he grimaced with pain. Grimes walked around to the driver's side and sat behind the wheel. In the closed space the smell of smoke on his clothes was vile. Luther gave him the keys and Grimes turned the engine over. He switched on the lights and reversed onto the driveway through the bushes. At the end of the drive he started to turn north.

'Where're you goin'?' said Luther.

'There's a medical centre in Houma. They'll keep you alive until we can get you to City General,' said Grimes.

Luther caught his arm in a fierce grip. 'The hell we are. Not this side of the border. I'm not going back to prison. Ever again. Take me home.'

'You'll die without surgery,' said Grimes.

Luther lifted the Magnum pistol from his lap.

'You aren't going to use that on me.'

'No,' said Luther, 'but if you take me to any fucking hospital I'll kill the first three people I see and blow my own brains over the inside of their emergency room.'

Grimes knew he was capable of what he said. Luther gasped as a spasm of pain doubled him over.

'Drive,' he said. 'South.'

Grimes swung the car left out of the driveway and ploughed through the storm. The road was empty but vision was poor. His hands hurt and he had difficulty concentrating. To avoid killing them both he kept his speed down.

They were both silent for a while. Luther fidgeted in the seat and in the way he twisted his fingers and cracked his knuckles Grimes felt a head of tension building up.

Finally Luther said, 'I got to know.'

'Know what?' said Grimes.

'Don't jerk me off, Eugene. Did you fuck her?'

Grimes pulled his face. It was weird. He actually felt guilty and embarrassed. After all these years of hate; after a thousand fantasies of cutting and stomping and torturing; of seeing Luther crippled, incontinent and blind; now, face to face, Grimes didn't want to hurt him anymore.

He said, 'Don't ask me that.'

Luther jammed the Magnum into Grimes' crotch.

'You sanctimonious cocksucker. I ought to blow your balls off. Say it. Tell me.'

Grimes squeezed the steering wheel. The pain in his scorched palms helped him stay calm. He shook his head.

Luther's lips were swollen with malice and contempt. 'You wanna know about fucking?' he said. 'Like sexual intercourse? Dolly could tell you plenty if she were still here. All the while she was seeing you, she still needed me inside her.'

Grimes groaned. His cock was erect and aching.

'She used to tell me all the bullshit love-talk you gave her. It turned us both on.'

Grimes squeezed the wheel as hard as he could but all he could feel was the lust and jealousy rolling against each other in his guts.

'The night before you got married she was in my bed, squealing underneath me, pleading for all the cock I could give her . . .'

Grimes' right arm left the wheel like a triphammer and his elbow smashed into Luther's chest. The car swerved and Grimes' foot slipped from the gas pedal. He hit Luther again and Luther blurted a cupful of blood across the windshield. Grimes struggled to keep the skittering car on the road and shouted.

'Okay!'

He grabbed the wheel in both hands again and the car straightened up.

'I fucked her. She fucked me. We fucked each other. I stuck my tongue up her ass. She sucked my cock. What do you want to hear?'

He stopped the car and rested his forehead on the wheel. His hands began to hurt again. He looked across at Luther who was slumped forward, moaning.

'Jesus Christ,' said Grimes.

The anger was gone. His voice was weary. He wasn't sure which planet he was on anymore. He reached over and pulled Luther upright and wiped blood and mucus from his face. Luther took shallow breaths and wouldn't look at him. Grimes turned back to the road and drove on.

From the shotgun seat Luther said quietly, 'The turn is up ahead on the right. A dirt road. Take it slowly or you'll miss it.'

Grimes couldn't see through the rain. He slowed down and concentrated and the turn-off appeared in the headlights. The tyres crunched as they left the blacktop and bit into the soft dirt. As the road took him deeper into the swamps Grimes lost track of time and distance. Dancing raindrops rolled under the headlights. Dripping vegetation loomed first from one side, then the other, brushing the roof of the car. Luther coughed and suddenly Grimes had a picture in his mind: of Luther, alone, sitting on the edge of his bed, taking off his boots and picking fluff from his toes, wishing Callie were there so he could run his fingers through her hair and whisper sweet nothings in her ear. Just a man; nothing more or less than any of the rest of them.

Grimes shook his head at the darkness and when the cabin came into sight he was grateful. The cabin lights were dim, disappearing for a second behind a stand of trees. Outside stood a Japanese hatchback and a Dodge station-wagon. The Dodge was splashed with mud and had a dent in the rear fender.

'Ever see a bird on a string, Eugene?'

As he finished the sentence Luther slumped forwards in a faint, his head banging against the window. Grimes leaned over and took the Ruger Blackhawk from his lap. No one stopped him. No one threatened him or beat him or dragged a bag over his head. Rain lashed his face as he wound down the window and threw the gun out into the mud. He found the sawn-off shotgun in the pocket of Luther's combat jacket and threw that out too. Then he checked Luther's pulse. One hundred and ten. His blood pressure was just holding up. Grimes got out into the rain.

The wind slapped his pants around his ankles and plastered his shirt and jacket against his back. He shivered. He reached back into the Camaro and sounded the horn three times. Then he went and stood in the car headlights with his arms raised above his head. A shape hovered by the window and a moment later the cabin door opened.

'Is that you, Grimes?'

She sounded surprised and nervous, but hopeful. She stayed out of sight and Grimes imagined her crouched in the doorway, holding her gun in both hands.

'Yeah, it's me.'

Nothing happened.

Grimes said, 'If I were Luther or Jefferson you'd be dead by now.'

Callie appeared in the doorway pointing an automatic with her right hand. When she saw him she let the arm holding the gun fall to her side. She was wearing a denim shirt with the tails tied in a knot over her belly and a pair of white panties. There was a blood-stained length of sheet bandaged around her right thigh. Grimes walked up to her and she fell against him, her face pressed to his chest. It felt good and he wanted to believe her. He brushed the backs of his fingers against her hair.

'I didn't think you knew about this place,' she said.

'I didn't. Luther brought me here.'

Callie pushed herself away from him and raised her gun. Grimes couldn't help flinching. Callie's face flickered as she scanned the darkness beyond the car lights.

'He's in the car,' said Grimes. 'Bleeding to death. I'm going to bring him inside and look him over.'

'No way, Grimes.'

Grimes said, 'I'm bringing him in. You want to shoot us both as we come through the door, go ahead. You'd be doing me a favour.'

He went back to the car. Luther's face was a pale disc behind the rainwater and blood on the windshield. Grimes opened the door and Luther fell against him. Grimes shoved him back and then pulled his legs outside. Luther's head flopped around. Grimes tried to get the body over his shoulder. Kirk Douglas and Earl Holliman. But Grimes couldn't get underneath him and his feet kept slipping in the mud. He noted that Luther's body still had some tone to it, wasn't quite as heavy and dense as a completely unconscious man would be. He pinched the inside of Luther's thigh, hard, and Luther jumped.

'Come on, bastard, give me some help.'

Luther opened his eyes blearily and mumbled something Grimes couldn't hear. He shuffled himself to the edge of the seat and Grimes hooked his arm around Luther's waist.

'Let's go,' said Grimes.

He lifted and Luther stood up and leaned heavily into him. Grimes skidded and caught his balance by resting his back against the roof of the car. His ribs hurt. Like two drunks they staggered across the muddy ground and through the cabin door. Once inside Grimes paused to lean against the wall and look around. He was still supporting most of Luther's weight.

The cabin formed a single long room stretching away from the front door. In the corner to Grimes' left was a small stove and an aluminium sink screwed into the wall. Connected to the stove by a rubber pipe was a gas cylinder. Beyond the stove were two straight-backed hardwood chairs set on either side of a wooden crate. The crate was marked with old coffee and food stains. Against the wall between the cabin's only two windows was a bed and a second crate. An oak table with another straight chair filled the space beyond the bed and against the far wall was a chest of drawers and a dresser with a mirror. The room was illuminated by three butane gas lamps, one on the stained crate and two on the dresser. On a shelf above the sink burned a coal-oil lamp with a glass chimney and base. Callie was standing by the bed chewing her lip and still holding her gun in her right hand.

Grimes adjusted his grip on Luther and half-carried him towards the bed. Luther dragged his feet as if he were deliberately trying to make the job harder. As they got closer Luther looked straight into Callie's eyes. He parted his lips and let a mouthful of bloody drool spill down his chest.

'Callie, baby. Sugar. Help me.'

On Callie's face, sympathy and guilt struggled against cold reason. She threw her automatic onto the bed and stepped forward, arms reaching out to help. Luther's legs started to go and Grimes struggled not to drop him. He fought for balance. Then suddenly Luther was gone and Grimes found himself choking and going down, gagging for air as the edge of Luther's hand hit him in the throat.

The bastard had suckered him again.

CHAPTER TWENTY-THREE

Things went sour for Jefferson from the moment Grimes climbed out of the car.

After the long ride from the city Jefferson's right knee was frozen with pain. He could not bear weight on it without gasping. As he struggled out of the car to follow Grimes he told himself that he was stupid, that he should grab the radio and call in assistance and drop the whole bucket of slop on the State Police. But he didn't have a choice. He had to see it through. The panic of a lover contemplating rejection churned in his belly. He didn't like it. This wasn't the place to deal with feelings he knew nothing about. It was a fucking outrage. Rage was another emotion he normally had no use for: now it too crept along his limbs and poisoned his blood.

He called Artie over and used him as a crutch, leaning his left arm across the ex-con's thin shoulders. It helped some, but not a lot. After a few paces Artie complained about his ribs hurting and how, Jesus, he wasn't built to carry such a big guy as you, Captain.

Jefferson bent forward and hacked Artie in the groin with the edge of his right hand. Before Artie could fall Jefferson grabbed him by the throat and forced him to his knees. Artie's eyes filled with tears as they darted about between the clumsy strips of plaster on his face. He whimpered through the fingers squeezing his neck. He did not understand. His eyes were bright with incomprehension and terror.

Jefferson choked on a great wedge of disgust. Artie was the world. Artie would always be the world. He, Jefferson, was wasting his fucking time. He, the three-hundred-pound shithammer, had lost the losing battle. His last, best hope was wandering around in a fucking inferno trying to get himself killed. A woman and a bunch of goddamn clowns were getting the better of him. He was hurting bad. And Artie was the world. Saliva flew into Artie's face as Jefferson spoke to him.

'Don't think. Don't speak.'

Jefferson paused between each pair of words to inhale some self-control.

'Just o-fucking-bey. Now stand up and walk.'

He dragged Artie to his feet and together they limped towards the farmhouse. Struggling against the wind they must have looked like a fat old woman and her skinny husband trying to get home before the storm. Jack and Mrs Sprat. They should have been moving through the trees lining the driveway, using stealth and cunning and other good shit, but with the bad knee he wasn't fit enough to make it worthwhile. They were completely exposed. Stupid, incompetent fucks. With every step he increased the distance between himself and the rational control that was his power. Violence bubbled into his throat, scalding his tongue. He could not walk. He could not see. He could not breathe. Grimes had defied him without effort. Somehow it had all slipped away from him.

And Artie was the world.

When Grimes stumbled from the house with smoke coming from his hair and clothes Jefferson could not contain the violence any longer.

'Grimes!'

Lightning threw a web of shadows across the ground. Thunder drowned out his voice. A squall of rain lashed his face with the force of birdshot and he closed his eyes against it as he bellowed again against the wind.

'Grimes! You fucking ass-ho-le!'

He opened his eyes and thought he saw Grimes pointing towards a tree. The simple son of a bitch. Jefferson looked at the tree but the rain was as dense as a bead curtain and all he saw was a fucking tree bending in the gale. A second blast of lightning struck and two yards to his right Jefferson saw a phantom floating in the rain: a lean face with a skeleton's grin. From below the face a sawn-off shotgun pointed at Jefferson's belly.

Jefferson shoved himself away from Artie hoping that the phantom would choose the wrong target. He was falling sideways and squeezing the trigger of the Python when a blast of sound and flame cracked the world open at his feet. He soared backwards and saw a cascade of dark water falling towards him. Then his shoulders gouged into the ground and he lay still without breathing.

His mind became clear, as it always did when he'd been wounded. He was badly hurt. There was no pain yet, or none that he could distinguish from that already searing his face and chest and knee, but any force that could throw him like that must have damaged him. His wind returned. He breathed slowly – slowly – so that the movement of his chest wouldn't be noticed. The mental effort required to do it was enough to levitate a beer truck. Two gunshots sounded nearby. Bangbang. So that was the way the world ended after all. He was too stunned to flinch. Magnum loads. He was sure he hadn't been shot with a Magnum. For one he was alive. For another he was just receiving the first messages from the mutilated nerves in his skin and the news was of widespread damage. He was hurting from nipples to knees. Sure. He'd seen the shotgun. Both barrels in the belly.

Jefferson had faith in his belly. He had a chance.

He opened his eyes and stared at the cascade and the silhouettes of the trees jerking above him. The sound of the storm thrashing the leaves and branches filled his ears and blocked out anything else he might have heard. He counted off sixty seconds. No more gunshots. No kicks in the ribs to see if he was still alive. He gave the phantom another minute to come and finish him off. When he didn't, Jefferson began to turn his head at the same speed that he was moving his chest.

His limbs jumped as the Magnum blammed a third time. So much for controlling his body. Bye, bye, Dr Grimes. When the roll is called up yonder you'll be there. His guts churned over. Sorrow? Real sorrow? He was losing his mind. Fuck this. He had to survive. Recuperate. Then search and destroy.

He continued his turn to the left. He was lying on the northern border of the driveway with his feet pointing towards the house. The flames threw enough light for him to see a figure rise from the ground. Dressed in black. So the good doctor was still alive. Grimes took a step forward and another figure moved away from him. The second figure must have been standing there all the time. Jefferson hadn't noticed him until he moved. Camouflage jacket. Tiger stripes. The phantom. It had to be Luther Grimes. The Tough Bullet. It certainly wasn't that other stupid incompetent fuck who'd tailed them from the city on a white charger. To serve and protect. Maybe Joe Gags had met Luther before they arrived.

The two men disappeared into the trees bordering the southern side of the drive. They seemed to be talking like old buddies. Grimes' arms swung free of his cuffs. The third shot. Bastards. Jefferson felt betrayed. He licked raindrops from his lips. Jealousy. Jesus Christ, he was turning into an asshole. A car engine started and Joe Gags' Camaro reversed into sight, turned and drove towards the road.

Jefferson rolled over onto his belly in time to see the Camaro's tail-lights pull out of sight heading south. He allowed himself the luxury of a great roar of pain. A stream of obscenity gushed from his mouth as he pushed himself to his hands and knees. Rainwater and blood dripped from his body into the grass. He clambered to his feet and let instinct take over: he needed a weapon. He had lost his revolver when he'd been shot and had no time to search for it. He tested his legs out. They didn't like it but they'd work if he told them to. He staggered the forty feet to Artie's corpse and found the Colt .45 Automatic tucked into the waist of Artie's jeans. He checked the .45 and found a cartridge already chambered. In one of Artie's pockets he found a spare clip of shells.

Jefferson straightened up. Against the tree that Grimes had pointed out he saw another corpse, this one with a gash in the side of its neck and a baseball cap on its head. The poor asshole should have stuck to playing poker. On impulse Jefferson cocked the .45 and blew off the top of Joe Gags' head.

'Because it feels so goddamned good,' he said to himself.

He shoved the Colt into the holster on his hip and walked back to his car. As he walked he stomped his feet down harder than he needed to, hurting himself, daring his body to give in. His body didn't have the guts. With his hands he explored the extent of his injuries.

His Hawaiian shirt was shredded beyond repair. A collector's item too. The dealer who'd sold it to him swore that the shirt had been worn by Ernest Borgnine during the making of 'From Here To Eternity'. Jefferson didn't believe him. Ernest didn't take a size fifty-six chest. But it was a fine piece of work, or had been, and he was sorry to feel it come away in pieces in his hands. At several points the buckshot had carried the shirt through his skin without ripping the cloth: the shirt was stapled to his body with lead rivets. Well, no one ever died of rayon poisoning that he'd heard of. But his tugging on the shirt hurt so he stopped. No sense in unplugging the holes anyway. Most of the wounds were on the right side of his body, maybe half a dozen holes in his lower right belly and a couple more in his thigh. He ran a hand over his genitals and found a full set. He was aching in so many places that he could not be sure, but he didn't think the bucks had penetrated anything vital. A thin man would have been trying to thread his bowels back through the holes. Jefferson's belly had not let him down.

A carbohydrate intake fit for a seed bull maintained the six-inch layer of body fat. Underneath the fat were more inches: iron hard muscle built by doing thousands of sets of ten-second Roman chair sit-ups with a forty-pound barbell held behind his neck.

These things made a difference.

His confidence began to return and he stoked it. He reminded himself of who he was. He couldn't be killed. He couldn't be beaten. He was the self-made man: built one brick at a time from the granite of his own will. As an adolescent he should have been doomed: to dogmatism and imbecility by an expensive education: to blandness and bigotry by his family; to the Chinese water torture of a good career, a steady job. He had battered his way out. From will alone he had created the machine he needed to realize his ambition: to be complete; to be free; to contain within himself – himself alone – everything he needed to exist in this shitpool that was Earth. He had done it. He feared no one, he felt for no one, he needed no one. His car was in front of him. He raised his fists above his head and smashed them down like mallets on the roof of the Eldorado. He rested his forehead on his fists as if he were praying and, scooping up the pain of his body, he said:

'I have beheld the infinite Abyss, fiery as the smoke of a burning city. And I have driven my cart and plough over the bones of the dead.'

Water ran down his neck and across his shoulders. He raised his head and the collar of his shirt pressed into his hair.

'And I will not fall in the tangled roots.'

He turned his face to stare into the blackness marking the road that Grimes had taken. He could go find him tomorrow, he thought. Or the next day. The self-made man wiped water from his eyes. No. Find him now. Find him now or let go of it for good, one or the other. He opened the Eldorado's door and got in. He started the engine.

Find the bastard now and take it home.

CHAPTER TWENTY-FOUR

Grimes held onto the back of a straight hardwood chair and tried to cough. He wanted to vomit, swallow and breathe all at the same time. His vision was blurred. Through the blur he watched Luther pull a long combat knife from his belt.

Callie screamed and Luther lunged at her, grunting and snorting as he aimed a vicious slash at her face. Callie stumbled backwards and fell onto the bed. The slashing motion made Luther cry out in pain and he curled his arms across his body. Grimes straightened up, his breathing noisy and coarse as Callie rolled across the bed and scrambled for her pistol. As she slid off the opposite side of the mattress and stood up, the pistol tangled in the sheets and she dropped it. Luther took the knife by the blade in a throwing grip.

Grimes picked up the chair, one hand gripping the back, the other the seat.

Luther pulled his arm back to let fly and again hesitated as his body coiled in with pain. Grimes stepped forward and swung through a hard, tight arc, all hips and shoulder, with the chair held close to his chest, its outer leg making a short blunt spear. He shouted and Luther half-turned, his reflexes dulled by blood-loss and pain. The turn took him into the arc of Grimes' movement; and Grimes, finishing the move, rammed the leg of the chair through Luther's skull.

During the instant of contact Grimes felt bone crumple and give way then the force of the blow knocked Luther's head to one side. Luther dropped to the floor and lay still. Grimes lowered the chair but kept hold of it and looked at Callie. Callie walked around the bed holding her gun by her side. She was looking at Luther.

'What's happening to him?' she said.

Grimes followed the direction of her pointing finger. Luther was flat on his back. The right side of his face was twitching. As they watched the twitching became more violent, more grotesque, and spread down into the muscles of the neck. His right arm and shoulder started moving, then his leg, until the whole right half of his body was shaking and writhing. The left half of his face and body remained limp and still. Over his left temple was a large swelling.

Grimes put the chair down and sat on it, staring at Luther. It was the first time in his life he'd beaten him down. He waited for it to feel good.

Callie said, 'Jesus what's wrong with him?'

There was a concern in her voice that triggered the old hatred in Grimes' heart.

'I wish the bastard was awake so he could feel it.'

'It's horrible,' she said. 'Do something.'

'It's not enough,' said Grimes. He tried to will himself some sense of triumph or satisfaction but all he felt was horror.

Callie said, 'I'm going to stop it.'

She pointed her gun at Luther and snapped off the safety catch. Grimes stood up and grabbed the gun, twisting it from her grip.

'I said it's not enough.'

'Well it's enough for me!'

Callie screamed the words in his face.

'You're meant to be a fucking doctor.'

'I'm nothing.'

'Then give me the gun and let me finish it.'

Grimes stared at her. Birds on a string, like Luther said. There was a high frequency noise in his head as of machinery and circuitry about to explode. He looked at the gun in his hand. He'd never used one on a living

210

object, but it was a way of stopping the noise. That was what they wanted. He put her gun on the chair and squatted down beside Luther.

'You're right,' he said.

He was a doctor. The fact had never given him much pride or satisfaction before; now it was the only thing he knew about himself that felt real and wasn't all bad. He just had to prove it. He worked his arms beneath Luther's thighs and shoulders and grunted as he stood up. The convulsions were powerful and he almost dropped the jerking body.

'Come on, you fucker.'

He caught his balance and staggered down the cabin past the bed. He slung the body onto the table, knocking a glass and a bottle of whiskey to the floor. Neither broke. He brought one of the gas lamps over to the table and held it out towards Callie.

'Hold this for me.'

Callie hesitated.

Grimes said, 'Please.'

Callie came over and took the light from his hand.

'Here,' said Grimes, 'so I can see his head and face.'

Blood ran down Luther's neck from a wound above and in front of his left ear. Grimes bent forward and peeled back Luther's eyelids. The right pupil contracted to the light; the left was blown wide open and didn't respond. He let the eyes close and examined the lump ballooning over Luther's temple. The skin was broken and bleeding. The main source of haemorrhage was beneath the scalp and the swelling was tense with blood. Underneath the haematoma he detected the grinding of broken skull fragments with his fingertips. The seizure continued unabated.

'Tell me what's happening.' Callie sounded sick.

'It's an extra-dural bleed.'

'In English.'

Grimes rubbed his hands over his face. 'I've given him a depressed skull fracture, punched in a piece of bone like hitting a hard-boiled egg. The bone fragments have

211

ruptured an artery on the inside of his skull and he's bleeding. The pressure on his brain from the bone and the haemorrhage are causing the convulsions.'

'Can you do anything?'

Grimes took his jacket off. It was wet through and stuck to his shirt so that he had to pull the sleeves inside-out. He tossed the jacket onto the bed.

'Leave the lamp on the table and bring me his knife.'

His hands were trembling and he wrung them together. The burns were still sore. Callie handed him the knife and he tested its edge with his thumb. It wasn't scalpel sharp but it would do. He asked Callie for a kitchen fork and she brought it from a drawer in the chest behind them.

'Thanks,' said Grimes. 'I know you don't have to do this.'

'I must be out of my fucking mind,' said Callie.

Grimes nodded. 'I need you to hold his head still.'

He took Luther's head and turned it so that its right side was flat against the table.

'Callie?' said Grimes.

Her face was rigid with anxiety. She held her hands in front of her at waist height and flapped them in the air.

'I can't,' she said.

'Sure you can.'

He took her hands and placed them, first gently then with firm pressure, on Luther's head, one against his jaw and the other against the back of his skull. Callie closed her eyes and took a deep breath through her mouth.

'Keep him absolutely still.'

Grimes took the knife by the blade, his forefinger pressing against the upper edge. He stretched the skin around the lump taut between his left finger and thumb and made a large C-shaped incision through the scalp. The main edge of the incision curved past the eye and the lump sat in the jaws of the C. Blood rushed over his fingers and into Luther's hair as he turned the flap of skin backwards, exposing the shattered bone. Easy.

The chair leg had been driven in at the skull's weakest

point, directly over the H-shaped suture lines where different parts of the cranium knitted together. A large irregular fragment an inch in diameter and three smaller splinters had been smashed in. Blood oozed rapidly through the cracks and mixed with that leaking from the cut edges of the scalp.

Grimes straightened and rolled his shoulders to loosen them. His hands were no longer shaking. He hadn't lost his touch. The rumour circulated his mind that he wasn't one hundred per cent scumbag after all. It was hard to believe but the rumour helped. He wiped his brow on his shirt sleeve and bent back over the wound.

He changed his grip on the knife so that he was holding the blade like a pencil and used the point to gently prise up the tip of one of the small splinters. The chain of the broken handcuffs dangled in his way. He took the protruding splinter between thumb and fingernails and, edging the knife underneath it, gradually worked the splinter loose and pulled it out. Blood flowed freely from the hole left in the skull. With more space in which to work, the second and third splinters came away more readily than the first.

Callie said, 'He's stopped shaking.'

She had the hushed, awe-struck manner that dealing with a medical emergency often induces in the uninitiated. Grimes spoke without looking at her.

'The pressure's been released.'

He picked up the fork.

'I just need to lift out this last big fragment.'

In places the circumference of the big fragment was jammed into the surrounding bone. His tools were cumbersome, and trying to free the bone without shoving an inch of metal into Luther's cerebral cortex was painstaking work. Twice Grimes stopped to wipe his face and shake cramp from his hands. His mouth was terribly dry and his back ached. His concentration was poor. Pictures of Jefferson and of Artie Mann's butchered face kept flickering through his mind and at those moments he stopped and closed his eyes until they disappeared. Callie said nothing to disturb him. Finally he got the tines of the fork and the tip of the knife under opposing edges of the fragment and lifted upwards. Nothing moved. His hands quivered with the strain. Jesus. The bone was impacted. The fork slipped loose. Grimes resisted the urge to scream and bang his fists on Luther's head. He relaxed for a moment and tried again. Suddenly the fragment sprang loose and flipped up into the air. It hit Grimes on the chest and fell back onto the table.

'It's done.'

Grimes put the knife and fork down.

'If you want to take a look at your lover's brains here's your chance.'

Grimes took a look himself. The outer covering of the brain, the dura, was intact. Grimes wondered what was going on in there. He watched Callie brush a strand of hair from Luther's face. Her hand lingered on his cheek. It was a bad moment. Grimes' balls contracted and he turned away from the mixture of emotions on her face. Cocksuckers. The relative calm that concentrating on the work had brought him evaporated and for an instant he wanted to kill them both. Bury them one on top of the other with Luther's flaccid cock jammed in her mouth. With a massive effort he turned back towards her.

'Help me take his clothes off,' he said.

'What for?' she said.

Grimes pushed his chin at her across the table.

'Because his body's full of holes, honey. Your holes. I need to find out where they are.'

'Don't shout at me, okay? This is hard enough.'

Together they stripped off Luther's combat jacket and T-shirt. His body had a sallow, deflated look and the tattoo on his shoulder stood out sharply against the bloodless skin. There was an exit wound high in his belly: just below his right rib cage a couple of inches from the sternum. There was a second exit wound in his right flank. Neither wound was bleeding anymore.

Grimes said, 'Fucking hell,' and shook his head. 'Help me turn him.'

Blood oozed from the holes as they rolled him onto his right side. Luther groaned and moved his head.

'He's coming round,' said Callie.

She sounded frightened.

Grimes examined the hole in the left side of Luther's back then leaned over to look at the first exit wound again, trying to gauge the path the bullet had taken. Lung, certainly; maybe a nick in the pericardium; stomach, probably; liver – and this was the downer – almost definitely. A ruptured left lobe of liver meant heavy internal bleeding and bad news even in a fully-equipped operating room. There was a second through and-through wound to the muscles of Luther's right flank and a third in his right thigh below the buttock crease, but these hardly mattered.

'Shit and bloody balls,' said Grimes.

'It's bad then,' said Callie.

Grimes turned and stared at her silently, trying not to think. After a second tears began to prickle his eyes. He turned away from her, shading his eyes with his hand. Jesus. There was nothing more he could do. Roughly he dragged Luther onto his back again, banging his shoulder into the table top.

Luther groaned and said, 'Callie.'

His voice was slurred and his eyes were closed.

'Jesus, Grimes, take it easy.'

Grimes rounded on her. His voice was a choke, barely audible.

'Mind your own fucking business, lady.'

'You'll hurt him.'

Grimes raised his arm six inches and chopped Luther across the belly with the edge of his hand. Luther groaned and pulled his legs up. The legs flopped back down.

'Grimes!'

'Fuck you both.'

'Baby, please.'

215

Luther mumbled and opened his eyes, twisting his head from side to side. It was clear to Grimes that he was unaware of where he was or who they were. But then Luther had always been the lucky one. Callie pushed Grimes' arm out of the way and bent over Luther's face, her hands stroking his shoulders.

She said, 'I'm here, sugar.'

What the fuck was this?

'Why don't you put your hand on his dick?' said Grimes.

Callie slapped him across the face. Grimes grabbed her hair and pulled her across the table, cocking his fist. His head was bursting. His arm shook. He wanted to fuck the whole fucking world until its bloody shit-filled guts ran down its legs. He bellowed formlessly into her face and she cringed away, raising her hands in front of her.

'Goddamn all you bastards,' said Grimes.

He let go of her and held onto the edge of the table. His head hung down and he spoke into his chest.

'I hate.'

He shook his head and tears fell from his eyes.

'It burns.'

'I know,' said Callie.

Her voice was quiet now, aching.

'He told me why. I'm sorry.'

Luther's eyes were closed again and he was mumbling words they couldn't understand. Grimes picked up the knife.

'Don't,' said Callie.

'I don't want him to die,' said Grimes.

Once again he climbed down and pulled the ragged edges of his senses together, but he didn't know how much longer he could keep it up. He took Luther's wrist and felt his pulse. One hundred and thirty and thready.

'He's bleeding into the lung and belly and I think he's ruptured his liver. If I open him up there's a minimal chance I can pack the liver and staunch the bleeding until I get him to hospital.'

As he spoke he considered what he was suggesting and

216

his shoulders sagged. Another pipe dream; the latest of many. He ran a hand over Luther's abdomen. In the gaslight the skin was the colour of an old porcelain piss pot. Grimes put the knife down. With his left hand he checked Luther's neck for the carotid pulse. With his right he pinched the bridge of his own nose and rubbed his eyelids. Crusts of blood crumbled from his fingers and stuck to his face. His mind drifted across a great space where he thought and felt nothing. It seemed to take a long time to reach the other side. When he did he realized that the flesh beneath his fingertips was cold and still.

Grimes took his hand from his face and looked at Luther.

'He's dead,' said Grimes. 'And maybe better off that way.'

'You said you might be able to save him.'

Grimes turned away from her and walked over to the bed. 'Looks like I was wrong about that too.'

He sat down on the mattress.

'After a while you get used to it.'

He began to pick clots of blood from under his nails. He could feel the small muscles round his lips and eyes quivering and didn't dare look at her in case he lost control again. He wanted her to come over and hold him. He wanted it very badly. But there was no way he could ask.

He watched Callie pull a pair of men's jeans on over her bandaged leg and roll up the bottoms. She walked towards and then past him and a moment later he heard her pouring water from a jug into the sink and washing her hands. Suddenly Grimes felt empty.

He looked up from his hands and saw a photo hanging on the wall above the bedstead. It was in colour and showed three men in the uniform of the 101st Airborne Division with Ranger patches on their shoulders. Luther, his hair cropped down to the wood, stood on the left of the group. Their faces were serious: all bone and tanned, tight-looking skin. Their chests and shoulders struck proud poses against a blue sky. There was a handwritten message on the picture that Grimes couldn't read. He took the photo down. The writing said:

'The courageous violent slashing themselves with knives. 1967.'

It was signed: 'Still waiting for a visit. Regards, Al Beckett, Montana 1979.'

Behind him Grimes heard Callie say, 'I'm leaving.'

CHAPTER TWENTY-FIVE

He was lost.

The water and the night formed a labyrinth of pain. Jefferson knew. He'd left his own bloody footprints over every aching inch of it. Dark creatures walked the labyrinth with him: fear and madness; failure and death. The night and the water and the creatures had done everything they could to bring him to his knees and break him. Now, as he lay bleeding and shivering in a slough of stinking mud outside the cabin, he clenched his fists until they hurt and scooped down into the darkest bilges of his spirit. He was the prodigy. He was the will. He couldn't be killed. He could walk the burning lava where strong men screamed and died. The scumbags and grovellers had failed. All of them.

He was here and his hand was on their balls. His body shook with pain as membranes and fibres popped inside him. But Jesus Christ, how come it had cost him so much?

When Jefferson started his car at the foot of the farmhouse driveway the rain was torrential and turned the windshield into a plate of pebbled glass an inch thick. He switched on the wipers. Every two seconds a hole appeared through the glass for an instant before vanishing again. He put his headlights on and stomped on the gas pedal. Driving on the winding blacktop with twenty per cent vision would have had its dangers in a horse-drawn cart. At the speed Jefferson drove it was suicidal. Bubbles of adrenalin sparkled through his blood and he wondered if it would make the bleeding of his wounds better or worse. He used the excitement to sharpen his awareness. He had to make up time. This was moonshine country and there were turn-offs and trails all the way along this road that would never make it onto any map. Grimes and his brother might take any one of them.

Miles passed in the tunnel of rain before suddenly there they were: a pair of red tail lights shining through the piss pouring down his windshield. Jefferson flicked his own lights off and slowed down as quickly as he could without losing control of the car. For a moment he thought himself mistaken as he stared over the steering wheel into the swirling filth, then he saw the twin red glow again, and beyond the red the edges of a pair of headlight beams. Outlined between the red and the white light was the bulk of the Camaro. There was a good chance they hadn't seen him in this shit. If they had, well, fuck it, he was ready to shoot it out; even with the Tough Bullet.

The driving took all his concentration and he was glad the Camaro didn't go above thirty. Eight miles down the road the Camaro's brake lights came on and took a sharp turn to the right and Jefferson was left peering at the blur on his windshield trying to find the cut off. He slowed down and switched his lights back on. Still he was blind. Suddenly he was right on top of it: less a road than a muddy track just wide enough for a single vehicle. He braked and turned the wheel then braced himself as he felt the car slide out of control. On a decent road he would have made the corner easily enough but the rain had given the surface of the track the consistency of cottage cheese. The dirt crumbled beneath his tyres and the car slid away from him. Its front end ploughed sideways and forwards into jungle foliage at the side of the track. The back end swung around in an arc, the tyres skating over the water on the blacktop until the right rear wheel left the road and fell into the ditch.

He grunted as the steering wheel jammed into his left rib cage. Pain lanced through his innards as if a buckle had burst open deep inside his body. The engine cut out.

He left the front and rear lights on and took the keys from the ignition. Gathering himself he shoved the door open and climbed out into the mud. The Eldorado wasn't damaged – that he could see – but a look at the rear wheels told him he would never drive it out of the ditch. He was confident that on a good day he could have lifted the rear of the car back onto the road by himself. But this wasn't a good day.

He ran his hand over his face. His fingers found a strand of wet gauze hanging from his nostril and he pushed it back in with his pinky. He stared down the track, thinking. In this part of the state a dirt road like this could be two miles long or twenty. But more likely two, he told himself.

He opened the trunk of the car and dug out a flashlight. There was an automatic shotgun in the trunk but he couldn't see the use of hauling it. He opened the First Aid kit. Tucked inside amongst the pressure packs and tape were four small plastic sachets of pure heroin. A man never knew when he might need to discover some evidence. As a rule Jefferson didn't use pharmaceuticals, at least not on himself, but at that moment he needed all the help he could get. Sheltering his head as best he could under the lid of the trunk he tore one of the bags open and poured the heroin into his mouth, spilling a good deal down his chin. He held the powder under his tongue until his mouth was so full of saliva that he had to swallow. He had no idea of the effective dose he had taken. The heroin he absorbed through the membranes of his mouth would get straight into the blood. He guessed that most of what he swallowed would be digested before it did much good. He put the other sachets into his pocket and found the two pill bottles he'd taken from Grimes' bathroom. What the hell. He shook out six tablets of dexedrine and two of dihydrocodeine into his palm and threw them down his throat in one handful. Beat that, Presley. He closed the trunk and leaned back into the car to turn off the lights, then started walking along the dirt track.

It felt like the road to Calvary. The idea amused him. Clarence Christ. Jesus Jefferson. He'd have to ask his wife what she thought of that.

The flashlight was a consolation. Without it he would have wasted energy and patience that he could not afford by slipping down a hole here and blundering into a bush there. The tyre tracks of Grimes' car crumbled and melted as he walked and after a hundred yards he could no longer make them out at all. The rain glittered in the beam of light and hissed in his ears. Lightning still came and went but the thunder was moving away from him and the heart of the storm was elsewhere. Even so the wind was strong. Jefferson was surprised at the physical toll exacted by the thousands of raindrops splatting into his body. He could feel himself weakening under the barrage on his head and shoulders. Or was it the junk? Or the mud dragging at his feet and the wind blowing from his left, throwing that little bit of extra weight onto his injured right knee? And he was still bleeding. When he dipped the palm of his hand into the front of his shirt and looked at it in the flashlight it was fresh blood that ran away in the rain. With his best efforts he couldn't manage more than one pace per second. Two miles an hour and bleeding. For the first time he realized that he could die out here after all.

He should have gone back to the car and sat still out of the rain: given the blood a chance to congeal and cranked up the radio. Or waited for Grimes or Luther or both to come back down the track and taken them out with the shotgun. He turned and shone the flashlight back the way he'd come. The beam made a sparkling tunnel which faded into the blackness. The footprints leading towards him were full of water. Fuck it. Suddenly he had no idea of how far he'd come or how long it had been since he'd left the car. All his concentration had been focused on placing one foot down in front of the other. Double fuck it. He turned round again and kept going.

He wished he knew some marching songs but he didn't.

Should've joined the infantry. He became aware of an improvement in the pain. The junk was working. He was feeling faster too. He'd walk all night long if he had to. He was able to quicken his pace. The dexedrine had hit the spot just in time: to quit now would have been insane. There was still everything to play for. No pain, no gain. He even remembered a marching song, or the tune anyway. Colonel Bogey. Eat Jap. Now that would have been a mission to remember. A single fucking bomb. He started whistling as he walked. From time to time he broke off his whistling to laugh.

If only his mother could see him now.

The only fond memories he had of her recalled his Sunday visit to the nursing home where she'd spent the last year of her life. A stroke had nailed her speech centre, amongst other things, and a formless noise ending in a drool was all the vocalization she could manage, but her doctors assured him that she could understand well enough and he could tell from her eyes and the half of her face that still moved that they were right. He spent many hours talking to her on the balcony of her room overlooking a flower garden. Freed from the imbecile interjections and inane thoughts by means of which she'd previously denied him any chance of communicating with her, Jefferson was able to talk honestly for the first time in his life. She sat drooling and crying while he described his inner life: his beliefs and insights; Vietnam; the contempt in which he held her and his two sisters and the reasons why; the vapidity and worthlessness of her own life; and the theory and practice of his work: the killing, the extortion, the lies. All the while her hand had fluttered up and down in her lap. When he'd exhausted all he had to say he'd kissed her on the cheek, turned her wheelchair to face the garden and walked out of her room. He never went back. She'd died nine months later and his sisters had wrapped her in a copper coffin and buried it in the marble monstrosity that contained his father.

As soon as he thought of his father the conditioned

reflex of four decades switched his mind onto something else. Jefferson's own will and testament ensured that he would never rest amongst the copper caskets. Medical students would cut his heart out and dissect the attachments of his muscles to his bones, marvel at the number and variety of his scars and examine the contents of his eyeballs and the inner surface of his bladder. And then they'd open the top of his skull and lift out his brain and maybe one of them would stop a while to ask himself what had gone on there when it had been alive. Finally his fragments would be collected together and burnt and the ashes presented to his wife in a brass urn engraved with the words:

There is no justice. There's just us.

He laughed to himself again then dropped the flashlight into the mud and doubled over grabbing his belly as another buckle burst inside. He waited, regulating his breathing as best he could until the pain wore off. Then he picked up the flashlight and let the rain wash it clean and continued up the road. He had trouble keeping the flashlight pointed in front of him. It felt like an eighty-pound dumb-bell at the end of a set of concentration curls. He would transfer it to the other hand and after a few minutes that arm would feel the same way and the light would droop down until it rested against his leg, spilling its beam down the leg of his pants.

By the time the lights at the cabin appeared his mind and body had started to part company. The dexedrine revitalizer and his compulsion to find Grimes had driven his body to perform above and beyond the call of duty. Now that his body had brought him here its job was done. He could finish the rest himself. His mind was a turbine; his body wanted to lie down in the rain and die.

Not yet. There it was, for Christ's sake, beyond the bushes a few yards away: a squat brick-shape set at an oblique angle to the track. He wanted to run; at best he could stagger. Pale light came from two windows in the long side of the cabin. The light was strongest from the far window. More light flooded the building from the headlamps of a car parked outside. He shifted his body forward to take a step and his right leg turned into a tube of jelly underneath him. He collapsed to the ground in a spiral motion and landed on his face.

All in all it was fucking humiliating.

Just beyond his vision now, behind the trees, were three cars: the Camaro with its lights on, a Dodge stationwagon and a Jap hatchback. All three cocksuckers were in there: waiting to be scooped in and squashed. And he couldn't even stand up. He seethed with frustration. He grovelled in filth. He raised his head and dug his palms into the earth and tried to push himself off the ground. Sheets of delicate tissue ruptured within. He ground his jaws together and strained harder. The sound of the ocean swelled in his ears. His vision failed. His arms gave way and he slopped back into the mud. His head was full of molten metal. He could feel the suture lines between his skull bones cracking apart under the pressure. Blistering fluid leaked onto his scalp. He wanted to tear his hair out, ram his fingers into his eyes, chop his hands off.

He was lost.

Calm yourself, boy. The voice spoke to him from firmer depths. He was weak. He'd lost more blood than he'd thought. His body needed rest, a chance to recover. Ten minutes. Do it. Do it now.

He did it. He lay in the mud and stared into the dark. A place where all the lights were dim. The clouds had shut out the stars. In the city, even in the darkest alley, there was always a glow from the street lights. The darkness reminded him of the hole. Ten minutes. The terminal fatigue melted from his limbs. He told his arm to move and it obeyed. He hoisted his right haunch from the hollow his weight had created and pulled Artie's .45 from the holster. It was covered in shit but the army hadn't used it for seventy years out of nostalgia. The Colt would keep shooting through mud and grit. And when a man got hit with a .45 there wasn't much else he could do but die. He held it up to the rain, turning it around until it felt clean. A stranger's gun but it still felt sweet. Pointability. He thumbed off the safety. He'd point the fucker all the way up Luther Grimes' ass.

Getting to his feet wasn't as easy as drawing the pistol but he took his time and made it. His wet clothes cleaved to the folds of fat around his middle. The flashlight lay on the ground but he hadn't the heart to bend down to pick it up. Anyhow, he didn't need it anymore. From here on in he knew his way.

He shambled twenty paces closer to the cabin and leaned against a tree. The rain was a drizzle now and the wind a breeze. From within the cabin came roars of psychic pain and the sound of breaking furniture. A large iron gas cylinder crashed through the cabin window and rolled towards him through the mud. Jefferson started for the cabin door.

At the best of times he wasn't a man to scuttle around from one piece of cover to the next, posing fancifully with a pistol grasped in two hands. In the shape he was in it wasn't an option. He watched the door and windows and stumped forwards on legs he couldn't feel, slowly raising and lowering one foot and then the other. When he reached the cabin he leaned against the wall for a while, resting. The door was an inch ajar. Softly, he pushed it open with the back of his gun hand and peered inside.

At the far end of the room Grimes was leaning over an empty table, naked to the waist, talking to himself. Callilou Carter was standing by the wall, watching him. A clear shot.

The bitch was dead.

CHAPTER TWENTY-SIX

Callie picked up the Samsonite suitcase filled with money and turned back to look at Grimes. He sat on the bed without moving: just sitting, staring at a photograph in his hands. She wanted to leave it all behind, to walk out of the door and drive to hell and be gone. Instead she put the suitcase down on the floor and walked over to the bed. Why was it so damned hard to say 'No'? They'd always found it easy enough to say it to her. She sat down beside him and put a hand on his forearm. Grimes didn't move.

'Grimes?' She squeezed him.

Grimes didn't answer.

'You okay?'

She knew it was a stupid thing to say but she didn't know how to comfort him. God knew why she wanted to but she did. Or felt that she ought to.

'Listen,' she said. 'You can't stay here. Come away with me.'

Grimes' eyes flickered up to the right then looked straight at her, staring.

'Come away to what?'

'Christ, I don't know. Maybe this isn't a good time to talk about it.'

Grimes took hold of her wrist. She tried to pull away but he was too strong.

'Let me go.'

'I love you,' said Grimes, quietly.

'No.'

Callie pulled again, harder, and this time he let go.

'I told you before,' she said, 'I'm not going to be a part of anybody's fantasies but my own. Don't be like all the other limp dicks I ever met. Don't be like Luther. I never lied to you. We fucked; it was pretty good; it helped me feel better. End of story. I didn't ask you to get involved in all this. "It's too dangerous for a woman to do it alone." Sure. When things got dangerous – and I mean fucking terrifying – you weren't there for me. Shit. If you'd seen your psycho brother doing his one-man-army act you'd have been goddamn glad you weren't there.'

Jesus this wasn't doing anyone any good. Grimes put his face in his hands. Whatever she owed him it wasn't love. If that was what he expected he was as crazy as he looked. But she did owe him something. She shook her head and tried again.

'I'm sorry,' she said. 'You helped me. When I was scared and sick and crazy you made me feel safe. Not many people could have done that. Now let me help you. Christ knows you look like you could use it. But if you plug me into some kind of crazy movie you've got running inside your head you can forget it. You're hurting more than enough as it is. And so am I.'

Grimes said, into his hands, 'I love you.' Then, 'I don't love you.'

Callie closed her eyes. The world was a gigantic brothel full of clients who didn't want to pay their bills. I love you. She heard her father saying the same thing to her mother an hour after he'd cut his knuckles open on her teeth. And Cleveland Carter saying it to the fallen woman he'd saved for Jesus. And Luther: to whom the word meant, 'Me.' Nothing else, just 'Me.'

She said, 'You don't know what the word means.'

Grimes didn't answer and Callie blew her breath out.

'Maybe I don't either.'

She felt sad and hurt. And angry. She stood up and walked over to the chair Grimes had used to brain Luther

228

and picked up the Browning automatic. She pushed the pistol into her belt.

'I've got to go.'

Grimes turned towards her and for the first time she felt scared of him. His face was a mask, as brittle-hard as bone china. Behind the mask his eyes were without pity.

'Don't, Grimes,' she said. 'No one can hate himself as much as you do and stay alive.'

'You'd better go,' said Grimes and stood up.

'Limp dick,' he said quietly to himself and nodded.

He took the neck of the bloody shirt he was wearing in both hands and with a series of vicious jerks tore it apart as if he wished it were his own flesh. He stripped the rags from his arms and threw them on the floor. Then Callie watched him take the room apart.

He stood before the dresser and tilted it towards him, looking at his reflection in the mirror. She flinched as he rammed his head into the mirror and shattered it. Splinters of glass pocked his forehead with blood. The dresser crashed forward as he stepped sideways and turned and pitched it into the floor behind him. He pulled the drawers out of the chest and dashed them apart against the chest's edges, scattering their contents about his feet. Squatting down he picked the chest up, raised it above his head and caved it through the back of the dresser. The bed he turned over, the wooden crates he smashed apart with his feet. As he pounded the crates to pieces he started to bellow wordlessly, repeatedly, as if he were making love to his rage. Callie backed up against the wall by the window and waited.

Grimes walked past without looking at her and tore the aluminium sink away from the wall. Veins stood out from his arms and shoulders as he threw it the length of the room to land amongst the broken furniture. He ripped away the rubber hose connecting the stove to the gas cylinder, hoisted the cylinder into the air and heaved it through the window beside Callie's head. She blinked and shied away as broken glass tumbled past her face. When

Grimes started back down the room she put her hand on the pistol and cocked the hammer but he seemed unaware of her. He stopped by the table where Luther's body lay and bent over the corpse's head. With his left hand he grabbed Luther's hair and lifted the dead face up towards his own.

With his right hand Grimes punched Luther in the throat and Callie's stomach rolled over with the sound.

'You turned my life into a world of shit.'

Grimes punched Luther again, this time in the face, and at the same time shouted through gritted teeth, 'Didn't you?'

He took a ragged breath. Saliva dangled from his chin.

'You knew how much she meant to me.'

His fist struck again.

'Didn't you?'

Luther's head slipped from his grip and banged down onto the table. Grimes grabbed another handful of hair.

'You fucked her. You took her away. You never thought about me.'

And again the fist.

'Did you?'

Tenderly, he cradled Luther's head in the palm of his hand.

'I loved you both. So fucking much. You knew it.'

Grimes smiled and his voice turned gentle and Callie felt goose pimples break out on her skin.

'You knew it. But you couldn't let it be.'

And again he rammed his fist into the dead man's face.

'Could you?'

With the last punch Luther's body slid from the table and fell to the floor in a tangle of limbs and blood. Callie struggled with a surge of nausea. Grimes bent forward and rested his forehead against the bloodstained oak. He placed the palms of both hands on the table on either side of his head and dug his fingertips into the wood. Callie heard his nails breaking.

'You hurt me.'

The muscles between his shoulder blades bunched up and squirmed, shiny with sweat in the light of the lamp.

'You all hurt me.'

After a moment's silence Grimes began sobbing softly.

It was more than she could handle. She'd already tried harder than he had any right to expect. She pushed herself away from the wall. She'd given it her best shot and there was nothing she could do to make him feel better. Nothing. Anyhow, he was supposed to be the expert on this stuff, not her. She turned her back on him to get her case and found a monstrous figure covered in blood and filth grinning at her from the doorway.

Clarence Jefferson showed her the muzzle of his pistol and spoke over her shoulder.

'Say goodnight to the lady, Grimes.'

CHAPTER TWENTY-SEVEN

Grimes straightened up slowly from the table. His body was drained and his mind was empty. The rage and pain were finally exhausted. He wasn't worried anymore. With neither dread nor resignation he stared across a twilight world of smoky yellow light and shifting shadows at the grotesque police captain propped against the door jamb.

Jefferson's face was a collection of fleshy lumps. Some of the lumps were soft and pink. Others were hard-looking and shone dark blue. Strips of damp brown gauze hung from his nostrils, and his hair glistened in the light. The creases between the folds of fat around his neck were black with dirt and as he moved his head drops of muddy water squeezed out of the creases and ran down his chest. His shirt was full of holes and caked with blood and filth. Here and there, between the holes, a seagull flew across a patch of blue sky. Where his body showed through the shirt it was a red mass of wounds. This time Jefferson didn't need to hold up a mirror. Grimes felt a terrible sorrow for them both.

'Say goodnight to the lady, Grimes.'

Jefferson's voice was wheezy.

'I want you to let her go,' said Grimes.

He couldn't make out Jefferson's eyes but the Captain seemed dreamy, not altogether there.

Jefferson looked from Grimes to Callie and back.

'Why?' he said. 'She sold you out.'

'No,' said Grimes. 'I sold myself out, long time before I ever met her. You too.'

After a moment Jefferson jabbed his .45 at Callie's belly.

'The gun, honey. Take it from your belt, slowly, and toss it through the window behind you.'

Callie's face was pale and her body was tight. When she'd convinced herself that she couldn't use the automatic and win she pulled it from her belt and pitched it through the broken window. Jefferson nodded his approval and they all waited for what seemed like a long time. Then Jefferson jerked his head over his shoulder at the door.

Callie looked at Grimes uncertainly, wiping the palms of her hands against her jeans. They had nothing to lose. Grimes nodded to her and Callie started to walk unsteadily. Halfway to the door she couldn't help glancing sideways at the Samsonite suitcase on the floor by the chair. Jefferson caught the glance and stopped her with a gesture from his gun.

'All this excitement the consolation prize slipped clear out of my mind.'

He pointed at the case.

'Open it, bitch.'

Callie raised her hands, palms open.

'I can't. The key is in Luther's pocket.'

Jefferson stared at her. He craned his head to see the body crumpled on the floor behind Grimes and the table.

'So you got that bastard after all,' he said to Grimes. 'Congratulations. Now find that key for me. Any tricks, she dies first.'

Grimes squatted down beside Luther's body, trying not to look at his face. The front pockets of Luther's pants were empty. Gently, he rolled the body over to get at the back pockets. Lying on the floor underneath Luther's thigh was the combat knife. As he felt in the pockets Grimes glanced over at Jefferson. The table blocked most of the cop's view. Without hurrying he picked up the knife in his right hand. With his left he found the key to the case and held it up above the table.

'Found it,' he said.

As he spoke he slid the knife into the back of his pants and stood up.

Jefferson said, 'Throw it to the woman, gently now.'

Callie turned to face him and Grimes tossed the key. She caught it in both hands. Without any fumbling she bent over the case, unlocked it, set it flat on the floor and opened the lid.

'Stand back,' said Jefferson.

Callie moved back to the wall. Grimes stepped from behind the table.

'You too,' said Jefferson.

Grimes stopped moving. He felt slightly sick and his heart was racing. The length of the knife was heavy and clammy against the moist skin of his buttock and back. He had to control the weapon in Jefferson's hand – the weapon before the man. The distinction mattered. Even if he was dying the cop would take them down if he was still armed.

Jefferson pushed himself away from the door and swayed. When he got his balance he shuffled across the room. From the shelf over the sink he took the coal-oil lamp in his left hand and held it over the open case. The stacked hundred-dollar bills reflected a flickering grey-green light. Jefferson bent forward painfully and looked at the money.

'Some of this could be yours, Grimes, if you want it.'

Grimes said, 'I don't.'

Jefferson straightened up with a grunt.

'Goddamn it, Doc, you make it too hard. Every time I offer you my hand you take a loose shit in it. My patience is all wore out.'

'The good ole Louisiana boy talk won't help you anymore,' said Grimes. 'All that talk about being a friend and a partner. I thought it was part of the performance but you meant it. You're alone. Solitary confinement for life.'

'That's enough,' said Jefferson.

'You want me to come into the cell with you and you

234

thought I just might do it because you saw me pacing up and down inside a prison of my own.'

Grimes needed to regain a fragment of Jefferson's trust. He took a step forward and held out his left hand, open, just in front of his stomach.

'You made the prison real. You made me bang my stupid head against its walls. The problem is that it's easier in there than it is out here. Out here there's no one else left to blame. Just me.'

He took another step forward and in the light of the coal-oil flame he could see Jefferson's eyes. The pupils were pin-pricks. Morphia. That explained the slurred, dreamy quality. It would make him more susceptible to suggestion. Maybe this time he would let Grimes in.

Grimes said, as if from nowhere, 'Who hurt you?'

The tension in Jefferson's body became extreme. His face trembled and the glass chimney of the lamp he was holding rattled as his arm shook.

'I can't go back,' he said. 'Things gonna be simple again.'

His voice cracked at its edges.

'The bitch dies. You die. I take my money and go.'

'Go where?' said Grimes, quietly.

Jefferson looked at him and didn't answer.

'They say,' began Grimes, tentatively, 'that the only ones who ever really hurt you are your own family. Other people only hurt you when they push old, old buttons that are already there, waiting to be pushed.'

Jefferson took a deep breath and blew it out. He glanced at Callie, who was still pressed against the wall, and then looked back at Grimes.

'I know that,' he said. 'How do you think I was able to break you?'

'I know you know it,' said Grimes.

He presented the suggestion bluntly and hoped.

'Maybe your Ma . . .'

Jefferson's face twisted in a spasm of contempt.

'That old bitch was too weak to hurt me. I wouldn't give her the credit. She never forgave me and I was glad.'

His legs quivered.

'Jesus,' he said. 'I'm tired.'

He stepped past the money and sat down slowly on the straight-backed chair. He rested the lamp on his knee and stared at the flame.

'What was there to forgive?' asked Grimes.

Jefferson was just about in range now – a half step, drawing the blade, blocking the gun hand – but Grimes couldn't do it. He knew that this story was being told for the first time, like his own, and somehow – training or instinct or both – he couldn't bring himself to interrupt.

'I must have been about seven, eight years old when it started,' said Jefferson. 'I was big for my age. Tall . . . Fat even then. The second Sunday of every month my mother took the girls over to visit her sister for the day and my father . . .'

Jefferson stopped and, without looking at her with his eyes, said to Callie, 'You can go. Get out.'

Callie looked at Grimes uncertainly and didn't move.

'Out!' said Jefferson.

Grimes felt a tug of fear as he felt the moment slipping away. He jerked his head at the door and Callie, stepping slowly amongst the wrecked furniture as if she didn't dare make a noise, left the cabin.

'I couldn't tell this with a woman here,' said Jefferson.

He looked at Grimes uncertainly, as if for reassurance.

'It's difficult,' said Grimes. 'I know.'

Jefferson looked at the lamp again and his eyes filmed over and shone.

'My father would run me around the garden playing football, softball, that kind of thing. One day, after the game, he got into the bath-tub with me. We just splashed around, I guess. All I remember is thinking how big his cock was compared to mine. It became a regular thing. In a way it was fun.'

Jefferson stopped and his fingers quivered against the

glass base of the lamp as if he would shatter it. He swallowed hard and Grimes felt him using his rage to squash down the tumour of anguish in his throat.

'I don't know why I knew it wasn't right when he started jerking off. I guess he sure as hell knew it wasn't right and maybe that's what I picked up on. He told me if I ever told anyone about it I'd be taken away and put in a home . . .'

He paused to grab his breath and the words were hard to catch now, ground out through gritted teeth. Tears rolled down the gutters in his swollen face.

'I didn't tell anyone. I wanted to please him . . . I wanted to be a good boy . . . but when he soaped his cock and started to fuck me in the ass it hurt and I screamed and asked him "Don't, Daddy!" But he did it anyway and it hurt and he told me never to tell anyone and I never did . . . I never did. Even when he fucked me again . . . and again . . .'

His voice broke into sobs and for a moment the three-hundred-pound shithammer was just an aching fat boy crying alone in the dark and biting his pillow.

He was at Grimes' mercy.

Part of Grimes told him to seize the chance and cut the bastard's head off. Do it. But he wasn't about to kill an eight-year-old child. He didn't even want to kill the shithammer. Not anymore.

Grimes let him be and waited while Jefferson collected himself together. Jefferson's voice took on a harder edge and he blinked the tears away.

'I knew it would work because it had happened by accident to one of the kids at school and they'd warned us all about it. Next time my mother went away I told Dad I wanted to listen to the ball game while we played in the tub and he said okay.'

Jefferson's lips curled.

'So I fixed up the portable wireless, and plugged it in, and when Dad got into the tub I dropped the wireless into the water with him and stood crying while I watched him die.'

He nodded, his eyes distant.

'There wasn't much fuss. Cardiac arrest. Too much exercise. Middle age. That kind of shit. No one had any reason to suspect me. But my mother knew.'

He half-smiled, a mixture of satisfaction and disgust.

'She found the wireless where I'd hid it and she knew. And she knew why I done it. I saw it in her sickly weak scumbag woman's eyes. But she never talked about it and she never asked me and you know something, Grimes? She never touched me – ever again – until the day I finally touched her, when I kissed her on the cheek the last time I set eyes on her.'

There was a long pause and a silence and then a noise and by the time Grimes spotted Callie crouching in the doorway Jefferson was up and moving and pumping shots from the .45. Suddenly the room was crammed with violent noise. A shower of blood and cloth and skin erupted from Jefferson's hip. He staggered sideways shouting 'Cocksuckers!' and Callie screamed and disappeared from view as a cloud of wood splinters exploded from the door frame.

Grimes pulled the knife and stepped forward. Jefferson turned to face him and Grimes held his hand out and shook his head.

'No!'

'All you bastards the goddamned same!'

It was too late. As Jefferson levelled the .45 to shoot him Grimes stepped to one side and swung the knife down with all the strength of both arms. The blade cut through Jefferson's wrist at the base of the thumb and severed his hand. Hand and gun fell together to the floor. Jefferson roared with pain and without missing a beat punched Grimes in the face with the bloody stump of his arm. The raw bones gashed Grimes' brow open and he fell to his knees, dazed and half-blinded. Jefferson raised the lamp in his left hand and Grimes lifted his arms to protect himself but Jefferson powered the lamp down behind him, dashing it to pieces against the edge of the open suitcase. Flames of blazing coal oil flared across the room and the money started to burn. Through the fog in his head Grimes felt Jefferson's good hand close about his throat.

The hand squeezed with tremendous strength and Grimes' ears filled with blood. He almost blacked out as Jefferson gave his head a great wrench and dragged him three feet across the floor. Heat. Skin. The smell of burning flesh. Blisters tightened and popped across his back. Jefferson was bending and twisting him backwards across the pyramid of flame rising from the suitcase. The pain brought him round enough to clench his fists against it and he realized he still held the knife in his right hand. With a great grunting jerk he dragged one leg from underneath him so that one foot was planted firmly on the ground. Through the blood running into his eyes he looked up at the face hovering above him and locked Jefferson's gaze.

'Don't,' said Grimes.

His voice was less than a croak but Jefferson heard him. Maybe the word made him think of the lonely fat boy screaming in the tub; maybe he realized that only mercy would set him free; or maybe he was just too tired and doped and wounded; but just for a second the relentless pressure on Grimes' throat eased, and in the gap that opened between one death and another Grimes lunged upward, using the last coiled strength of arm and leg to stand and thrust, driving the knife deep into Jefferson's belly and into the vital organs beyond.

The two men reeled backwards. Together they stumbled against some wreckage and fell to the floor, Grimes landing on top, still clinging onto the knife. For a few seconds he could hardly breathe and his vision flickered in black and red flashes as the blood flow returned to his head. When he could see again he raised himself up until he was sitting across Jefferson's waist. A great shudder rippled through the body beneath him and the hilt of the knife rose and fell as Jefferson panted in shallow gasps.

Jefferson stared at the planks in the cabin roof.

'RED . . . DUST . . . FIRE . . . TWILIGHT . . . BONES . . .' he whispered.

He shook his head as if telling himself he should have known better. After a moment he looked into Grimes' eyes.

'I played it wrong . . . right from the beginning, didn't I, Doc?'

His voice was faint, almost drowned out by the crackle of flames behind them. There was a tightness in Grimes' throat as he nodded.

'Sometimes it's hard not to,' he said.

'All these years . . .'

Jefferson broke off and coughed and brought up a scumtide of red mucus that slithered down the bulges in his neck.

'All these years . . . you're the only one I ever let close . . . the only one who ever . . . tempted me back . . . inside Bad City.'

He shook his head and blinked through ancient tears. He smiled brokenly.

'Look what it did to me.'

'I'm sorry,' said Grimes softly.

Jefferson grabbed Grimes' hand and squeezed it as his great body buckled hugely with pain. He hauled his head and shoulders from the floor until their faces almost touched. Grimes tensed his arm to take the weight.

'Tell me you don't hate me, Grimes.'

Jefferson's eyes were startlingly clear and Grimes realized that this was the only moment that really counted. There was nothing left inside him but the truth. He squeezed the hand back.

'I don't hate you,' he said.

Jefferson, looking up at him, knew that he meant it and nodded. His body shivered violently.

'Who'll have mercy on such as we, Grimes?'

Grimes couldn't find any words and for an instant Jefferson's face was crenellated with mystery and terror. Then his expression relaxed and his head fell back and a bloody froth foamed over his bottom lip.

'Baa. Yah. Bah,' he said.

And Clarence Seymour Jefferson was dead.

CHAPTER TWENTY-EIGHT

Grimes reached out and closed Jefferson's eyes. For a second his fingers lingered on the dead man's face, then he shook his head and stood up.

The room was filling with smoke, and fragments of charred money swirled about on the draught from the open door and the smashed window. The fire had spread to the broken furniture but it wasn't yet out of control. Grimes could have dragged the bodies outside the cabin but he couldn't see the point. Instead he kicked shut the lid of the suitcase, stifling the flames, and shoved the case along the floor with his foot, away from the fire. His suit jacket lay on the floor by the bed, and he picked it up and pulled it on. The sleeves dragged on the broken handcuffs at his wrists and he flinched as the movement aggravated the burns on his back, but the cloth was wet and cool and with the jacket on he felt better.

From the overturned mattress he grabbed a sheet and wrapped it around the hot case. Lying nearby were a bottle of Jack Daniels, half-full, and the photograph of Luther in the army. The glass covering the photo was cracked. Grimes took the whiskey and the photo in one hand and a fistful of the sheet in the other. Dragging the case like swag he made his way to the door and stepped outside.

The rain had stopped and Callie was standing behind the station-wagon with her pistol held in both hands at arm's length. There was blood on her cheek where splinters of wood had pierced the skin.

'Is he dead?' she shouted.

Grimes nodded.

'You sure?'

He nodded again and she lowered her gun and stepped around the car.

'What about you?' she said.

Her eyes flickered up and down his body.

'I guess I'm okay.' He took a step towards her.

'No, Grimes. It's better you don't come too close. There's too much here I don't understand. Don't take it personal but I don't really want to understand. I just want to be somewhere else.'

He didn't blame her. He felt no anger, just wonder at the scale of his own need, the nature of the emptiness inside him that he should ever have believed himself to love her.

He kept his face tight and said, 'You left this behind.'

He hoisted the smoking bundle into the air and swung it gently across the eight feet that separated them. The movement made his back sting. The case landed in a puddle of muddy water with a splash. Callie licked her lower lip and looked up from the case at her feet to Grimes.

'You saved the money.' She sounded surprised.

'You should be able to salvage most of it,' said Grimes. 'There was too much blood on it to leave it burning.'

The irony might have been nice, but Grimes wasn't much in the mood for irony. He saw that Callie wasn't listening. She was looking at the three cars parked outside the cabin – Camaro, hatchback, station-wagon – and thinking.

'If I was you I'd take the hatchback. No one will be looking for it.'

Callie said, 'Thanks.'

She walked over to the Japanese car and opened the back, then returned to the case and bent over to pick it up. She winced as the wound in her leg hurt her.

'Here,' said Grimes, stepping forward, 'let me.'

He picked up the bundled swag by the neck again and

243

carried it over to the car. He heaved it into the trunk, the sheet wet and filthy now, and watched a few last wisps of smoke escape on the wind. Callie shifted nervously and gestured towards the bundle.

'You want some of this?'

Grimes shook his head.

'You worked for it. You enjoy it.'

Callie still held the automatic in her left hand. She looked at it and stole a glance at Grimes and he saw the thought cross her mind.

'Why not?' he said.

He wondered if he had the speed left to stop her. Probably. It didn't seem that important.

'Superstition, maybe,' said Callie. 'The others knew the rules, they just didn't play a tight enough game. You were in a game of your own, you and Luther. I've got this feeling that if I killed you for the wrong reasons something bad would happen and I'd never get to enjoy my retirement. Enough's enough.'

'Yes,' said Grimes. 'Sometimes it is.'

Callie shifted around again, looking at his chest instead of his eyes, and said, 'Look I meant it earlier on when I said you could come along. No strings, yeah? Maybe we'd be good for each other.'

Grimes wondered what calculation she'd just made; the wound in her leg perhaps. Whatever her reason it wasn't important. Grimes didn't have the time. He shook his head.

'I don't think so.'

Callie shrugged defensively and closed the back of the car. Avoiding his eyes she climbed gingerly into the driver's seat and closed the door. Grimes walked over and she wound the window down.

'Good luck, Grimes.'

'Same to you, Callie. I'm glad you got what you wanted.'

Callie switched on the engine and paused with her hand on the gear shift.

244

'I'm sorry I'm not what you need.'

She was staring straight ahead through the windshield.

Grimes bent down to the window. It was funny but he didn't want her to leave feeling badly about herself. There was no reason why she should.

'Hey,' he said. 'We did all right. For a while.'

'I guess. Maybe some other time, then,' she said.

'Sure,' said Grimes.

Callie tilted her face towards him and there was a moment when, if either of them had made the move, they might have kissed each other. But neither of them did and the moment passed.

'Goodbye, Grimes.'

Maybe the moment only existed in his imagination anyway.

'Goodbye, Callie,' said Grimes.

And then she and her money were gone and he watched the car disappear into a silence that made his chest ache.

Grimes took a deep breath, held it and let the breath out. Then he opened the door to the station-wagon and climbed inside.

From the pocket of his jacket he took a fresh pack of Pall Malls, turned on the ignition and lit a cigarette with the dashboard lighter. His chest hurt when he inhaled and he took a long pull from the bottle of sour mash to kill the pain. As he drank and smoked he watched the fire, and the motion of his thoughts crumbled and subsided, collapsing slowly inwards like the walls of the burning cabin.

The photo lay in his lap and he picked it up and held it in front of him. The courageous violent slashing themselves with knives. Courage. He closed his eyes and a picture of a barefoot boy with a coloured bird tied to his finger came into his mind. Before he could place it the picture was gone and he found his head falling forward onto his chest. He shook himself awake.

He wanted to sleep for a hundred hours but he had too many miles to go. His father would be waiting for news and Grimes owed him at least that much. Hauling himself up in the seat he put the photograph down beside him and jammed the bottle of whiskey between his thighs. As he put the engine into drive and swung the car onto the dirt road, the whiskey sloshed around inside the bottle. The flames of the cabin reflected in his rearview mirror and then were gone, swallowed up by the jungle and the night.

It was midnight on the Mississippi Delta as Cicero Grimes stopped at the parish road to drink another shot and listen for the chimes he'd yet to hear.

Silence.

Not even thunder.

As he lowered the bottle from his lips he clenched his teeth against the bite of the alcohol and tried to fashion a tough grin through the aching deep inside him. He had the blues and he had them bad and he'd no direction home except the City.

He trod on the gas and the car started to move.

It seemed like it had been a long time, but maybe, if he tried hard, he'd be able to find his way back.

After all, Eugene Cicero Grimes had been there before.

GREEN RIVER RISING

Tim Willocks

'The best thriller since *The Silence of the Lambs*'
Daily Telegraph

THE DAY HELL CAUGHT FIRE . . .

After three years' hard time, minding no-one's business but his own, Ray Klein wins his parole. That same day, the disciplinary perfection of Green River State Penitentiary is torn apart by tribal war, and the prison falls into the hands of its inmates.

As the River sucks them all towards the abyss, Klein must choose: whether to claim his freedom and leave the ones he cares for to die, or risk everything and fight . . .

'Brilliant . . . a phenomenal piece of fiction . . . *Green River Rising* is magnificent'
Jane Shilling, *Sunday Telegraph*

'Breathtaking . . . the best suspense thriller of the year'
New Woman

'*Green River Rising* is a stunner – and maybe the best prison novel ever'
James Ellroy

OTHER BESTSELLING TITLES AVAILABLE

☐	Green River Rising	Tim Willocks	£5.99
☐	Bloodstained Kings	Tim Willocks	£5.99
☐	Dirty White Boys	Stephen Hunter	£5.99
☐	Black Light	Stephen Hunter	£5.99
☐	Black Dahlia	James Ellroy	£6.99
☐	The Big Nowhere	James Ellroy	£6.99
☐	L.A. Confidential	James Ellroy	£6.99
☐	White Jazz	James Ellroy	£6.99
☐	Players	Eugene Izzi	£5.99

ALL BOOKS ARE AVAILABLE THROUGH MAIL ORDER OR FROM YOUR LOCAL BOOKSHOP AND NEWSAGENT.

PLEASE SEND CHEQUE/EUROCHEQUE/POSTAL ORDER (STERLING ONLY) ACCESS, VISA, MASTERCARD, DINERS CARD, SWITCH OR AMEX.

EXPIRY DATE .... SIGNATURE..

PLEASE ALLOW 75 PENCE PER BOOK FOR POST AND PACKING U.K.

OVERSEAS CUSTOMERS PLEASE ALLOW £1.00 PER COPY FOR POST AND PACKING.

ALL ORDERS TO:

RANDOM HOUSE, BOOK SERVICE BY POST, TBS LIMITED, THE BOOK SERVICE, COLCHESTER ROAD, FRATING GREEN, COLCHESTER, ESSEX CO7 7DW.

NAME..

ADDRESS ....

....

Please allow 28 days for delivery. Please tick box if you do not wish to receive any additional information ☐

Prices and availability subject to change without notice.